"Mary, may I come in?"

Russ stood in the doorway, his arms behind his back.

"Please," she said. "My feet are getting cold standing here on this bare tile."

Keeping his back hidden from her, he sidled into the living room as she closed the door. They stood several feet apart, motionless.

"Russ—"

"Shh." He hesitated, then withdrew his hands from behind his back and held high in the air a bedraggled clump of twigs covered with small, pale green leaves and gray-white globules hanging in bunches. "I've brought you flowers."

She stared at him, pressing a hand over her spontaneous smile. "Flowers?" she managed.

"They don't look like much, do they?" He appraised the sorry bouquet. "But I like them." He lowered his hand to let her examine the gift. "This, Mary, is the official flower of the state of Oklahoma, and I've spent the last half hour climbing a tree in the dark to get them for you."

She studied the tiny oyster-colored berries. "Why, it looks—" she raised her face to his twinkling eyes "—like mistletoe!"

He laughed aloud. "It is." Holding the bouquet over her head, he grabbed her with his free arm and pulled her close just before he bent his mouth to hers.

Dear Reader,

For me, Christmas is magic—a time to celebrate traditions, family and belonging to that special place called "home." The holidays inspire nostalgic side trips to my childhood where, through the scrim of years, all is tinsel, colored lights and breathless wonder. Best of all is the giving and receiving of surprising, unexpected gifts of love.

Whether through serendipity or by design, I have been a privileged listener to the stories of several sensitive, courageous young women. Though blessed by loving adoptive families, each felt a need, insistent and intrinsic, to locate her birth parents—to "come home" to the fullness of her heritage. What struck me most about their experiences was the mystery of synchronicity, far beyond mere coincidence, propelling them to seemingly preordained discoveries. Call it déjà vu, ESP or grace. In each case, though, an angel whispered to a waiting heart.

And...they came home, not necessarily to joyous reunions, but to a place that restored the self to wholeness. Out of such journeys the theme for *This Christmas* was born.

Whenever we reach out to others, whenever we welcome home family and friends, whenever we heal broken relationships, we affirm that most amazing mathematical paradox: Love never divides; it only multiplies!

This Christmas, and always, may the love in your lives increase a hundredfold!

Laura Abbot

P.S. I enjoy hearing from my readers. Please write me at Box 2105, Eureka Springs, AR 72632-2105

Laura Abbot

THIS CHRISTMAS

Harlequin Books

TORONTO • NEW YORK • LONDON
AMSTERDAM • PARIS • SYDNEY • HAMBURG
STOCKHOLM • ATHENS • TOKYO • MILAN
MADRID • WARSAW • BUDAPEST • AUCKLAND

ISBN 0-373-70721-5

THIS CHRISTMAS

Copyright © 1996 by Laura A. Shoffner.

This edition published by arrangement with Harlequin Books S.A.

® and TM are trademarks of the publisher. Trademarks indicated with ® are registered in the United States Patent and Trademark Office, the Canadian Trade Marks Office and in other countries.

Printed in U.S.A.

Dedication

For Mother and Dad

With much love and many thanks for the rich sense of family you provided me

Acknowledgments

To Diane, Tracy and Deborah for inspiring the character of Mary.

To my dear friends Betty and John for their gracious assistance.

To my editor, Paula Eykelhof, for being such a perceptive and patient teacher. And to Wendy Blake Kennish, with thanks for her insights and her help.

The inscription that appears
on Mary's necklace:

ᚻᛁᛚᚷ

CHAPTER ONE

THERE WAS THAT LOOK again—the disturbing one that arced across the dining room table between her parents. It was intense, unsettling.

Mary Fleet toyed with her dinner roll, slowly tearing it into small pieces. She cleared her throat. "I had hoped this would be a celebration."

Her father set his fork on the china dinner plate and peered at her over the rim of his glasses. "As far as I'm concerned, there's nothing to celebrate."

Mary lowered her eyes, then turned to face her mother, who sat motionless, her goblet poised halfway to her lips. "Mary, your father didn't meant that the way it sounded."

Silence followed—strained, unnatural, broken only by the discreet clink of silverware.

Mary stared at the special meal Helga, the housekeeper, had prepared for her farewell dinner. But the tightness in her stomach had destroyed any vestige of appetite. The candles flickering in the silver candlesticks and the elaborate centerpiece of fall flowers swam in front of her eyes. It didn't have to be like this. "Dad, say something."

Her father stopped chewing and stared at her. "Like what? I'm delighted you're moving to...Oklahoma?" He intoned the name as if it were a distasteful epithet.

"Can't you be pleased for me? I've told you what a wonderful job opportunity this is."

"You had a perfectly good job right here in St. Louis and another offer in Jefferson City. You must realize how disappointed your mother and I are." He paused. "You have everything here—family, friends, a future."

She'd spent her whole life trying to please them. But this was different. Even if her parents didn't understand, she was twenty-eight and more than ready to be on her own, to accept a new challenge. Buying time to control herself, she sipped from the Waterford goblet before patiently beginning yet another explanation. "It might've taken years at the main bank here to get the opportunity I have in Oklahoma to work in the trust department. It's the goal I've been aiming for ever since grad school. I just can't get excited about the Jeff City loan department position." Was the need to justify her decision the price of years spent as the model daughter? She confronted her father. "Why are you so opposed to Oklahoma?"

She saw her parents momentarily exchange that look again.

"Charles." Phyllis Fleet spoke quietly, her body willed to dignity. "Please let's not spoil Mary's final evening at home. What's done is done."

"Besides the job," Mary went on, "I love the place. Ewing is a far cry from a dusty oil town. It's a beautiful little city with lots going for it culturally. When I went for my interview, I couldn't have asked for a friendlier, more comfortable reception." She leaned over and placed her hand on top of her father's. "Please, Dad, be happy for me."

He grunted skeptically and removed his hand. When he spoke, his tone was cool. "It's bad enough you're moving to Oklahoma. Then you had to hit us with that other business."

Mary eyed the crème caramel quivering on the plate Helga had just placed before her. *Here it comes.*

"Where have we failed you? From the moment we adopted you, we've done nothing but love you!" She saw the hurt and frustration on his face.

Mary pushed her untasted dessert aside. "I know you both wish things were different, that I'd come to some other decision about trying to locate my birth parents. It has nothing to do with what you did or didn't do. You've been wonderful parents, and I've never doubted your love." She glanced at her mother's face and read the pain in her clouded eyes. Her father shifted nervously in his armchair. When she resumed, there was pleading in her voice. "I just feel . . . incomplete. Is that so hard to understand?"

They were both silent, hoping no doubt that she would change her mind about everything and continue fulfilling their long-held expectations for her—the right marriage, the obligatory volunteer activities, a home nearby in Ladue, the upscale St. Louis suburb. She knew their wishes and knew, therefore, how heartbroken they were about her decision to search for her birth parents. How could she make them them understand that neither the move to Oklahoma nor her need to know who she was took anything away from the love and gratitude she felt toward them. "Let me say this just once more. You two will always be my family. Nothing is going to change that." She weighed her next words carefully. "I *need* to know who I am, where I came from. I wish I didn't feel this way—it'd be a lot easier for all of us. But ever since I was a little girl, something's been missing. And that *something* has grown to an emptiness, a void I can't fill any other way. Maybe I'll find out about my past, maybe I won't. But I have to try."

Her father's eyes reflected more than bafflement—a detachment, as if he'd withdrawn to an inaccessible place. "You've tried to explain, but...I still don't understand *why*."

Mary looked to her mother for support, reassurance. Instead, her mother sat, head bowed, face impassive.

"Mom?" Mary choked out the word.

Her mother raised her head, blue eyes filmed with tears, studied her husband for a long moment and then slowly shook her head.

It was more than disappointment Mary saw in their faces. Her stomach cramped. Fear. They were afraid—of what? Surely not of losing her? No, something else, inexplicable and powerful.

Her mother spoke into the strained silence. "What time will you leave in the morning?"

"Six."

"So early?" Mary heard dismay in her mother's voice.

"I need to get to Ewing in time to pick up the key from my landlord. I'll phone when I arrive."

Helga entered the room and stood expectantly beside Phyllis. "Pardon me, ma'am, but the hospital's calling for Dr. Fleet."

Her father shoved back his chair and got to his feet. As he strode toward the study, he patted his wife's shoulder.

"Not again!" her mother said ruefully. "I'd hoped we could spend this evening together."

"It's fine, Mom. We're used to the life of an obstetrician. Besides, I still have some packing."

Phyllis bit her lower lip. "Mary, although your father and I have significant reservations about your move and about your…other decision, we're not trying to run your life. You're an adult. But you'll always be our daughter, and parents never outgrow their protectiveness."

Mary rose and put an arm around her mother's shoulders. "No child could've been as loved and protected. I'm very lucky." She dropped a kiss on her mother's perfectly coiffed silver-blond head.

Her father reentered the room, quietly observing his wife and daughter. "I'm off to the hospital. There's an emergency."

Mary went awkwardly into her father's outstretched arms, feeling the familiar scratchiness of his worsted sport coat rubbing against her cheek, inhaling the antiseptic cleanliness of his starched shirt. His embrace, like all his gestures of affection, was restrained. She didn't want to part like this. "Will you get home before I leave?"

"I doubt it." He sighed. "Have a safe trip." He kissed her forehead, dropped his arms, then turned abruptly and left the room.

She resisted the impulse to call him back, to say she'd stay, she'd change her plans, anything to break through the barrier of his reserve.

She deeply regretted that she couldn't please him. By staying in St. Louis. By convincing herself that she *was* in love with Todd Maples, the promising young associate in his clinic. And, most of all, by abandoning her decision to try to find her biological parents. Perhaps his disapproval of her move to Oklahoma was merely a smoke screen for his deeper distress—the implied threat that locating her birth parents apparently posed for him.

Her mother stepped to the center of the table and gently blew out the candles. "Give him time, honey. It's hard for him."

Mary heard in her heart the "And for me, too" that her mother failed to voice.

MARY PAUSED in the doorway of her old bedroom. Leaving all this familiarity, launching in a new direction and risking the emotional consequences of change was daunting. But there was no turning back now, only a giant forward leap of faith.

The warm glow from the porcelain bedside lamp cast shadows on the daintily flowered drapes and striped wallpaper, color-coordinated in pastel pinks and blues. Except for the neat stacks of clothes lying on the bed beside the open suitcase and several stuffed animals sitting in the white wicker rocking chair, the room was anonymous in its tidiness.

A large corkboard on the wall gave the only testimony to the life of the girl who had grown up here. Mary sighed, flipped on the overhead light and walked over to the display, where her history, in photographs, hung before her. One of the earliest showed an intense, dark-haired seven-year-old in ballet slippers and a knee-length pink tutu smiling a shy toothless grin. The next few pictures, taken at Lakewood Summer Camp, portrayed Mary giggling with her cabin mates, standing precariously on the high diving board and receiving the Most Improved Camper Award.

Amid faded corsages, report cards and certificates of achievement in high school mathematics were candids of a diffident young woman, dressed in evening gowns, standing beside a variety of adolescent escorts.

Her eyes fell to several photos of her in her track uniform tacked above a variety of medals and ribbons, most of them blue. Only running had given Mary a sense of herself, a feeling not just of control but of freedom. She smiled at the memory of her mother's horrified response when she'd adamantly refused to attend any more ballet classes and insisted on trying out for the track team. What was the origin of this need to churn her legs, to feel the wind whip her face as she raced faster and faster? Maybe as a child, she'd accepted the notion, literally, that anyone named Mary Fleet was the swiftest. Whatever the reason, she'd always known running was a destiny rather than a choice.

She picked up one of the faded blue ribbons, drawing the silky length through her fingers. No parents could've provided a child with more opportunities. They had spared nothing in giving her a loving, privileged childhood, from the best schools to enriching trips and specialized lessons.

Mary sighed, letting the ribbon slip from her hand. She'd hurt them. It wasn't the first time her stubbornness had collided with her father's advice, but this latest disagreement had the potential to be the most devastating.

She gently removed a photo of her father beaming down with pride and embracing his cap-and-gown-clad daughter. This was a favorite picture—one of the few times the camera had captured her father bestowing a spontaneous hug. She tucked the photograph into the side pocket of her suitcase and then extracted from it the faded legal-size envelope she'd placed there earlier. Sitting on the edge of her bed, she pulled out the yellowed parchment and studied it under the light of the bedside lamp. Her birth certificate from the state of Colorado.

So few clues. Date and time of birth: January 10, 1968; 8:10 a.m. Place: University Hospital, Denver. Attending physician: Dr. James P. Altmuller. Mother: Phyllis Marie Jackson Fleet. Father: Charles Adam Fleet.

Mary sighed heavily. No matter how difficult, no matter how lengthy, this quest could no longer be deferred.

AFTER HER SHOWER the next morning, Mary peeked into her parents' bedroom. Her father's side of the bed was undisturbed and her mother lay turned away from the door.

Later, sitting cross-legged on her own bed, drying her hair and stifling a series of yawns, Mary wondered, not for the first time, if she'd made the right decision in accepting the transfer to Ewing. Maybe she was experiencing normal job-change jitters. Too late for second thoughts, though. Besides, the appointment to the trust department was a rare opportunity.

Stepping into red slacks and pulling a striped T-shirt over her head, she felt a wave of exhilaration. She put her cosmetic bag into the suitcase, glanced around the room and then closed the lid with authority. *Ready or not, Ewing, here I come!*

"Mary?" Her mother stood tentatively in the doorway. "May I come in?"

"Of course. I was going to wake you before I left."

Phyllis Fleet gathered her satin quilted robe and sat on the edge of Mary's bed. "I haven't been asleep since three-thirty." She was strangely still.

Mary crossed the room and sank down beside her. "Oh, Mom, I hope you're not worried about me."

Phyllis, eyes downcast, took one of Mary's hands, absently stroking the back of it with her thumb. "Every mother worries, but that's not what's kept me awake."

Mary waited, puzzled by her mother's serious tone.

Phyllis looked up. "I'm taking a step that may hurt your father terribly and will betray a trust." Her face, devoid of makeup and drawn with worry, looked haggard.

"Mother, you don't—"

"Hush," Phyllis interrupted. "I know I don't have to. Frankly, between your needs and my loyalty to your father, I feel torn to shreds. I love you both, and no matter what I do, someone will suffer." She paused, shoulders sagging.

Mary covered her mother's hand with her own, sensing her emotional turmoil.

Phyllis straightened, clearing her throat. "Your father and I never made a secret of your adoption, nor could we have loved a child of our own making any more than we love you. Quite simply, you are the joy of our lives." She paused. "When you were little and began asking us about your birth mother, we told you the truth. You were adopted privately, and your mother was a college graduate born in Oklahoma. She chose not to reveal your father's identity. That's all."

Mary spoke quietly. "I know. It's not much to go on. I may never discover any more than that. Nothing will ever change my feelings for you and Daddy, but Mom, a whole piece of me is missing. I have to search."

"No matter how much it hurts your father?" Mary remained uncomfortably silent, unable to respond to the painful question. Her mother continued, "He's lived in fear this day would come. He's unable to accept the fact that he can't do enough or love you enough to make you feel complete." Phyllis's fingers twisted her wedding ring around and around. "In his mind, your moving to Oklahoma where your mother was born simply adds insult to injury."

Mary bowed her head. "What about you, Mom? How do you feel?"

Phyllis pondered the question. "I'd rather you didn't pursue it. Not just because it's somewhat threatening to me as your mother, but more importantly because I don't want you to risk getting hurt. Yet, in my heart of hearts, I suppose I understand."

Mary, tears glittering, sought her mother's eyes. "Thank you for that."

"Your father wouldn't approve of what I'm about to do. It's the only time in our marriage I've consciously gone against his wishes in an important matter."

Phyllis tipped Mary's chin up and plumbed the expression in her eyes. "You're absolutely determined to begin this search process?"

Mary gazed steadfastly at her. "Yes, Mother, I am."

"Very well." Phyllis reached into the pocket of her robe. "I want to give you something." She withdrew a silver chain, suspended from which was a marbled agate stone.

Mary leaned closer to study the pendant. It was engraved with tiny, unfamiliar hieroglyphics. "What is this? Where did it come from?"

Phyllis sighed. "I can't give you many answers. "This was sent to us along with the adoption papers. Perhaps it belonged to your birth mother." Phyllis dropped the necklace into her daughter's hand, closing Mary's fingers around the smooth cold stone. "Godspeed, my dear," her mother whispered, drawing Mary into her arms.

Mary held her thin body close, aware that in some way she didn't fully understand, her mother had taken a huge risk. "I love you, Mom," she murmured. Beneath her hands, she felt the tremors of her mother's sobbing.

CHAPTER TWO

RUSS COULTER heaved his rangy, six-foot-two frame out of the conference chair next to his father's massive desk in the Ewing offices of Sampson, Davis and Coulter, Oil and Gas Attorneys. "It may be spitting in the wind, Dad, but I'm gonna give Buck Lloyd a try. It's mid-October. I can't wait any longer. I've got to make some decisions about how many cattle I can feed during this next grazing season and how much money I'll need to borrow."

J. T. Coulter laced his hands behind his head and leaned back in his chair, swiveling to follow his son's restless pacing. "Sure you're not biting off more than you can chew?"

"If I'm going to expand the ranching operation, I'd like it to be on adjacent land, not on acreage scattered throughout the county."

"Think you can service your obligation to buy out the rest of the family *and* acquire more land all at the same time?"

Russ heard the deliberate neutrality in his father's voice. When his grandfather, Benjamin Coulter, died, he'd left the ranch to his grandchildren. Neither Brian, Russ's younger brother, nor Janie, his kid sister, had the slightest interest in managing it. Russ had never considered any life *but* that of a rancher and was gradually buying out his siblings' shares. He knew his father was concerned he'd overextend himself financially, but through careful management, he thought he could accomplish both goals.

He stopped pacing and picked up his Stetson, slowly rotating it between his fingers. He looked at his father. "Yes, Dad, I can. And I'm going to start by talking to Buck Lloyd about buying that fifteen hundred acres."

J.T. stood and rounded his desk. "Son, I know it's important to you to get that land for your cattle operation, but Buck Lloyd is not about to sell it to you—at any price. And he can be a very dangerous man." He draped an arm around his son's shoulders. "I wish things were different, but a leopard doesn't change its spots. Buck's too old to give up his grudges at this late date. Our troubles with him go back too far and cut too deep. You may have to settle for another parcel of land."

"Not without sounding Buck out. He's partial to the smell of money." Russ clamped his hat onto his head. "I admit, though, I'd rather walk blindfolded into a stampede."

J.T. slapped Russ on the back. "Go get him, son."

"Damn right." Russ gave his father a thumbs-up, left the law office and strode down the street to the Oilman's Tower. Nothing ventured, nothing gained. Though a portion of the fifteen hundred acres would have to be cleared of the pesky Eastern red cedars, there were some fine stands of little bluestem and switchgrass. Financially, it would be tight but buying this land was worth the risk.

He paused before entering the offices of Lloyd Exploration. Mother Nature and the fluctuations of the cattle market posed plenty of obstacles. He didn't need an intransigent Buck Lloyd.

"May I help you?" The grim-faced receptionist scowled, as if he were an annoying pest.

"I'm Russ Coulter. I'd like to see Mr. Lloyd."

"Do you have an appointment?"

"No."

"Then he won't see you."

Russ looked down at her, his jaw set. "I called to make an appointment and you wouldn't give me one. But Mr. Lloyd won't see me without one. Right so far?"

She nodded, her eyes dissecting him.

"So—" he leaned on the edge of her desk "—it would seem we're at an impasse. Now, you can either arrange an appointment or—" he gestured toward the leather couch in the reception area "—I intend to set up camp right there. Sooner or later, he'll have to come out, and I *will* talk to him."

"See here, Mr. Coulter—"

"No, *you* see here. This can take as short or as long as you want." He sauntered over to the couch, selected an oil-and-gas journal from the stack on the coffee table and sat down. "It's up to you." He crossed his legs and began to read.

An hour passed, the stony silence broken only by the riffling of magazine pages, the soft clicking of the computer keyboard and occasional phone calls.

An attractive, trim woman in a business suit, shiny black hair just brushing her blouse collar, entered the reception area and, after a brief conversation, was ushered into one of the offices. The receptionist's not-so-subtle one-upmanship.

One journal article later, Russ saw the same woman, cheeks flushed and dark eyes blazing, emerge, anger apparent in her clenched fists and rapid stride.

He set the magazine aside and got up to open the door for her. "That bad, huh?"

Her deep-set brown eyes threw off sparks. "If he's typical of Oklahomans, I'm transferring to Devil's Island."

"No call to let old Buck ruin your day."

"I guess I'm not accustomed to crudity and rudeness in the business place." She brushed past him.

Her heady cologne filled his nostrils. Watching an attractive woman—even one under a full head of steam—beat the hell out of reading. "Not so fast. Heaven help us if you judge the fine people of Oklahoma by the likes of Buck Lloyd."

She stood in front of him, all five feet three or four, staring directly into his eyes. Then her face relaxed into a tiny self-deprecating smile. "You're right. Mainly you are 'fine people.'" She nodded at the stenciled name on the door. "But he's an exception." She started down the hall. "It's been lovely chatting with you, but I need to get back to work."

He watched her walk away, appreciating her trim legs. "Don't go away mad, ma'am," he called after her. For an answer, she waggled two fingers over her head in farewell.

Russ smiled, reentered the office and sank back on the couch. Whoever she was, that woman looked like she could give as good as she got.

Russ's stomach growled and he checked his watch. Eleven forty-five. He'd missed breakfast and didn't relish bypassing lunch, but damned if he'd desert his post.

At twelve-thirty, he heard heavy footsteps coming down the hall. He glanced up. Two hundred fifty pounds of Buck Lloyd stood glaring at him, paunch straining against the buttons of his dress shirt, his florid complexion blotched with liver spots. His shrewd eyes assessed Russ with all the warmth of a Brahma bull. The receptionist backed out of the room. Buck yanked one beefy hand through his sparse reddish-gray hair and barked through teeth clenched around a cigar, "What in hell are you doin' clutterin' up my office, boy?"

Russ tossed the magazine on the table and took his time standing up. "I've got a business proposition for you, Buck."

"I don't do business with Coulters."

Russ planted himself, feet apart, hands folded behind his back, swallowing the bile that threatened to choke him. "Never knew you to turn down an opportunity to make money. I want to buy the fifteen hundred acres you own west of my place and I'm offering a fair price."

With his tongue, Buck shifted the cigar to the other side of his mouth. His face was beet red. "Goddamn it, boy, you've got your head straight up your ass. You're gonna pay *me?* There isn't enough money in the entire Oklahoma oil patch for me to sell you one clod of dirt. Blood money, that's what it'd be."

He circled the receptionist's desk and stopped in front of Russ, glaring straight into his eyes. Russ held his ground, returning the stare. "I'll never be interested in doing business with a Coulter." He removed the cigar and blew smoke into Russ's face. "Now get your ass outta my office and stay out."

Russ gathered up his hat, took hold of the door handle and then turned back. "Let me know when you change your mind." As he closed the door, he heard Buck's muttered expletive.

So. Nothing gained. For now. He'd just keep chipping away. Meanwhile, he'd have to lease additional pasture elsewhere. For the time being he wouldn't have a consolidated operation, but he had a good, loyal crew and somehow they'd manage.

He rubbed his hand over his short-cropped sandy hair and put on his hat. He hated throwing money into a lease when he could be buying land. But he was realistic. Might as well slip over to the bank while he was in town and sound out Gil Genneret about a loan.

As he entered the revolving doors of the Wheatland Bank, he saw, standing at the elevator, the same attractive brunette who'd stormed out of Buck's office. He tipped the brim of his hat with his index finger. "Howdy." She nodded, pivoted and decisively punched the Up button.

She must still have a burr under her saddle. Thin, intense types like that didn't interest him anyway. His preference tended toward dimpled, pale-complexioned cream puffs—all generously endowed. Still, her slim athletic grace and clean-cut features would appeal to some men. *Keep your mind on business.*

He shifted his attention to the young loan department receptionist and smiled engagingly. "Gil in?"

As she picked up the interoffice phone, he began mentally rehearsing the pitch he needed to make to the loan officer.

AT THE END OF THE DAY Mary slipped the file folder into a desk drawer and sat back contentedly, surveying her small, tastefully appointed office on the second floor of the Wheatland Bank. She'd been on the job nearly a month and already felt right at home. Her framed print of Monet's *Water Lilies* hung over the credenza, and behind her desk she'd arranged four botanical lithographs of English garden flowers. Several framed certificates and diplomas hung inconspicuously near the door. Small photos of her parents were the only accessories on her desk, other than the computer monitor, a leather-bordered desk pad, the telephone and a walnut In-Out box. Mary approved of the results—simple, orderly, understated. Just the way she liked things.

When she'd come to work that first September morning several weeks ago, she'd been keyed up. Happily, the transition had been smoother than she'd anticipated. She thrived on the challenge of managing personal trusts, and her fellow employees had demonstrated their eagerness to help. Every day had justified the initial impressions she'd formed at the time of her interview. Ewing offered a nice blend of sophistication and hominess, and she'd experienced none of the guarded big-city reserve she was accustomed to.

Gwen Van Dyne, a personal loan officer, had made a particular effort to welcome her, and from their first introduction, Mary had been drawn to Gwen by her laughing hazel eyes and infectious good humor. Mary couldn't imagine the crisis that could daunt Gwen, who coped with a full-time job, civic responsibilities, a husband and two children with the equanimity of a Mona Lisa.

The only disappointment had come this morning when she'd made the rounds of offices in the Oilman's Tower soliciting support for the Annual Charity Horse Show, one of the local philanthropic projects the bank supported. She shuddered as she contrasted the welcome she'd met elsewhere with the reception she'd received at

Lloyd Exploration, Inc. The gargoyle of a receptionist had been intimidating enough, but Mary's face burned as she recalled the tongue-lashing she'd received from Mr. Lloyd. "What idiot sent you over here? I've never supported that damn horse show and it'll be a cold day in hell before I ever do. Tell George over at the bank I don't appreciate him sending you over here to sweet-talk me." That'd been bad enough, but then he'd administered the coup de grâce. "Now get your twitching little fanny outta my office."

Had the man never heard of sexual harassment? Certainly he'd never heard of manners. She supposed every Eden had its serpent and, as far as she was concerned, Buck Lloyd was Ewing's.

A further unsettling footnote to the morning was that tall, lanky cowboy in Buck's office, the same one she'd seen later at the bank. Despite her best intentions, she couldn't help noticing his outdoorsy good looks and cocky grin. She should've ignored him, but something about him and his undeniable charm had made her spill her frustrations. After all, she was on bank business and discussing Buck Lloyd had showed poor professional judgment.

She stood, carefully positioned the desk chair and adjusted the window blinds. Leaning over to pick up her purse, she heard Gwen in the doorway. "What time shall I pick you up this evening?"

Mary straightened, the butterflies rising with her. She knew her appearance at the kickoff dinner for the horse show committee members was expected—it went with the job—but the thought of meeting so many strangers all at once was a bit intimidating. "You decide. You're the one who has a family to consider."

"Ted's delivering Jenny to a friend's house and taking Jeremy to his Scout meeting. I should be all set by 6:45."

"Fine. Should I wear anything special?"

"It's a nice-casual affair." She put her arm around Mary's shoulder and gave her a little hug as the two started down the corridor. "If I looked like you, I wouldn't worry."

But later, driving home, Mary did worry. She'd never enjoyed big parties, especially where she knew very few people. Small talk was not her forte and balancing food, drink and poise all at the same time was virtually impossible. It had been at Gwen's urging that she'd volunteered for the horse show fund-raising committee, since bank employees were expected to contribute time to civic groups. She gripped the wheel more tightly. She knew she could do it. After all, she needed to get better acquainted in Ewing.

She concentrated on the scenery. The boulevard ran along the river. Nestled in the gentle valley, the small, bustling city boasted a modern downtown anchored by the twelve-story, glass-paneled Emerson Oil Building. Delineated by graceful, curving streets and tasteful landscaping, the residential areas rose from the valley into the gentle hills. The community exuded spaciousness and prosperity—a place where the good life was being lived. The caution light ahead turned red. While Mary waited at the intersection, she noticed the well-tended grounds and two-story brick building of the Sooner Arms Retirement Community. She mentally filed the location. One of the reasons her boss had welcomed her transfer was his expectation that she would develop more trust business with female and elderly clients. She genuinely enjoyed older people. Except, of course, for Lydia Belle Fleet, her great-grandmother.

What an unpleasant, superior old woman! When the Fleets had made their obligatory treks to Evanston for stuffy family Thanksgivings, the octogenarian cowed Mary. With a long, bony index finger she would beckon the little girl close, holding her with talonlike fingers and inspecting her through cold, rheumy blue eyes. "Charles, Charles," she would rasp imperiously. "Who *is* this child?" Mary's father would answer resignedly. "You know who this is, Grandmother. This is my daughter Mary." Then would come the indignant snort, fingers digging into Mary's flesh. "Nonsense, Charles. This can't be your daughter." The old lady would lean even closer, studying Mary's face. "Why, look at those eyes, that bone structure. She doesn't look a thing like the Fleets." And despite her father's reasoned explanation of Mary's adoption, Grandmother Fleet would turn away, harrumphing her displeasure.

Mary shook her head to dispel the memory. No wonder she'd always questioned where she belonged. But she refused to let Grandmother Fleet, Buck Lloyd *or* that flirtatious cowboy ruin her good mood. She'd do her best to enjoy her first social outing—the kickoff dinner at the Coulter ranch.

WHEN GWEN PULLED UP outside the condominium at precisely quarter to seven, Mary glanced one last time in the full-length mirror, hoping the autumn-hued gauze skirt with the yellow silk blouse belted over it fit the "nice-casual" category. She tucked her chin-length hair behind her ears, picked up a small purse and headed out to Gwen's station wagon.

"You look gorgeous!" Gwen's effusiveness went a long way toward calming Mary. "We're off to the ranch."

"A real ranch?"

Gwen deftly turned the corner and laughed. "Oh, it's real all right." She looked at Mary. "Haven't you been beyond the city limits yet?"

"Not in this direction."

"Well, sit back and enjoy. You're in the heart of oil and cattle country."

They drove west, rising gradually from the timbered river valley, vibrant with the yellows and crimsons of early fall foliage, onto the upland of cedar-covered hills, glittering farm ponds and cleared pastureland. Occasional palatial homes surmounted small rises, barns and outbuildings clustered below.

Mary craned her neck to look back at the skyline. In only a few miles they'd exchanged a civilized, familiar world for the raw, expansive countryside.

Mile after mile of low hills and fenced pasture, broken by stands of dense scrub oak, stretched to the far horizon, tinted only by yellow-brown prairie grasses, outcroppings of red rock and the sandy, rust-tinged soil. Cattle grazed in the distance and occasional loading pens bordered the side roads.

"I had no idea the countryside was so different west of town."

Gwen grinned. "The river divides the flatlands to the east from this rolling country."

Up ahead several vehicles were turning through a stone entry. "Is that it?" Mary could see a rambling stucco, Spanish-style ranch house and in the yard a large party tent bedecked with strings of brightly colored lights. Her clammy fingers toyed with her skirt. "This looks like a big event."

As if sensing her nervousness, Gwen stilled Mary's hands with one of her own. "You'll be fine. You already know some of the guests and I'll introduce you to a lot more. They won't bite, I promise."

After parking the car, Gwen maneuvered Mary through clusters of people conversing on the front veranda. At the door stood a tall, tanned gentleman with graying hair, his arm casually circling the waist of a ruddy-faced, redheaded woman whose green eyes twinkled in her smiling face. She spotted Gwen. "I'm delighted you could come." The woman welcomed Mary, extending her hand. "I'm Carolyn Coulter. I don't believe we've met." She indicated the man beside her. "My husband J.T."

Mary paused, struck by the obvious affection between the two. "I'm Mary Fleet. I work at the bank with Gwen. Thank you for having us to your home."

Carolyn laughed. "Technically this isn't our home. It was built by my husband's grandfather. We live in town and our son lives here now. But it's a great place for parties. The food's out in the tent, but please look around inside if you'd like." She turned to greet the next guest.

Gwen nudged Mary. "You really need to see the house. They don't make them like this anymore."

One step down from the tiled entry hall was a huge room with high, beamed ceilings and wood-planked floors. Colorful Navajo rugs were strewn amid the strategically placed pieces of massive Southwestern-style furniture. A sleepy-eyed collie sprawled on the leather couch; when they entered, he raised himself up, grunted and then rested his head back on his forepaws. A native stone fireplace dominated the far wall, and Mary crossed the room to study the magnificent painting above it. "It's a Wilson Hurley," Gwen whispered. "J.T.'s father was quite a collector of Western art."

Mary spun around, eyes shining. "This is wonderful. I can't take it all in." She fingered the bronze of a cowboy roping a calf, which stood on an intricately carved library table.

Gwen smiled. "Russ Coulter always talks about being art-rich and cash-poor, but I don't think the family could ever let these things go."

"Who's Russ? The son?"

"Yes. He was a few years behind me in school. I've known him forever. C'mon, let's mingle with the tent crowd."

Sombreros, strings of chilies and woven turquoise-and-magenta runners decorated the tables set up in the tent. A strolling guitarist ambled through the crowd and, outside, the bar was doing a thriving business. A man from the credit department at the bank, whose name Mary couldn't remember, pressed a margarita into her hand.

She took a quick sip of the salty drink. She'd been introduced to a cast of thousands. All of them seemed to know each other and assumed that she, likewise, knew everyone. Conversation surged around her. Gwen, engulfed by the crowd, was clear across the tent, animatedly talking with an older couple. Clutching the margarita, Mary withdrew to a small bench beneath a nearby tree. From that vantage point, she tried to put faces together with the names and scraps of information she'd been told.

Her eyes blurred as she tried to sort everyone out. Suddenly she sat up straight and stared. Leaning against the bar, one elbow propped on the counter, was the cowboy she'd run into earlier in the day. In khaki pants and a blue oxford cloth button-down shirt, he looked even more attractive than she'd remembered. His tanned face was wreathed in a broad grin directed at a curvaceous blonde who crowded close to him and hung on his every word. Mary watched the woman rise up on tiptoe and whisper in his ear. He threw back his head and laughed. As he did so, he spotted Mary. He raised his glass in recognition and winked over the top of the blonde's head.

Mary had seen enough. She stood abruptly, determined to make her way through the throng to Gwen. Just as dinner was announced, she found her. Thankfully, they sat at a table with bank people. After the business meeting, J. T. Coulter and his wife graciously invited the guests to stay and mingle.

Mary was ready to leave, but Gwen, thoroughly enjoying the party, excused herself to meet briefly with the chairman of the promotion committee. At loose ends, Mary retreated to the house. There, at least, she could enjoy more of the artwork.

Wandering around the great room, Mary appraised each painting, marveling at the artists' use of color and texture in depicting the American West. A small acrylic of an Indian maiden bathing in an arroyo particularly entranced her. She could almost feel the water droplets on the sun-warm brown skin.

Slowly she wandered down a wide hallway lined with pen-and-ink sketches of scenes from cattle drives. At the end stood a fabulous Spanish conquistador's chest. She brushed her fingertips over the distressed wood of the lid.

"Wonderful piece, isn't it?"

Mary jumped at the husky sound of the male voice and whirled around to find herself face-to-face with the good-looking, too-confident cowboy.

"It's quite old." He leaned against the wall, one foot crossed over the other, arms folded. "Like it?"

Mary smiled. "Yes. It's beautiful, just like the art." She gestured down the hall and started to move toward the living room. "The Coulters seem like very special people."

"They are." He stood erect, barring her way. "Are you trying to get away from me?" In his twinkling gray eyes Mary saw a clear challenge.

"No, er, yes." She went on the offensive. "Is it just my imagination or have you been following me today?"

"Well, it wasn't my intention but it's kinda worked out that way." He winked. "I don't mind—not at all. Do you?"

With nowhere to look but into those playful eyes, Mary felt trapped. "No one's ever going to accuse you of being bashful."

He chuckled. "True. I've been called many things, but that isn't one of them. I've got you sized up, by the way."

"Oh?"

"I'll bet you've always been the 'good girl' in your family."

"Meaning?"

"That you use the right fork, always send thank you notes and never take up with a man to whom you haven't been introduced."

"That's exactly right, so now if you'll excuse me, I'll—"

"Mary? There you are." Gwen approached them, beaming with satisfaction. "Good, you two have already met."

"No, we haven't." Russ bent over to peck Gwen on the cheek. "But I sure would like to be—" he grinned and sent Mary another impudent wink "—properly introduced."

Gwen raised her eyebrows. "In that case, let me do the honors. Mary Fleet, meet Russ Coulter."

Russ Coulter? No way. In her confusion she couldn't remember what she'd said. Had she insulted their host?

Russ took her hand. "I'm delighted to make your acquaintance. Now, do you think that'll do for an introduction?"

Mary faltered. "Yes . . . well, yes."

Gwen looked anxiously at her watch. "Mary, we've got to get going. I promised to pick Jenny up by nine-thirty."

Russ put an arm around their waists and walked them toward the living room. "Gwen, why don't you let me take Mary home?"

"You're sure you don't mind?"

"No." When Mary blurted out the word, they both stared at her. "I mean, it's late. I'll just go with you, Gwen."

Gwen broke away from Russ and faced her. "Nonsense. I've known Russ a long time. He may act like Casanova, but he's a pussycat at heart." She purred up at Russ. "Aren't you?"

He held up his hands. "Not a dangerous bone in my body."

"There. It's settled. Besides—" Gwen murmured to Mary "—I wanted to introduce you anyway."

"But—"

"No 'buts' and no arguments. Take good care of her, Russ. See you tomorrow, Mary." She breezed out the door and left Mary standing there woodenly, feeling distinctly manipulated.

"YOU DON'T SEEM entirely happy with this arrangement," Russ said as he drove onto the county road leading toward Ewing. He studied Mary surreptitiously. She sat gazing straight ahead, hands folded primly in her lap, appearing maddeningly self-contained.

A smile twitched her lips. "Does the word *railroaded* mean anything to you?"

"So you like being in control?"

She turned to look at him. Her triangular face, with its molded chin, full lips and high cheekbones, made a delicate setting for the huge eyes that burned like black coals beneath her straight, full brows. "Yes. I like to make a plan and stick with it.

"Don't you believe in spontaneity?"

"Not if I can help it."

He chuckled. "No wonder you're annoyed."

She shifted slightly in her seat. "Not annoyed, exactly."

"You just don't like surprises. And I'm a surprise."

"Something like that."

He patted her hand. "Whaddya say you make the best of it?"

She smiled tentatively. "I have a choice?"

"Let's start by your telling me what brings you to Ewing."

"I'm a business development trust officer at Wheatland Bank."

"'Trust' as in all that complicated stock market knowledge?"

She threw him an indignant look. "We women *are* capable of higher-level thought, you know."

"Ouch! I guess I deserved that. It's just that—"

"Looks and brains can't go together?"

He groaned inwardly. She certainly had the looks. Though not a classically beautiful face, hers was arrestingly different, almost exotically attractive. He liked the way her ebony hair, faintly highlighted with auburn, bounced above her Audrey Hepburn neck. "In your case, they obviously do. I'm really not some male chauvinist creep."

"What a relief!"

He heard a teasing tone in her voice. Damn, it was hard to penetrate her thoughts. "What took you to Buck's office this morning? Bank business?"

Warming to a less personal topic, she related the story of Buck's rudeness, finishing with his insensitive remark about getting her fanny out of his office. Russ hit the steering wheel with the flat of his palm. "It figures. You came up against the Buck Lloyd we all know and somehow have to tolerate."

"Have to tolerate? Why?"

Russ frowned. "Buck's a Ewing institution, arguably one of the wealthiest, most influential men in the area. He has a finger in every pie—city government, state politics, the Chamber of Commerce, you name it. Believe me, he enjoys using his clout and exerting financial leverage. But he's a bigoted rattlesnake of a human being. If you're in business in this town, there's no getting around him. You have to tolerate him." His voice softened. "Mary, I'm sorry you had to encounter him."

"I've certainly had more pleasant meetings." She pointed down the street. "Make a left at that next corner and then a right at the first intersection."

Observing her covertly, he fumbled for words to describe her. Reserved? Sedate? Certainly not transparent. A private person. Something mysterious about her intrigued him.

She spoke softly. "You have lovely artwork in your home. Eleanor Davies's acrylic is especially nice."

"Funny, some guests never notice the art." He turned the corner. "I'm glad you liked it."

"It's an impressive collection."

"My great-grandfather made some money in the early days of the Oklahoma oil boom. He appreciated quality. He's the one who built the ranch house. He always said 'big' wasn't as important as 'good.' So he built a reasonably sized house and furnished it with things he loved."

"You treasure them, too."

It wasn't a question. She understood. Russ smiled quietly in the dark.

When he shut off the ignition in front of her condo, she reached for the door handle. "Wait," he jumped out, skirted the truck and helped her down.

She paused on the porch, extending her hand. "Thanks for the ride, Russ. Good night."

He took her hand. "Don't I deserve at least a cup of coffee for the taxi service?"

She cocked her head skeptically. "It's late. Tomorrow's a workday."

"And maybe you don't know me well enough to ask me in?"

"That crossed my mind."

He rocked back on his heels. "I can remedy that. To-morrow's Friday. How about dinner on neutral ground—a restaurant?"

"I don't know, Russ."

"Sure you do. I'll pick you up at seven."

She studied his face. The hint of a smile gleamed in her brown eyes. "I guess it's safe."

"Great!" He dropped her hand and pointed a finger at her as he backed down the steps. "And caution—that's a good characteristic in a banker, Mary."

MARY SPOONED UP the last bit of the Grand Marnier soufflé she'd shared with Russ. Her dinner had been excellent and the intimate bistro atmosphere of the restaurant appealing. It usually took her several dates to feel comfortable with a new man, so she was surprised at how quickly she'd relaxed with Russ. Maybe it was because he seemed so at ease himself.

He handed his credit card to the waiter and sat back in his chair watching her, a twinkle in his eyes. "So what do you think? Up to St. Louis standards?"

"Did I sound like a snob? I have to admit that not only this restaurant but everything in Ewing has surpassed my expectations." She glanced around the dining room. "This is equal to St. Louis's finest."

He leaned forward on his elbows. "Seriously, what's been the most difficult adjustment?"

She thought about it. "Missing friends, family. I've lived there all my life, except for college. It would've been easy just to stay and live the life that was all mapped out for me."

"Like?"

"Like marrying a man from the same social set, joining the clubs my parents belong to, enrolling my children in the right private schools."

He studied her, his expression serious. "So why the move? Why not do the expected?"

She considered his question. "I was feeling stifled. I had such a sense of—" she paused, needing to explain to herself more than to him "—life passing me by. Of passive acceptance, instead of—"

"Adventure?"

She smiled. "Adventure." She rolled the word around in her mind. "That's it. *Adventurous* was never a word used to describe me."

He signed the credit slip and stood up. "I think it's about time to test that theory." She felt a delicious shiver of anticipation as he took her hand and escorted her from the restaurant.

WHEN HE WALKED her up to her porch, Russ knew just how to begin the test. "Well? What's the verdict?"

She fumbled in her purse. "Verdict?"

"Am I harmless? Do I get invited in?"

"I haven't made up my mind about 'harmless,' but in the interest of good manners—and adventure..." She opened the door, flicked on the lights and led him inside.

He studied the tasteful but somewhat barren room. "Nice place. Maybe a bit sterile."

"I've just moved, for heaven's sake. Give me some time. Anyway, I like simplicity." She laid her purse on the end table. "Do you want something to drink? Is tea all right?"

He rarely drank tea. "Great." He sat on the low sofa and stretched out his legs. Glancing around the room, he noted that the few prints on the walls lined up precisely. She'd probably used a level. The magazines—*Vogue, Time,* and *Travel and Leisure*—were stacked on the spotless coffee table, carefully overlapping.

"Herbal or regular?"

"Regular." He watched as she filled the teakettle, then gracefully set out the cups. The soft peach of her blouse highlighted her smooth tan skin. Her absorption in her task and her fastidiousness amused him.

The teakettle shrilled. *Take it easy. She's not your type. Not at all. Still ...*

She carried the tray to the coffee table, set it down and handed him his cup. "Sugar? Lemon?"

"No, thanks." He took a big swig. Tasted like boiled aluminum.

She settled at the other end of the sofa. He held up the sugar bowl for her. She shook her head. I prefer mine plain."

"Like everything in your life?"

"Does it show? Yes, I do like everything simple, neat— my surroundings, my finances, my business—"

"Your personal life?"

She raised an eyebrow. "Where I come from, it's considered impolite to probe into someone's personal life."

"Well, where I come from, we're pretty open. Cards on the table. Now me, my personal life's *neat.* Love 'em and leave 'em, no entanglements, no ugly farewell scenes." He grinned lazily.

"Neat for you. What about the victims of your, uh, charm?" She pursed her lips.

"They go in with their eyes wide open." Even to himself he sounded like a jerk.

"How perfectly businesslike." There was no missing her sarcasm.

"I guess we're each businesslike in our own ways." He took another sip of the offensive brew. "In fact—" he set down his cup and raised both hands to his head in swami fashion "—I'll bet you're so organized that your spices are arranged alphabetically." He leapt up and moved with exaggerated strides to the kitchen.

She stifled a chuckle. "Cabinet to the right of the sink."

He flung open the door. "Aha! My powers are intact. Allspice, basil, cinnamon..." Before she could utter a defense, he returned to the living room, pausing in front of the bookcase. "Let's see about the books." He ran a finger along the spines. "Sure enough. Austen, Christie, James—Henry, *then* P.D.—Kesey, Maugham..." He straightened up abruptly and faced Mary accusingly. "How could you?"

Mary blinked in bewilderment. "How could I what?"

"Leave out L'Amour?"

"What does love have to do with books?" She eyed him suspiciously.

He threw back his head and roared. "Not that *l'amour, ma petite.* Louis L'Amour!"

Stupefied, she stammered. "Louis L'Amour? Who's he?"

He crossed the room, knelt before her and seized one hand. "Your education's been neglected. An oversight I will hasten to correct. Louis L'Amour is only the greatest author of Westerns this country has ever known."

Still holding her hand, he got up to sit beside her on the sofa. "I'll bet you can't sing 'Ragtime Cowboy Joe' either. You probably don't even know all the words to 'Oklahoma.'" Puzzled, she shook her head. With his index finger, he turned her chin so she was facing him. "Now that you're a resident of this state, you need a mentor."

She stared at him with those huge eyes and he heard her breath catch. "You?"

He leaned forward until their noses nearly touched. "Yeah, me. And I think it may take quite a long time."

She didn't look away. "A long time?" she echoed dreamily.

"Right, podner." He dropped a light kiss on her warm cheek and reluctantly stood, pulling her up with him. Damn, he'd come *that* close to giving her a much bigger Oklahoma welcome. She was dangerously near to him, and it took willpower to restrain himself. He cleared his throat. "I'll be going now, but you take care."

She walked him to the door. "Russ—" she seemed to be searching for the correct words "—I really enjoyed the dinner. Thank you for inviting me."

She was so earnest it required effort to keep from grinning. "You're welcome, and, Mary—" he brushed one callused hand over her satiny hair "—you haven't seen the last of me. Good night." He closed the door softly.

CHAPTER THREE

DRESSED IN running tights and a baggy sweatshirt, Mary sat the next morning, hands cupped around a mug of hot tea, savoring a stay-at-home Saturday. She tried to concentrate on the papers spread out before her—a sheet listing adoption clearinghouses and support groups, documents from the Colorado Department of Vital Statistics, a brochure outlining approaches to obtaining information about birth parents or children given up for adoption.

But she was finding it hard to focus. During the night a northerly wind had brought cooler temperatures and gusty clouds. Tree branches rasped against the living room windows. She took a sip of the hot, soothing tea. Russ. She'd already spent entirely too much time daydreaming about his lanky, hard-muscled body, his mischievous, strong-jawed face, and the sexy challenge in those teasing gray eyes.

She shivered involuntarily, brushed back her half bangs and took another gulp of the tea. Even if she wanted a relationship—which she didn't—Russ wasn't her type! He was way too fun-loving for somebody as serious as she. And there were more important things to do than sit here mooning over a cowboy with a Casanova complex. Things like getting on with her search.

She picked up the letter from the Denver hospital administrator and reread it for the umpteenth time. In stilted prose he informed her that he wasn't permitted to release any identifying records pertaining to the circumstances of her birth. Only in life-threatening medical emergencies might such information be made available and then only as a result of complex legal maneuvering. She stuffed the offending letter back in the envelope. It was so unfair! Who had a better right to know about her own mother than she did?

For so long she'd been haunted by mysteries that hovered just beyond her reach. Why had her birth mother given her up? How could she have? Had there been any other choices?

Had her birth mother been a victim who sought to rid herself of an unwanted child, perhaps conceived under painful or violent circumstances? Or had she been a young woman of great compassion and strength who'd given up a beloved infant in the hope that the child would have a better life than she could give it?

Was there someone out there right now who wondered where her child was, how she looked, whether she'd been happy and loved? Or someone who lived guiltily every day in the fear that a past indiscretion would turn up to challenge a carefully built fabric of half truths?

She carefully opened a manila envelope and withdrew the necklace Phyllis had given her. She rubbed her fingers idly over the smooth, worn surface of the gray stone, mottled with streaks of mauve and cream, and then laid it out on the table, willing it to supply answers. Where had it come from? What was the significance of those three strange characters etched into the surface? She traced them with her forefinger. What clue did they hold? Were they Arabic, Hebrew, or Cyrillic? Indian hieroglyphics? Coptic symbols?

Meticulously she copied the mysterious letters on her notepad. She picked up the necklace again, feeling the heft of it in her hand. Holding the stone, she sensed an uncanny attachment, a kind of summoning. *Ridiculous.* She'd always prided herself on being practical, rooted in reality. Yet today, as if she had no choice, she felt a compulsion to wear the necklace close to her heart. She hesitated, then slipped it over her head.

She sat for a few moments thinking of her adoptive parents. At what personal cost had her mother made the decision to give her this one tangible link to her past? Her parents had always been a partnership. She couldn't remember a time when they'd argued in front of her or presented anything but a united front, whether establishing her high school curfew or setting the limits of her college budget.

Even when she'd tried to explain her deep, abiding need to locate her birth parents, her mother and father had banded together in their mutual hurt and concern. So it was difficult to imagine the pain of her mother's struggle to relinquish the necklace. Subsequently, there had been no mention of it, not in their phone conversations or her mother's letters. Her father's tone, when they had spoken since, remained polite but detached.

So many puzzles. From the time she was old enough to conceptualize, she'd catch her reflection in the mirror—wide brown eyes staring back at her, olive-skinned face framed by silky black hair—and wonder. Who did she look like? Where had she come from? Had her birth mother been Hispanic, Native American, or possibly Mediterranean? Was there someone, somewhere, who had the same high cheekbones, long nose and generous mouth? Someone who thought what she thought, laughed as she laughed, loved what she loved? As an adult, she still wondered.

She sighed and scanned the brochure. Where to begin? With the doctor in Denver? With these ethnic possibilities? Skimming the booklet, her eyes came to rest on one passage. Because of the Indian Child Welfare Act, it read, tribal adoption records were quite thorough. What if her birth mother was Native American? But what tribe? Mary's momentary excitement swiftly dissipated. She was grasping at straws. But what else did she have? Straws and a necklace.

She scooped the papers into a stack and drained her mug. Her head told her she might never find the answers she so desperately sought. Yet not knowing was a canker eating at her heart. Patience and persistence. She didn't care how long it took.

She carried the mug to the kitchen. Standing at the sink, she gave a gasp of pleasure as the clouds parted and the sun illuminated the brilliant maple tree in the back yard. It wasn't going to rain, after all. She kicked off her slippers and pulled on her running shoes. She needed a run. What a glorious day to leave her worries behind and explore Ewing on foot!

She'd just pocketed her key and turned for the door when the phone rang.

"Hi, Mary. It's Gwen. Just checking to see how it went last night." Mary could sense the grin on Gwen's face.

"Oh . . . fine, thanks."

"What do you think of Russ?"

"Is this a loaded question?"

"Maybe."

Mary leaned on the counter, cupping the phone to her ear, gathering her thoughts.

"You're not answering my question."

"Pushy, pushy. He's pleasant enough." Pleasant enough? She didn't dare tell Gwen she thought he looked like a grown-up version of Tom Sawyer. Or how much she loved his happy-go-lucky smile. Or that she found him the most naturally relaxed man she'd ever seen.

"Pleasant? That's all?"

"I think it's adequate to describe a man who, by his own admission, has a fickle streak."

Gwen laughed. "That's our Russ, all right. Nobody's been able to rope him in. But he's a great guy and I think you'd be good for him."

Mary straightened and tried to project firmness. "Gwen, I appreciate your concern for us both, but I'm not, repeat *not,* in need of any matchmaking."

"Okay. 'Nuff said. But he is nice, isn't he?"

Mary shrugged resignedly. "Yes, Gwen, Russ Coulter is nice." She giggled. "You don't give up easily, do you?"

"Nope. Have a great day. See you Monday."

Mary hung up, more eager than ever to go for a run—and to dispel unsettling thoughts of Russ Coulter. She didn't have time for this.

Once outside, she fell into an easy stride, adjusting her breathing and pumping her arms. Her weekday runs, of necessity, were abbreviated, but today she could indulge herself. Take as long as she pleased, go wherever she wanted.

Her route took her through a lovely, tree-lined neighborhood, past a sprawling middle school and into a large park. From the boys on the playground to the young couples wheeling baby carriages, everyone spoke to her. She found herself waving and returning their cheerful remarks, her natural reserve thawing.

She felt better already. No need to concern herself with Russ. Sure, she'd see him around, but that was all. Her heart thudded against her rib cage and perspiration dampened her forehead. She rounded the small pond in the middle of the park and headed for home, exhilarated. A great new job, wonderful people and the freedom to explore her origins. What more could she ask?

Feeling infinitely better, she slowed her pace as she neared her condo. All her silly little worries had evaporated. Then she noticed her front porch.

Completely obscuring her door stood a six-foot-tall live fig tree surrounded by half a dozen small wrapped packages. Mary approached curiously. Fastened to the trunk of the tree was an envelope inscribed with her name. She pulled it off and opened it. "Too Spartan. Your home needs growing things and good literature. Welcome to Oklahoma. Russ."

She blushed, remembering his assessment of her living room, and then chuckled softly as she began unwrapping one Louis L'Amour novel after another. She was embarrassed by the conspicuous generosity of the gift—and secretly pleased.

She opened the door and tugged at the tub in which the tree was planted. She could barely get the thing into her house. Panting, she pushed it into the corner behind the armchair and surveyed the effect. Darn it all, he was right. It was just what the room needed.

With a deep sigh, she sank into the chair. But it was not what *she* needed. She didn't want to feel obligated and she certainly didn't need any entanglements of her own. Todd Maples had cured her of that notion! She frowned remembering how close she'd come to marrying Todd—until that evening in the restaurant.

"WHAT DO YOU MEAN you can't marry me?" The tiny plush box lay on the table between them, the candlelight reflected in the sparkling facets of the large diamond set in a platinum band.

Painfully Mary raised her eyes to Todd's shocked face. "I'd do anything to avoid hurting you."

"Anything except marry me." His jaw worked. "Can you give me a reason? I mean, it's not like you didn't know this was coming."

"I'd convinced myself I still had time...time to make a decision." As she spoke, she realized she'd been trying to talk herself into saying yes. Why? Because she wanted to please—whom? Todd? Her parents? His family?

"Time? Mary, we've been friends since high school. We've been dating steadily, and I thought seriously, for almost a year. We've got everything in common—background, families, friends, a bright future." With a snap, he closed the lid of the ring box. "I don't understand."

Guiltily she averted her eyes from the pain in his face. "We're good friends. And I don't want that to change." She ignored his skeptical expression and plunged on. "This is so hard." She forced out the words. "Todd, I like you, I respect you a great deal, but...I don't love you."

He raked a hand through his thick brown hair. "Where did I go wrong? There's more to this! Even our parents expect us to walk into the sunset together."

"Maybe that's part of it. Think about it. Are we doing what feels right for *us* or are we going along with our parents' expectations?"

He threw down his napkin. "I don't believe it. You're blaming this on our parents? Come on, Mary. I love you. What's so complicated about that?"

Her stomach churned. "Todd, please don't make this any more difficult."

"Difficult!" He studied her as if she were an alien being. Then his eyes widened in understanding and he leaned forward, hands clenched on the table. "It's that adoption business, isn't it?" He stared at her. When she didn't answer, he pounded one fist. "Mary, it's not that important." He spoke emphatically. "*I don't care who you are.* It doesn't matter."

Mary held both of his taut hands in hers. "It matters to me." Her voice took on a pleading quality. "I need to know my history. Even *I* can't explain exactly why. I wish I could. It'd make life a lot simpler. This...black hole in me isn't just emotional, it's almost a physical sensation. I have to satisfy myself I've at least tried to find my birth parents. And if you're honest, you'll admit you have difficulty understanding all of that. Otherwise, you wouldn't have tried so often to talk me out of it." Mary flattened her hands over his still-clenched fists, then withdrew them into her lap.

His baffled eyes pierced hers. He shrugged his shoulders, picked up the box and dropped it into his jacket pocket. "Bottom line, you don't love me." He threw down a fifty-dollar bill, stood up and circled the table to pull out Mary's chair. "You don't leave me with much choice except to take you home so you can begin...finding yourself." The hurt in his voice was tinged with bitterness.

Even at the time, despite her regret about hurting him, Mary had been startled by how immediately she felt the release of a heavy burden.

AFTER HER RUN, she'd showered, changed, and just begun unloading the dishwasher when a loud knock startled her. She combed her fingers through her hair, tucking a wayward strand behind one ear as she crossed to the door and put her eye to the peephole. Russ! Her breath quickening, she opened the door. "What a surprise!"

There he stood, all six feet two of him braced against the doorway. He seemed taller in his boots, faded jeans, denim jacket and cowboy hat. He grinned cockily. "Where're your manners? May I come in?"

Flustered, Mary moved aside and, with a sweep of her arm, ushered him in. She lagged behind and stood quietly while he assessed the effect of the fig tree. "You really didn't have to do that," she said. "But the room does look better. Homier." She tentatively touched his sleeve. "Thanks for such a thoughtful gift. And the books—" She gestured to the coffee table. "But it's much too much."

"Not when you consider that your education's at stake."

"Which one should I read first?"

He turned and placed two broad hands on her shoulders. "It doesn't really matter. Not all your lessons about the West are going to come out of books."

His face was perilously close and he was trailing his hands slowly down her arms, sending shivers through her.

She barely managed the next words. "They're not?"

"No." His voice was husky, and his breath ruffled her hair. "They're not."

For a moment, with teasing affection, he just looked at her. She couldn't breathe. Then he tilted back his hat, ever so gently drew her to him and lowered his lips to hers, tenderly exploring. She should stop this nonsense, but...

He withdrew a few inches and intoned, "Statehood, 1907," and kissed her again. "Capital, Oklahoma City." She realized she was waiting for the next wisp of a kiss. "Site of the Cowboy Hall of Fame." He obliged, more insistently this time.

Just when she wasn't sure she could control what happened next, he grinned mischievously. "Book learning, hands-on learning—they're both good." He nodded approvingly. "But nothing beats a field trip. Want to go horseback riding?"

She struggled to regain her composure. "Today?"

"Sure, why not?"

"Did it occur to you I might have other plans?" She desperately needed to regain control of the situation.

"You and your plans! As a matter of fact, it did occur to me, but I like to live on the edge, act spontaneously."

"I've noticed." She gestured helplessly at the partially unloaded dishwasher. "Did you think you could just barge in here unannounced and assume I'd follow you anywhere?" Even as she uttered the words, she knew she was bluffing.

"Well, let's see." He loomed over her, smiling confidently. "I'm a respectable citizen, I have a character reference from Gwen, I'm even a customer of Wheatland Bank. And I'm not asking you to follow me just *anywhere*." He stepped to the hall closet and pulled out a windbreaker and tossed it to her. "Somewhere special. I want to show you my ranch. Do you own any cowboy boots?" She shook her head. "That's okay, your running shoes will do this time."

She gave up all pretense of resistance. "I haven't ridden in years, but I'd like to see the ranch," she said as she shrugged into the jacket he held for her.

Maybe she *would* follow him anywhere.

CHAPTER FOUR

RUSS LED MARY through the ranch house and into the cheerful kitchen. The collie lying on the rug struggled to his feet and limped across the floor to nuzzle Russ's hand. "Hey, old fella. Glad to see me?" The dog wagged his tail and then circled Mary warily.

"Who's your friend?" she asked, smiling. "We weren't introduced when I saw him at your party."

"Meet Casey Tibbs, named for my favorite rodeo cowboy. He's getting on in years, but you couldn't ask for a better buddy." Russ knelt beside the dog and buried his fingers in the collie's thick ruff. "It's okay, boy." He cocked his head at Mary. "She won't hurt you." Mary knelt beside Russ and stroked the dog's back. A sound as purrlike as a dog can make issued from Casey's throat. Russ looked up admiringly. "Isn't that something?"

"What?"

"He likes you."

"Is that so difficult to believe?"

"You have no idea. Casey has never been a ladies' man." Russ stood up and drew Mary to her feet. "C'mon, I think Mom's out here today cleaning up from the party."

In the garage, they found Carolyn Coulter, her arms full of sombreros. She wore no makeup and her short carrot-red hair had been hastily combed.

"Mom, you remember Mary Fleet?"

Setting down the sombreros, she smiled and extended her hand. "It's nice to see you again, Mary. Excuse the mess. I'm trying to get the decorations boxed up." She glanced quizzically at Russ. "You two going riding?"

"Thought we would. Do you keep any boots out here that might fit Mary?"

"You're welcome to the pair of sevens in the hall closet. I better warn you, though. You may have some company on your ride."

"Oh?"

"Janie's in the barn. I told her if she helped me with the lights, she could take Ranger for a run."

"Janie's my sister. Seventeen going on thirty."

"I'd love to meet her."

"Just don't let her bowl you over. She can be very outspoken," Carolyn said.

"Mom, that's a classic understatement."

"She's got you and your brother Brian as wrapped around her finger as she does your dad and me." She winked at Mary. "The trick is not letting her know that. Now then, let's see about the boots."

Later, while Russ rounded up the tack, Mary stood in the barn studying her borrowed footwear, hoping she wouldn't make a fool of herself. She absently petted Casey, who hadn't left her side. Although she'd told Russ she'd ridden before, she hadn't confessed that she'd ridden only English-style. When she'd asked him if cowboy boots meant they were riding Western, he'd laughed and said, "Yes, ma'am, leather-tooled saddles and all."

Surely she could handle it. A horse was a horse. The smells of saddle soap, hay, horse flesh and manure filled her nostrils, sending a pleasant shiver of déjà vu up her spine.

"Hi, who're you?" A tall, freckle-faced girl with laughing green eyes and a long reddish-brown braid emerged from the shadows at the other end of the barn. She had Russ's relaxed gait and easygoing mannerisms and Carolyn's puckish Irish features.

"I'm Mary Fleet, a friend of Russ's."

The girl stuck out her hand. "Hi, Mary. I'm Janie. Where's my sneaky brother been hiding *you?*"

Russ, shouldering a saddle, came out of the tack room. "I haven't been hiding her anyplace. I just met her Thursday." He shot his sister a warning look and entered a nearby stall.

Janie leaned closer and lowered her voice. "I don't even know you, but Casey approves—that's a first—and you're a step above what Russ normally brings home."

Mary couldn't stop herself. "What does he normally bring home?"

Janie furrowed her brow. "Let's see." She began ticking them off on her fingers. "He's brought home stray cats, assorted snakes, a positively deranged raccoon, Casey, of course, and—" she paused dramatically and glanced over her shoulder to be sure Russ wasn't eavesdropping "—dates that look and act like cotton candy. You know, all fluff and air." She shook her head as if cleansing her mouth of an excess of sugar. "You guys mind if I tag along for the ride?"

Carolyn was right. Janie didn't mince words. "We'd enjoy your company."

"Russ," Janie yelled over her shoulder. "Mary wants me to go along." She waited as if anticipating an objection. "Ranger's saddled. Who're you using for Mary?"

"Queenie. Would you be a big help and saddle Major for me?"

"Sure." Janie waved at Mary and disappeared into the tack room.

Russ led a chestnut mare out of the stall. "Meet Queenie. She's a sweetheart. Won't give you a bit of trouble." He checked the cinch and then turned, grinning. "Mount up. I need to adjust your stirrups." Mary's head came only to his shoulder. She had trouble focusing on his instructions. It was more fun to study his tanned profile beneath the brim of his worn cowboy hat. The hat and the surroundings changed him—he was more intense and—her heart skipped a beat—excitingly masculine. Tom Sawyer transformed into the Marlboro Man.

She placed her left foot in the stirrup and felt him steady her as she swung onto the mare. He gave her the reins and covered her small hand with his warm one. "Why are your knees bent?" She felt his hand clamp her ankle. "Just let your legs hang naturally." He rebuckled the stirrups and said, "Now stand in them." Stand in them? Then how was she supposed to hug the flanks with her knees? Western riding might require a few modifications.

He took off his hat and wiped a forearm over his brow. She spotted the hint of a cowlick at the crown of his head. She resisted the impulse to reach out and touch it.

"Ready?" Janie walked over leading two saddled geldings. She passed a set of reins to Russ, who mounted in one smooth motion. He gently spurred his horse. "We'll start off slowly," he said to Mary. "Just give Queenie her head. She'll treat you right."

Russ led the way, Janie and Mary falling in behind. Just outside the rear entrance of the barn Mary noticed a mysterious contraption partially covered with a blue tarpaulin. "Janie, what's that thing?"

Janie rolled her eyes heavenward. "Russ's ultralight."

"His what?"

"You know. One of those homemade gas-powered planes. Russ's latest toy. He's in his Red Baron stage."

"Red Baron stage?" Mary felt as if her legs were dangling helplessly.

"As in 'flying ace.' You've already missed his hang gliding and scuba diving phases." She grinned and clucked Ranger forward. "But you might be in time for snowboarding."

"Huh?" Mary concentrated on guiding the horse with her left hand. Her other arm felt useless. Maybe that was where real cowboys carried lassos.

"Russ has lots of interests. As soon as he figures out one thing, he goes on to the next. We can't keep up with him."

Without thinking, Mary blurted, "You mean like the women in his life?" Why had she said a dumb thing like that? Janie might think she cared about him.

Alerted, Janie twisted in her saddle to look at Mary. "Yeah, you could say so. But maybe you and I can work on that." She grinned conspiratorially and spurred her horse to a trot, leaving Mary and Queenie to follow.

Russ sat tall in the saddle, back straight, shoulders squared and, with a minimum of movement, directed and controlled his mount. Mary watched Janie's braid bounce up and down as she trotted ahead of her. From the rear, Russ and Janie bore a startling resemblance to each other—both long-legged, naturally athletic, confident.

For a moment the seed of envy she'd so often experienced took root in her mind. What would it be like to have a brother or sister? The Christmas when she was five, that was all she'd wanted from Santa—a baby brother or sister. The big red tricycle he'd brought, shiny and smelling of new rubber, was a huge disappointment.

But still hopeful, she'd looked forward to the next Christmas. She remembered clearly the day her dream shattered. With a single offhand remark, a worldly first-grade classmate had destroyed forever her illusion of Santa Claus, that jolly benevolent man in the red suit who would fulfill your wishes if only you were good enough.

Convinced she would never have a brother or sister, she'd shifted her focus to thinking about her birth mother. She'd imagined a joyous reunion—full of hugs and laughter. Betrayed by the childish myth of Saint Nicholas, she'd turned instead to an intercessor—the resplendent Christmas angel, robed in white satin, that adorned the top of the tree, her gossamer platinum hair creating a radiant nimbus. The angel's Madonna features—rosy cheeks, placid sapphire eyes, pink smiling lips—promised perfection. It was to her that Mary then addressed her prayers—if not for a brother or sister, at least for help in unraveling the mystery of her birth. Surely that was what guardian angels did! Each Christmas, she'd tell herself, "*This* Christmas. This will be the one." But it never was.

In fairness, her parents had bent over backward to make her feel special—their chosen only child. But when all you wanted was to be normal, "special" sometimes felt different. Lonely. When she was a teenager, her mother had explained about the hysterectomy she'd had before Mary was born and the difficulty of adopting another child. Even though she'd understood, Mary had still longed for a sibling—longed to be like everyone else. She would've loved a sister like Janie.

Lost in her thoughts, Mary was jolted back to reality when Queenie, in the effort to join her stablemates, broke into a fast trot. Mary grabbed the pommel. She was being tossed like a beanbag. Gritting her teeth, she tried to press her knees to the moving horse and post as she'd been trained to do. But her stirrups were too low. All she could do was hold on as, with each resounding slap of the saddle, the breath was being knocked out of her. What had Russ said? Just give Queenie her head? In a blur, Queenie overtook and passed Janie and Ranger before she slowed to a walk next to Russ. He'd reined Major in and was watching with amusement.

"Okay?" His laughing eyes offered reassurance. "You were an equestrienne, complete with jodhpurs and a little black hat?"

Mary, catching her breath, only nodded.

"First lesson. The trick of trotting Western-style is to hold your seat. Make yourself one with the horse. When she goes up, you go up with her. When she comes down, you come down. No daylight between saddle and posterior."

"You're kidding!"

"Try it. Just like rocking in a cradle."

On high seas, maybe. "Whatever you say." Janie rode on ahead and, sure enough, her fanny seemed molded to the saddle. Mary's legs felt like Gumby's.

"Cantering and galloping are easier. You ready?"

"Sure." Anything would be better than the miserable trot.

The moment Queenie shifted into a graceful canter, Mary relaxed. This was more like it. Eyes fixed on the rutted path through the pasture, she felt the wind streaming past her face and was soon oblivious to anything but the thrill of the pace. Gaining confidence, she prodded Queenie into a gallop and laughed aloud as an instinctive "Wahoo" escaped her lips. Somewhere behind her she could hear Major's thudding hooves.

Queenie pulled up short at the fence line and Mary slumped over her neck, petting her and smiling broadly.

Russ reined Major alongside. "Boy, once you got past the trot, it all came back to you."

Mary raised her flushed face. "Like riding a bicycle, just like they say. I'd almost forgotten what fun it is."

"It's not going to take you long to get the hang of Western riding. You're a natural." He nudged Major into a walk. Queenie kept pace beside him.

Mary swiveled her head to take in the pasture covered with gently undulating broom-yellow grasses, some heads drying to sepia, scraggly cedar trees defying the rocky soil by their proliferation, and in the distance a sandstone formation of boulder-size rust-colored rocks. Occasional racing clouds cast intermittent patterns of gray over the landscape. She inhaled deeply and gestured with a wide sweeping movement of one arm. She felt Russ's eyes on her. "It's so open, so free. St. Louis is beautiful, but this—" she regarded the scene again, squinting into the sun "—this is different. Exhilarating." She heard the comforting creak of the saddle and settled into Queenie's accommodating gait.

She observed Russ, who stared out toward the horizon. Only after several seconds did he face her. "This ranch is very important to me."

She knew he'd just revealed something special about himself, something personal. She spoke quietly. "I don't see any cattle."

The crinkly lines around his eyes eased and he chuckled. "Not yet. We won't be bringing them in to this pasture until January." He shifted in his saddle. "Know anything about ranching?"

"Not a thing—except you don't call steers cows."

"That's a start." Then, as the sun slipped beneath the rim of the far hills, he gave her a lesson in the types of cattle operations, explaining the risks involved, the cycles of buying, feeding and selling.

She tried to follow the intricacies of feeder operations versus cow-calf operations, but the animation in his face and the zest with which he described his work spoke of something she hadn't seen in him before. A seriousness of purpose and a determination nothing short of passion. Concerning the ranch, he was all business.

Mary swept her arm around. "Is this all yours?"

"Only to the top of that hill beyond the rocks. At the fence line, Buck Lloyd's property begins." He frowned. "The fifteen hundred acres I want to buy."

"That's why you were in his office Thursday?"

"That's why. Fat lot of good it did me."

"Isn't there other land for sale?"

"No desirable adjacent land. Anyway, his is the best piece around."

Across the pasture Mary could see Janie, bent low over Ranger, braid flying, racing toward them.

"Buck doesn't strike me as the type to give in without a fight."

Under his breath she heard him mutter, "Especially not with a Coulter."

"What do you mean?"

Grim-faced, he said, "Mary, a word of warning. If you have to do business with Buck, don't mention me or the Coulters."

"Why not?"

In the pounding of Ranger's hooves against the packed earth, she could make out only part of Russ's response. "...bad blood..."

"Hi, you guys." Janie grinned. "Race you back to the house."

Russ challenged Mary with his eyes. She nodded and they tore across the pasture after Janie.

"TOO BAD MOM and Janie couldn't stay for supper." Russ picked up a spoon, leaned over the kettle of chili and ladled up a taste. With an impish grin, he added a dash of Tabasco.

Mary turned from the oven where she'd been checking the corn bread. "Janie said I'd prolong my life by avoiding your chili."

He took another taste and smiled broadly. "She doesn't know what's good." Russ studied Mary's heat-flushed face, her warm brown eyes fringed by thick black lashes, one lock of sable hair brushing her jawline. Her pink turtleneck shirt defined her high shapely breasts and the jeans hugged her tiny waist. Seemingly aware of his scrutiny, she pushed back the strand of hair.

"Well, no one's ever called me a coward."

His eyes traveled down over her hips. She looked damn appealing. He'd had to laugh when she tried to post on the Western saddle, but once she got the hang of it, she'd been fearless—almost as if born to it. "Consider this supper your initiation as an Okie. Trial by fire, you might say."

He laughed aloud when, at the dinner table, she took her first spoonful of chili. He watched small beads of perspiration gather on her forehead. She grabbed her ice water, draining half the glass. "What's in this stuff, TNT?"

"Secret family ingredient." He nodded toward her bowl. "Go on. It gets easier. After *my* chili, I guarantee others will be disappointing."

"If I live to eat again," she sputtered. "Becoming an Oklahoman can be perilous."

No artifice. None at all. She came across as genuine, honest, employing none of the flirtatious conversational foreplay he was used to. *Easy, don't let your guard down. You don't want a repeat of some woman trampling on your heart.*

Janna Symington, his college sweetheart, had not only managed *that,* but had taught him more than he'd ever wanted to know about assumptions—and trust. He would never forget the horrified expression on her face when he'd asked her to marry him and move to the ranch. "The *ranch?*" She'd stared at him incredulously. "You can't be serious. Why, I naturally assumed we'd live in Dallas and you'd go to work with Daddy. I mean, I know everybody there." Condescension grew with each word. "Surely you can't expect me to live in the sticks! The ranch? No way!" And he'd thought she loved him!

With Mary, though, exercising caution would be easier said than done. After dinner, he showed her the artwork she hadn't seen at the party. Her eyes danced, and her intelligent questions pleased him. After the complete tour, they settled on the living room couch facing the huge stone fireplace in which a crackling fire blazed. "So you like this house?"

She hugged her knees to her chest and grinned. "It's fabulous! I've never seen anything like it." She stared into the flames. "And this is great country, too. This afternoon, riding Western-style—I loved it! I felt I could race clear off the edge of the earth." She turned to him, her eyes sparkling.

No makeup. Just smooth dark skin, full smiling lips and eyes like a Disney doe. He reached out and traced one finger idly down her cheek. "I might just hire you on as a hand out here." He'd meant the words in jest, but their full implication knocked the breath out of him. Damn it, she *did* fit here—as well as the Remington bronze or the Navajo sand paintings. He looked into her eyes, gauging her reaction.

"Anytime. I'll even muck out the stalls."

He tried to concentrate on something other than the faint sandalwood fragrance emanating from her neck and the swell of her breasts. He was sitting way too close. He couldn't remember when a woman had affected him so disturbingly. His runaway thoughts were causing an uncomfortable swelling in his jeans. *Do something, fella.* In the corner adjacent to the fireplace leaned his guitar. *Occupy your hands—and your mouth.*

"Ready for your Oklahoma music lesson?" He vaulted off the couch and removed the guitar from its case.

She clapped her hands. "A live performance?"

He sat cross-legged on the floor, the guitar hiding the evidence of his far from neighborly interest in her. He strummed a few chords. "Vince Gill, Reba McEntire and Garth Brooks are all Okies. Woody Guthrie was born in Oklahoma." He launched into "This Land Is Your Land."

Bathed in the flickering light of the flames, she sat motionless, rapt. At the chorus, she joined in with a light, lilting soprano.

Before he knew it, he'd taught her the words to "Cool Clear Water," "In the Oklahoma Hills Where I Was Born," and "Ragtime Cowboy Joe." Their voices rang louder and louder. Even Casey raised his head to howl in concert. Russ finally stood and laughingly set the guitar aside.

"Don't I get to learn 'Oklahoma'?"

"Next time. I promise."

She rose, facing him. "That was great! I'm sorry Janie and your mom missed all the fun."

He took hold of her arms, hearing the quick intake of her breath. He ran his hands up to her shoulders. "I'm not," he murmured shakily. They stood only inches apart, and he felt his control slipping away. The sudden onslaught of desire took him off guard.

Her small hands lay on his upper arms. "Neither am I, really." She gazed up at him with those dark liquid eyes. The air between them seemed charged. He smoothed one palm over the velvet of her hair, feeling it caress his flesh. She didn't move. Just kept looking at him. *What's a man to do?*

With his eyes never leaving hers, he lowered his face until her features blurred. His hands moved down over her shoulder blades. He sensed her hesitation, heard her tiny gasp. He pulled her to him, feeling her breasts flatten against his chest, and lowered his lips to cover hers, gently exploring. She didn't resist, nor did she advance. He reluctantly withdrew his lips, still tasting the faint wintergreen of her mouth, and tried to get hold of himself. Her trusting doelike expression undid him again. He found her lips, warm and responsive, and succumbed to the sensations coursing through his body. He could feel her relaxing against him as he unleashed into the kiss the ardor that had been gathering all evening.

When he pulled away, a quirky smile radiated from her mouth to the burning cinders of her eyes. "Does all this come with the welcome-to-Oklahoma lessons?"

He rubbed his fingers through his hair. "Almost as good as a Hawaiian aloha, huh?" He needed desperately to defuse this situation. The surge of emotions she'd elicited scared him. He wasn't accustomed to feeling out of control. This was no gal merely out for a good time. This was serious—and he needed to be responsible.

"I've never been to Hawaii." She looked demure, standing there dwarfed by the shadows flickering across the vaulted ceiling. She touched his hand. "Take me home now?"

"Sure." He went to the hall closet to get her windbreaker. Settling the jacket over her shoulders, it was all he could do to keep from wrapping his arms around her again.

She turned, her eyes luminous. "Russ, it's been a wonderful day. Thank you—" she winked "—podner."

"How about dinner and dancing Friday night?"

She appeared to be studying the proposition. "Russ, you don't have to, you know, just because of—" she nodded toward the living room "—what happened in there."

"I know I don't. I want to." As he said it, he knew he meant it.

Accompanied by the low, lovelorn sounds of a late-night country radio station, Russ felt quiet contentment as he drove Mary home. She offered the rare gift of silence—the kind that communicates more eloquently than words. It had been a good day and an even better evening.

On her porch, he paused, drinking in her soft expression. When he enfolded her in a protective hug, she snuggled against him and sighed. Then, as if a thought had just occurred to her, she raised her head. "Russ, what was it you said this afternoon about Buck Lloyd? About bad blood?"

Why had she brought that up? What a way to end the evening! "Let's just say there're long-standing bad feelings between the Lloyds and Coulters." He nuzzled her cheek and then released her. "I'll call you about next Friday."

She grabbed his arm. "Not so fast, Russ. You can't just say something like that and leave it. Besides, how could anyone not like the Coulters?"

"For Buck, it's easy." He shrugged. "It's nothing you need to be concerned with."

"I know I don't have to be concerned, but I do care about you—" she caught herself "—all of you, and—"

His voice softened and the flint left his eyes. "But you don't have to be burdened with ancient Ewing dirty linen." Couldn't she let it alone? Buck Lloyd was the last thing he wanted to talk about.

She opened the door, reached for his hand and drew him inside. "I live in Ewing now." She turned on the light. "And whatever the story, it won't be a burden." She led him to the sofa. "Anyway, you're my mentor. How can I trust you if you edit my education?" She freed his hand and sat down, pulling her knees up under her and folding her hands in her lap like an expectant pupil.

Russ laced his fingers and stretched both arms over his head, releasing them with a sigh. He didn't want to do this. Not tonight. But it wouldn't get any easier. Everyone else in town knew; she might as well hear it, too. "Okay, you win." He cleared his throat and took the plunge. "Buck Lloyd blames my father for the death of his daughter."

CHAPTER FIVE

IN A TYPICAL October flurry, stock market fluctuations kept Mary busy throughout the next week. She'd spent hours on the phone soothing concerned clients, several of whom were skeptical about having a new person—and a woman, at that—on their account. To add to the stress, she'd scheduled her first investment presentation for this afternoon at the Sooner Arms. She asked the receptionist to hold her calls, closed her office door and began rehearsing her remarks.

Halfway into the speech, she threw down the note cards. She'd never in her life done anything without careful preparation, but she was finding it next to impossible to concentrate. Why?

The truth? She sighed and gazed sightlessly out the window. Russ Coulter. She'd let him get way too close. Had the Todd Maples debacle taught her nothing? Any relationship with Russ would only add emotional baggage to her life and hinder her search, yet she found him nearly impossible to resist.

She recalled Russ's intense expression last weekend when he'd pointed to Buck Lloyd's fifteen hundred acres—the undisguised longing. "Fat chance," he'd said. Now she understood the futility in his voice. Incredible as it was, Buck Lloyd held a grudge. An unjustified one, based on Russ's version of the facts.

What he'd described had been an accident, pure and simple. How could Russ's dad, a young man himself, have prevented what happened? It wasn't his fault Ellie Lloyd got drunk at a Fourth of July party at the Coulter ranch. He had other guests. And when she suddenly decided to slip out to the barn, mount the stallion and go for a midnight ride, was J. T. Coulter supposed to have read her mind?

Mary shuddered as she recalled Russ's chilling words. "In the morning one of the hands found her. She was dead. Maybe the fireworks had spooked the horse. Whatever, she'd fallen or been thrown off and hit her head on a rock." Buck had needed a scapegoat, and he'd found one. Why had J.T. served so much alcohol, why hadn't he had someone take Ellie home, why hadn't he called Buck, why had he let her go to the barn?

Mary propped her elbows on the table, leaned over the desk and rubbed her forehead. She tried to imagine the drunken, confused young woman in the barn. With reckless abandon, Ellie had raced the stallion into the night. What had she been thinking? Feeling? A tragic story.

Mary shuffled the note cards in front of her. How bitter and vengeful Buck Lloyd must be. At least now she understood why he'd wanted nothing to do with the horse show.

She picked up her notes and got to her feet. Daydreaming wasn't getting the job done. She paced, delivering her speech and practicing her gestures. Better. She could do this.

THE SOCIAL DIRECTOR of Sooner Arms Retirement Community ushered Mary into the activities room and then excused herself. Mary glanced around. A peppermint-striped awning covered the snack bar, and floral country curtains enlivened the windows overlooking a small garden. Chairs with casters surrounded a speaker's podium. Near the door a bulletin board announced "Today is Friday, October 25. The weather is cool and sunny."

As Mary pulled a small table near the podium and spread out her materials, she heard the intercom. "Good afternoon, residents. In five minutes in the activities room, a representative from Wheatland Bank will present an estate planning seminar."

Mary positioned herself near the door to welcome the first resident, a thin, stooped woman with palsied hands and an acquisitive look in her eye, who identified herself as Bertha Mayhall and then said, "I'm surprised they'd send a woman." She sniffed indignantly but decided to stay.

A plump, grandmotherly lady introduced herself as Rose Farnsworth, sat down, pulled out a skein of yarn and began crocheting. She was trailed by Woody Higgins, who told Mary that although he didn't have a dime to invest, listening to her might "beat the hell outta settin' around watchin' that damn boob tube."

"Hot damn!" a tall, gaunt woman with thin flyaway henna hair uttered in a rasping, throaty voice. "'Bout time they sent a woman to talk business." With gnarled, arthritic fingers, she balanced herself on her walker. She nodded encouragingly. "Give 'em hell, honey. I'm Sal McClanahan. Never met a man who could get anything right."

Waiting directly behind Sal was a short, spry gentleman wearing maroon polyester pants, a wildly flowered Hawaiian shirt and a yellow polyester sport coat. He rubbed his hands together delightedly as he eyed Mary.

"Well, this is an unexpected pleasure. Mostly all we see around here are old people. You're already a hit, regardless of what you say." He extended a cool hand. "Chauncey Butterworth."

"I'm delighted, Mr. Butterworth."

"You single? Makes a man wish he were forty years younger." Chauncey winked, then strode to a chair right in front.

After several other residents took seats on the fringes, Mary walked to the podium. "Will more be coming?"

"Hell, no," Woody said. "The rest of 'em are too busy takin' naps or watchin' soap operas."

Chauncey joined in. "And some of us don't handle our checkbooks too well anymore, much less our investments."

Bertha gave Chauncey a disgusted sidelong glance. "Speak for yourself."

"Honey—" Sal waved her hand peremptorily "—just go ahead. Others may wander in and out—curious, you know. Just speak your piece."

Rose looked up expectantly, her fingers going like crazy with the crochet hook. Mary brushed back a lock of hair and nervously stacked her notes. It was difficult to tell who'd come as an alternative to boredom and who might be genuinely interested in the bank's services. She would just assume they all had millions lying around waiting to be invested and give them her best pitch. She smiled and began speaking slowly in a loud clear voice. "I'm sure you have all worked long and hard to achieve financial independence . . ."

Although one man dozed off after a few minutes, his snores providing a steady counterpoint to her remarks, the rest were attentive. Sal and Bertha, in particular, asked informed, pointed questions, which revealed an understanding of the market and tax implications. If these two already had funds invested elsewhere, it would take real salesmanship to convince them of Wheatland's advantages.

Chauncey Butterworth lingered after the others dispersed. "Mary Fleet, you're welcome here anytime. Would you give me the pleasure of your company for our Sunday brunch? It's turkey and dressing day. Food's not bad and I'd enjoy your pretty smile across the table."

Mary was touched. "I'd be honored, Mr. Butterworth."

"Call me Chauncey. I'll meet you in the lobby at 11:30. Don't be late. At mealtime, the troops line up like they're charging Bunker Hill."

"You've got yourself a date, Chauncey." Mary picked up her briefcase and followed the old gentleman down the hall to the elevator, pleased with her first presentation.

ON THE DRIVE HOME, even a traffic delay for the high school homecoming parade couldn't undermine the satisfaction Mary took in the day's work. On the contrary, the excitement generated by the marching band was contagious. She smiled to herself. Ewing—it already felt like home, like the place she belonged.

Her mood plummeted, though, when she arrived home and read her mail. Neither of the adoption registries she'd written had records of anyone attempting to locate a baby girl born on January 10, 1968. Although she'd expected this outcome, the reality hit like a stomach punch. Her remedy was an invigorating run, which, as usual, restored her equilibrium.

Now as dusk settled in, she peeled off her sweats and stood quietly for a few moments, contemplating this evening's date. Dinner and dancing. She started the water for her shower. Tonight she'd keep her wits about her—get a handle on her emotions. No way was she going to become another in Russ's string of conquests.

Stepping into the shower, Mary shivered as the warm water coursed over her body. She began shampooing her hair. No more embraces, no more kissing. Now *there* was danger. Danger in the curlicue of sandy hair on top of his head, in his skillful tapering fingers cradling the neck of the guitar, in his lips seeking hers, in the rapid escalation of her heartbeat—

Plunk. The shampoo bottle slipped to the tile floor. Fantasy was getting her nowhere, unless she counted the sweet urgency deep within her body. Toweling off, she reminded herself of Gwen's words. Russ wasn't easily "roped in," she'd said. Well, he'd have no worries on her account. She had set her priorities; a relationship, no matter how casual or fleeting, wasn't on the agenda.

Fine, then. So why are you standing in front of your lingerie drawer looking at the lacy bikinis and sheer chemise? Why not? She was the only one who'd see them, and besides, fine lingerie was her one clothing indulgence. She drew on the panties and pulled the soft chiffon chemise over her head.

Later, dressed in a simple but stunning black sheath, she tucked back the hair that always fell across her cheeks and put on onyx-and-pearl drop earrings. She switched on the porch light, then examined herself in the mirror. Not bad. Oh, for heaven's sake, who was she trying to impress? She glanced at the clock. He was ten minutes late. She fidgeted, straightening the already straight magazines and knickknacks. Fifteen minutes. Really. It was inconsiderate to keep others waiting. She peered out the window.

The ringing telephone shattered the quiet. "Hi, Mom.... I know. We haven't talked in several days.... At the bank? It's been a hectic week, but I love everything about it." She changed ears and listened to a recital of the Ladue Garden Club's latest fund-raising project. "Social life? Not much. I do have a date tonight, that is, if he ever shows up." Carrying the cordless phone, she walked to the front door to check. Nothing.

"Mother, is Dad there? I'd like to say hello." She waited for her father to come on the line. "Hi, Dad." She could hear weariness in his voice. "How are things with you?" His response was restrained, dispassionate. She'd hoped time would ease the emotional distance that had developed between them. Instead, she found it increasingly difficult to find neutral topics of conversation.

She heard a knock. "Wait a minute, Daddy."

She opened the door and clutched the phone to her chest. "Come in." She didn't know which irritated her more, Russ's lack of apology or the outlandish outfit he had on—black snakeskin boots, tight-fitting black jeans with a wide leather belt and huge silver buckle, a flamered cowboy shirt with black embroidery and a black cowboy hat with a beaded hatband. Hardly appropriate attire for a fancy hotel ballroom.

"Dad, are you still there?" Russ tossed his hat on the table and sprawled on the sofa, looking at her with amusement. What was so funny? "Sorry, what did you say?"

Her father's hollow voice echoed through the receiver. "I don't really want to talk about this," he was saying. "In fact, I'd vowed I wouldn't. But I'm making one last appeal. Mary, I want you to drop this cockamamy idea of searching for your birth parents. What's the point?"

"Dad—"

"Let me finish. *We* are your parents. What could you possibly want that we can't provide? Even if you *could* find them, they have no history with you. For whatever reasons, they gave you up. History, years of nurturing, love—that's parenting."

Mary pressed one arm to her stomach, trying to hold in the cramping pain provoked by his pleas. *Daddy, not now. Please understand.*

She racked her brain for the right words. "I don't mean to hurt you." She became aware that Russ had straightened up and was watching her with solicitude. Tears prickled the undersides of her eyelids. She turned her back to him. "Yes, I hear you, Dad. I can't explain it any more clearly than I already have."

"Then I guess what will be, will be." She heard dismissal in her father's voice.

"Please, Dad, it's not an option. I can't turn back." She heard his clipped "goodbye," and then the line went dead.

She clicked off the phone and stood there, shaken, a sob clogging her throat. She gulped and willed it back down. Trembling, she put the receiver in its cradle. She continued to stand, unmoving, her body rigid and tense.

Then she felt warm fingers gently kneading the bunched muscles between her shoulder blades and at the base of her bare neck. "Easy, Mary." Russ's deep baritone washed over her like soothing water. "Take some deep breaths."

She leaned into him and felt his strong arms encircle her. His chin rested on her head. "Wanna talk about it?"

He turned her around to face him, smoothing the hair from her forehead and seeking her brimming eyes.

His tenderness released her emotional turmoil. A sob seemed to split her open and she fell against him, tears dampening the front of his shirt. He held her, waiting, while the storm tore through her. *Daddy!* She wanted the Daddy she remembered—the man who scooped up his tiny daughter in a bear hug, soothed away the hurts and made the sun shine again.

Gradually, her tears subsided and she took deep breaths in an effort to regain control. "I—I'm sorry," she managed to whisper. She stepped back and swiped at her tearstained face. "I'm a mess." She started toward the bedroom. "I'll just be a minute."

Russ reached out, grabbed her by the elbow and pulled her over to the sofa. "Makeup isn't important." He put his arm around her. "I think maybe you need to talk."

She hiccupped and pushed a loose strand of hair behind her ear. He waited.

What could she say? Besides her mother and father, she'd never confided in anyone about her decision to look for her birth parents—except once. Todd Maples. And he hadn't understood at all; quite the contrary—not only had he tried to talk her out of it, he'd seemed almost embarrassed by the idea. The last thing she needed tonight was another sanctimonious speech about how selfish it was to cause her parents pain.

She sighed, rubbing her palms along her thighs, smoothing her dress. How could anyone who hadn't been adopted understand? Particularly someone with a made-to-order, all-American family like the Coulters? It was nobody's business but her own and she wouldn't inflict it on Russ. Nor would she open herself to his opinions on the matter.

She pulled away. "I'm really sorry, Russ. It's not a very happy start to our evening." She began to get up, but he restrained her.

"Whoa. I've had enough experience with Janie and Mom to know that if I ask what's wrong, you'll say 'nothing.'" He turned her face toward his so that she couldn't avert her gaze. "Mary, it's not 'nothing,' is it?" Concern filled his eyes.

She heaved another sigh and felt tears threatening her control. "No, it's not 'nothing.' But it needn't ruin our evening. I'm fine now, really." She tried to turn away, but instead felt her jaw cupped in his strong, warm hand and then she yielded to the gentleness of soft lips on hers. His other hand massaged the tender place at the nape of her neck. The sweetness of his kiss sent warm currents of comfort over the fragile hurts deep within. Then his arms went around her, crushing her to him. He withdrew his lips and planted tiny, deliberate kisses on her cheeks and temples. She felt his fingers comb through her hair in soothing, languorous strokes. As she snuggled into his warm chest, tension drained out of her, as if some lulling sedative had taken effect.

"Relax. We're not going anywhere just now," he whispered. She rested against him, aware only of the stillness inside her and the restorative power of his caresses.

Finally she reared back, seizing his hands. "Russ, I don't know what to say."

He smiled. "'Nothing'?"

"No, something." She stared down at their entwined fingers. Did she dare trust him? She looked up. The urge to speak gathered momentum under the intensity of his sympathetic response. "That was my father on the phone."

"Sounds like you two are at odds over some decision you've made."

She disengaged her hands and rose to her feet. "That's putting it mildly." She crossed to the far wall, straightening an already level print. "It's something I have to work out on my own."

He stood up, walked over to her and put his hands on her shoulders, pressing his forehead against hers. "You're mighty tiny and these shoulders—" he gave them a gentle squeeze "—aren't very broad. It might help to talk about it. I can be a very understanding, close-mouthed guy when necessary."

She laid her palms on his chest. The pain was too great. She *did* need to talk. "But what about the dancing?"

He led her back to the sofa. "Dancing can wait. Hurt can't. And you're hurting."

She curled up in one corner. He lounged at the other end. "I didn't even know myself how badly." She hugged herself. Then the words popped out. "I'm adopted."

"So?"

"So...so many things." The avalanche of words broke. "So I don't know who I am. Oh, I *know* who part of me is, but not the whole me. That's hard for Dad and Mom to understand, especially Daddy. They think they've given me everything—and they have. Everything within their power to give. And I wish it was enough. But it just isn't. They can't give me answers." She could feel the icicles of tension pricking her skin. She shuddered.

Russ sat quietly, his eyes signaling encouragement.

"It's like I'm—I don't know, different. As if I'm the missing piece in some cosmic jigsaw puzzle. Look at me." She gestured to her face. "Not one of the Fleets has brown eyes or dark skin or black hair. Strangers used to stop my parents and say, 'Why, that little girl doesn't look like she could be your daughter.' Sometimes they were even crueler. 'So look what the milkman brought to your house.' Do you have any idea how that made me feel?''

"Pretty crummy, I imagine."

"I need to know my roots, my genetic heritage. Not knowing—it's like some ravenous animal gnawing at me from the inside. For years I've tried to ignore the pain, but I can't anymore. I have this uncanny sense, I can't explain it, that if I just knew something, anything, about my birth parents, this out-of-focus dream I'm living would suddenly become clear."

He moved to the center of the sofa, placing his arm along the back, not touching her. "And the decision you mentioned on the telephone—the one that's 'not an option'...?"

"Is to find my biological parents. I know, I know—" she held up her palms to ward off objections "—it's a dangerous path for everyone. I've already caused Mom and Dad unhappiness, and even if I'm successful, I run the risk of creating a problem for whoever I find." She leaned forward. "But I've got to do it. Even if what I find is unpleasant, even if there's no chance of a reunion, I'll be more at peace than I am now."

His hand dropped to her shoulder. "What about you? What are *you* risking? Happiness? Rejection? What if you never discover any answers? Can you accept that? Can you be satisfied with yourself?"

Big questions. The same ones she'd been over hundreds of times. "I try not to think about failing. And I know I'm already so blessed in the family and friends I have." She wrinkled her brow. "Let me explain. It's like I'm chained to this big heavy anchor that's mired in the past and it just keeps tugging on me. And as long as it's tugging on me, I can't move forward. I can't move on."

He trailed a forefinger across her cheek. "How can I help?"

"You already have, just by listening." She glanced at her watch. "Our date! You must be starving."

"No problem. Let's just order some pizza, turn on the radio, and do some boot-scootin'."

"Boot-scootin'?"

He jumped up, retrieved his cowboy hat from the table, cocked it back on his head and grinned. "Country dancin', ma'am. Two-stepping, like this." Lustily singing "Two of a Kind," he helped her to her feet and sawed and dipped her around the room until she was breathless.

"Russ," she panted. "Stop!" She put both hands on her hips as recognition dawned. "Dancing. Country dancing? That's what was so funny."

"Funny?"

"When you came to pick me up. I'd worked all evening to make myself presentable. You might've mentioned you were taking me to a *saloon.*"

"I wouldn't exactly call the Red Dirt Café a saloon."

"I was supposed to wear cowboy clothes?"

"Begging your pardon, ma'am, cow*girl* clothes."

She began to chuckle. "Frankly, Tex, I thought you were dressed for a Halloween costume ball."

He laughed and then ran his hands over her back. She could feel the chiffon chemise riding up and down with his caresses. "Presentable? Oh, baby, you're more than presentable. You're about to drive this cowboy wild." He drew her to him, lifting her off the floor. She grabbed his cowboy hat just as his lips crushed hers in a kiss ripe with passion. She dropped the hat and clutched him around the neck, drowning in the comfort of his taut, lean body.

As he set her back down, his hands traced the curve of her hip, loitered at her waist and hesitated when he brushed the underside of her breasts, straining against the sheer chemise. Mary took a deep shuddering breath. Sweet God. What was happening?

She framed his face in her hands and, like a magnet wrenched from its mate, reluctantly withdrew her lips from his. Her voice was husky. "The pizza?"

He stole another kiss. "Pizza?"

Her knees were trembling. "I think it's a good idea."

He scooped up his cowboy hat. "You win." With elaborate ceremony, he placed it on her head. "But after that, we're gonna crank up the radio and do some country dancin'—right here."

TENTATIVE, MARY WAITED in the foyer of Sooner Arms the following Sunday morning, pulling her red wool sweater-vest down over her plaid box-pleat skirt. Like so many birds on a wire, several gray-haired dowagers perched on the chairs at the entrance of the dining room. Across the lobby Rose Farnsworth smiled and waved.

Behind Mary, Chauncey Butterworth emerged from the elevator. "There you are. Right on time."

Mary stifled a chuckle. Chauncey's kelly-green plaid slacks warred with his avocado-hued sport coat. "I didn't want to miss the meal. I've been looking forward to it."

Just then the doors opened and the residents surged forward. Chauncey escorted her into the cheerfully appointed dining room and gestured toward a window alcove. "That's our table."

"May we join you?" Sal McClanahan, vermilion hair flying, and Woody Higgins, a plaid flannel shirt tucked into high-water gray pants, stood looking eagerly at Chauncey.

"I'd hoped to have this sweet young thing all to my-self, but guess I shouldn't hoard the wealth." Chauncey puffed up like a peacock. "Sit down."

Mary smiled at each as they carefully maneuvered into the padded chairs. "I'm glad to see you both again."

"Honey, believe me—" Sal rolled her eyes balefully around the dining room "—the pleasure's all ours. Chauncey had a damn fine idea, inviting you. Hope the saltpeter in the mashed potatoes doesn't shortchange your fun."

"Sal, the very idea!" Chauncey covered Mary's hand with his and murmured to her, "Sal's pretty outspo-ken."

"That ain't the half of it," Woody hooted. "Never met such an opinionated woman in my whole life."

Sal sniffed. "Damn sight better than these dehydrated Southern belles around here who'll do anything to get a man's attention. Their conversation's about as interest-ing as listening to someone read the phone directory. No sir." She unfolded her napkin and placed it in her lap with a flourish. "I had me my man. Sure as hell don't need another. One good man is more than most women get."

The turkey and dressing were tasty, though blandly seasoned, and the green beans were overcooked, but the pumpkin pie was delicious and clearly a hit with Woody, who licked his fork of the very last crumb. Chauncey, with help from the others, entertained Mary with a run-ning commentary on the history of Ewing from its be-ginnings as a railroad town in the Indian Territory, to the discovery of oil and the boom era. Fluctuating eco-nomic conditions, they explained, resulted from Ew-ing's being a company town, dependent upon the ups and downs of the Emerson Oil Company.

"Times were a lot tougher for those of us out in the Oklahoma Panhandle, I can tell you. Like trying to scratch a living out of the desert," Sal said. "You boys sittin' up in those office buildings playin' geologist don't know the half of it."

"Whaddya mean *sittin'?*" Woody objected. "I was a driller. Damn hard work."

"Regardless, I'm glad I lived when I did," Chauncey said. "The oil business isn't half as exciting these days. About the most fun I have now is serving on the social committee here." He looked at the others. "Got any bright ideas for entertainment?"

"Some male strippers oughta liven up the joint." Sal laughed raucously at her own remark. Mary giggled.

"No, I'm serious."

Woody drummed his fingers on the table. "I don't have any suggestions, but I sure as hell can tell you what I *don't* want."

"What's that?" Chauncey asked.

"No more goddamn champagne music. If I hear Lawrence Welk one more time, I swear I'll puke." He shook his head in disgust.

Sal flapped a hand in his direction. "Why, Mr. Higgins, you'll disappoint all the sweet old ladies here."

"Ask me if I care. What about us cantankerous old men? 'Bout time we had poker and cowboy music instead of bingo and golden oldies."

Chauncey considered Woody's remark. "Why not?" He straightened up, a smile playing around his mouth, and turned to Woody. "Know any good banjo pickers?"

"Used to. All dead now."

The glimmer of an idea teased Mary's brain. "What kind of music?" she asked.

Woody elaborated. "Doesn't hafta be great—just cowboy tunes. You know, Eddy Arnold, Sons of the Pioneers, that kinda stuff."

It wouldn't hurt to try. The worst Russ could do was turn her down. "I might know somebody..." she began.

Woody interrupted. "Hell, get 'em over here. I'm dyin' of boredom."

Chauncey smiled warmly. "I knew there was more than one good reason to invite you to brunch. Could you check on your entertainer and let me know?"

Mary put her arm around his shoulders. "I certainly will." She leaned over and kissed him on the cheek. "Thank you for the lovely meal." She glanced at the other two. "And for your company. You've made me feel very welcome."

Sal eased to her feet, and Mary jumped up to position the walker for her. The scrappy old woman nodded approvingly. "I like you. You come back and visit us, hear? We don't get to see many young people. Does us a world of good."

Unexpected tears swam in Mary's eyes. "You can count on it." She supported Sal as the two began walking slowly toward the door, the men following along. At that moment Mary didn't care if she generated any bank business at Sooner Arms. These were, first of all, people she was beginning to care about and only incidentally potential clients. She'd talk to Russ soon. Surely he wouldn't refuse. She'd appeal to his pride. It was no small feat to outrank Lawrence Welk in a retirement center!

SAL McCLANAHAN carefully poured a cupful of sunflower seeds into the metal bird feeder and hung it back on the railing of her apartment balcony. She balanced against the sliding glass door and gazed out over downtown Ewing. Though the day was mild, leaves on the dogwood trees lining the avenue were deepening to wine red. In the distance she could see the pots of brilliant yellow chrysanthemums arranged at the four corners of the Emerson Plaza. She sniffed the mellow breeze of Indian summer. Yep, she'd made the right decision, returning after all these years.

Folks thought her brother, the only family she had, was the main reason she'd come back. Somebody to take care of her in her—what the hell was that expression?—*declining years*. Well, they had another think coming. She'd managed by herself for a good long spell out in the Panhandle after she was widowed. She had friends galore there, so one ornery brother wasn't any reason to come back. More likely she'd end up taking care of him.

No, there were other reasons. When you got right down to it, her roots were in Ewing. She'd missed the vegetation, the names familiar from long ago, the cultural advantages. Wasn't necessarily a mark of second childhood to want to come home. She snorted. Second childhood! Not if she could help it.

She steadied herself with the walker and turned to go into the apartment. A flash of red caught her eye in the parking lot below. She peered down. Mary Fleet. Sal chuckled. She liked that young woman. Reminded her of somebody, but darned if she could think who. The gal had spunk. Not only that, face it, she had compassion. Sal could spot a phony at fifty yards. No doubt Mary would like to get some senior citizen accounts, but today she'd proved she was as interested in people as she was in the bottom line.

Sal crossed the threshold but left the door slightly ajar. Now, where was that TV remote thingamajig? She didn't want to miss the Cowboys-Redskins game.

MARY PEERED AT the computer terminal. Another blue Monday for the stock market. The St. Louis office didn't seem too concerned, although even small changes in the Dow-Jones worried some clients, who'd bombarded her with calls throughout the day. She'd just hung up when the phone rang again.

"Good afternoon, Mary Fleet speaking.... Oh, hi, Chauncey." She swiveled in her chair to look out the window at the American flag flapping in the gusty wind. Chauncey was all business—entertainment committee business. "Yes, I did. He agreed to come play and sing but warns you not to expect too much."

Talk about understatement. Russ couldn't believe she'd suggested him and she'd had to do some real persuading. But after his razzing about country dancing, she figured he owed her one. Reluctantly, he'd told her to set it up.

"The first Saturday in November? Okay. What time? Three for the performance, four for a reception and five for supper?" Russ was going to love this—a lively Saturday with the geriatric set. She grinned. If he had his hands full *now* with all his women, just wait until the Sooner Arms vixens saw him! "Thanks for calling, Chauncey. We're looking forward to it, too." She twirled back around, hung up the receiver and sat staring into space.

Russ. What to make of Friday night? More confusion, much of it self-induced. What could've been a lighthearted evening out—albeit peculiar had they actually gone to the Red Dirt Café—had turned into a confessional. Then she'd started crying, and all Russ could do was try to put her back together.

So where did that leave them? Darned if she knew. The only thing she *did* know was she should never have let him soothe her. She'd been entirely too comfortable, too willing, too... aroused. What was it about the man? All the warning signs in the world couldn't keep her from succumbing to him. He'd disarmed her, pure and simple. Rubbing her back, he'd seemed sensitive, empathetic—hardly a Casanova.

She picked up her pen, idly tapping it on her desk. Why had she blurted that out about her adoption? About her search? She'd steeled herself not to confide. This was personal—her need, her journey, her identity. Daddy. God, his lack of understanding hurt. She couldn't have stopped those tears no matter who'd been with her. Maybe the price *was* too high. She couldn't bear the indifference in her father's voice, the chasm between them. Her pen clattered onto the desk. She glanced guiltily out her doorway; so new on the job, she didn't need to be caught woolgathering. She flipped through her address file and reached for the phone.

Four calls later, she gratefully hung up and applied herself to her correspondence, fingers flying over the keyboard. Late in the afternoon, Gwen stuck her head in the door. "You have plans for Saturday?"

Mary looked up. "What do you have in mind?"

"Ted's taking the kids to Tulsa for the circus. I've got some shopping to do. I thought maybe you and I could do lunch, as they say in the big city, and put smiles on the faces of Ewing's merchants. Sound good?"

"It sounds great. I need to get some things myself."

"Anything in particular?"

"Besides makeup and panty hose?" She wrinkled her brow. Then a sudden idea, accompanied by a rush of daring, swept over her. She smiled mysteriously. "Maybe. I'll think about it between now and Saturday."

CHAPTER SIX

THE RELENTLESS KEENING wind that rattled the storm door of her condo the following Saturday morning punctuated Mary's thoughts. She was reviewing the status of the search for her birth parents and making notes. Unless she physically confronted Dr. Altmuller in Denver, she saw no hope of gaining his cooperation. He was still practicing, but his office staff and answering service had referred all queries to him. She wrote a question mark next to his name. She'd had no response to her Internet request for information about a female born in University Hospital, Denver, on January 10, 1968. Another question mark.

The judge? The court? Her parents must have a record of the attorneys involved. She laid down the pencil and rested her chin on her folded hands. She could imagine her father's response to such questions. His whole attitude toward this business continued to puzzle her. He wasn't a person prone to overreaction. He'd surely anticipated that one day she'd become curious. Against her own judgment, her mother had risked more than she'd really wanted to by giving her the necklace. Mary's stomach felt hollow. Turning to her parents for help was a last resort, a desperate one. If only she could key in on the clue, something buried in the fear she'd seen pass like a current between her mother and father.

Cupping the pendant in her palm, Mary lowered her head to study the strange writing. Her perusal of a large unabridged dictionary had eliminated Hebrew, Arabic, Greek, Russian and even Sanskrit as explanations for the mysterious symbols. She fingered the smooth stone at the end of the chain. Again she felt that eerie rush of connection . . . to what? To whom?

She shook her head to clear the vision and let her mind drift to seeing Russ later this afternoon, to the reception and supper at Sooner Arms, and then—to the serious conversation she intended to have with him. Better to slow things down, permit them both some space.

She heard a car stop in front of her condo. Was it Gwen already? She checked her watch. She'd definitely lost track of time. Above the whine of the wind, she could make out the sound of a faint knock. On the porch, long chestnut hair blowing, stood Gwen. ''Welcome to Oklahoma,'' Gwen said as she ducked inside. ''About ready to go?''

''Just let me get this stuff put away.'' Mary began frantically gathering the scattered books and papers, furious with herself because her adoption materials were in full view. When Gwen started to help, Mary quickly reached for the stack she was holding. But the look on Gwen's face stopped her.

''Mary, I couldn't help noticing—''

Mary grabbed the papers, her face reddening. ''Gwen, I don't really want—''

''—to talk about it?'' Gwen gently placed an arm around Mary's shoulder and led her to one of the chairs, taking a seat opposite her. ''Please understand I'm not trying to pry. I have a reason for asking.''

Mary clutched the paperwork. She hadn't intended to involve Russ and certainly not Gwen.

"There's no tactful way to ask. Are you adopted?"

Mary raised her eyes and answered quietly. "Yes."

Gwen held up the adoption search pamphlet. "And you're trying to locate your birth parents?" Mary bit her lower lip and nodded. "You know, this is a subject I've thought an awful lot about."

Mary looked up quizzically. "Oh?"

"It's no secret, but I've had no reason to tell you before. Jeremy's adopted."

"And Jenny?"

"One of those situations that sometimes happens. Ted and I had difficulty getting pregnant, so we adopted Jeremy. Then, shortly after, I became pregnant with Jenny." She smiled at Mary. "Each child is unique, a special joy."

"Does Jeremy know?"

"Oh, yes."

Mary considered her next question. "How does he feel about Jenny? You know, resentment? Or like she's treated with preference?"

"Jeremy was so excited to have a baby sister. I think he knows Ted and I love him every bit as much as we do Jenny."

"From my limited exposure, I'd say you're doing a good job as parents. They're great kids."

"Thanks. We think so, too."

Mary released her tense grip on the stack of papers and took a deep breath. "What would you do if someday Jeremy decided to look for his birth parents?"

Gwen smiled sympathetically. "That's a distinct possibility. Ted and I have tried to anticipate it so that if it happens, we'll be in a position to be supportive."

"How would it make you feel?"

"Depends. I thank God every day for the woman who gave life to our son. If finding her would help him, complete him, I'd want that for him." Her large hazel eyes darkened. "But there are some ugly scenarios, as well. You've probably thought of that, too. Abusive relationships, rape, drugs. The mothers can't all be pretty high school girls who make one mistake and find themselves pregnant. I'd hate to see my son hurt."

Mary tapped her fingers on the table. Finally she said, "I know. I'm wrestling with that right now. My parents want me to give up looking. They're very reluctant, as if they're afraid of what I might discover."

"That's natural. And you? How do you feel?"

"Scared, but also determined. Nobody understands why I'm driven to do this when it might hurt my parents, hurt me."

"And?"

Mary looked at Gwen. "Maybe I never really had a choice. From the time I was small, I've always known I was different, that I had a made-to-order history given to me by my adoptive parents. That somewhere out there was someone who belonged to me. To whom I belonged." She paused. "I've always been curious, but for so long I tried to convince myself that the present and future were more important than the past. More and more I feel a...powerful *need* to know the past. And with all the stories on television about reunions, about birth mothers who want to meet infants they gave up for adoption, about...successes, I realized it was possible, even likely, I could unlock my own secrets."

She felt the enormous relief of expressing pent-up thoughts. "I saw this panel once on one of the talk shows. About adoptees. I couldn't get over how similar their stories were to each other's—and to mine. I'd always thought nobody felt like I did. Suddenly, here were four people sharing their innermost thoughts about being adopted, about feeling different, about the... compulsion to find answers. Gwen, any one of them could've been me." She patted the papers stacked in front of her. "Once I knew that, there was no turning back."

"Even if your scenario turns out badly?"

"I'm prepared for that, I think. No matter what, I'm committed." She faltered. "Unless..."

"Unless?"

"Unless I'm risking my parents' love."

"Your adoptive parents?"

Mary nodded. "My father's, in particular."

Gwen folded her hands over Mary's. "It's a balancing act, all right. On the one hand, there are *your* needs—both to preserve the relationships you have and to explore new ones. On the other hand, you can't ignore your parents' needs. God, I don't envy you. My advice—" she squeezed Mary's hands "—is to take it slow and easy." She smiled. "And to remember you've got a friend along the way."

Mary's fingers strayed to her chest, toying with the smooth stone suspended there. She found Gwen's empathetic eyes and felt a rush of affection. "Thank you. I think I'm going to need one."

Gwen nodded. "Anytime. Now, whaddya say? Ready to shop till you drop? Where shall we start?"

"Well..." With Gwen to bolster her resolve, Mary reached a decision. "Is there a Western store in Ewing?"

Gwen's eyebrows arched in surprise. "Yes, but why?"

Mary smiled. "I'm feeling so at home here I think, on occasion, I may want to dress like a native—boots, hat, the whole nine yards."

Recognition dawned on Gwen's face. "Why do I have the distinct impression Russ is behind this sudden urge?"

Faking a look of innocence, Mary shrugged. "I can't imagine."

RUSS CAREFULLY LAID the guitar case in the bed of his pickup and drove toward town. He must've taken leave of his ever-lovin' senses. It was one thing to strum for relaxation, quite another to perform. He tuned in a Tulsa C-and-W station and tried to forget how foolish he was going to feel. How in hell had he let Mary talk him into this?

Usually, with women, especially after ol' Janna had punted him, he'd have a good time, make his pleasant adieus and never give 'em another thought. Whooee! Mary was different. He remembered the other night— those deep teary eyes, like dark pebbles awash in spring water.

He cracked the window and let the cool autumn air fan his face. That adoption business was really eating at her. She'd made no attempt to minimize the issue or her pain. Damn, didn't she see she could get hurt? That there was a fifty-fifty chance whoever had given her up had, for all intents and purposes, abandoned her? That what she pictured as a joyous reunion could just as easily be self-destructive rejection? That who she was right now was plenty good enough?

Listen to yourself. You're getting involved. He'd guarded against this day, against being sucked into another relationship. The day he'd have to consider the future. It was hard to break the old patterns of distrust. Abandonment? He knew all about it. He'd insulated himself pretty successfully. Did he dare let Mary through his carefully constructed barriers? What in damnation was he thinking? His emotional reaction to Mary confused the hell out of him.

A woman who arranged her spices in alphabetical order!

Later, standing in front of the gathered residents, Russ adjusted the strap of his guitar and rolled his eyes at Mary, seated between a thin, red-haired woman and a plump grandmotherly type. The audience, prompt and expectant, filled the hush with titters, coughs and throat clearings. Chauncey Butterworth bustled officiously, first assisting a berouged lady to a seat near the front, now tapping the microphone repeatedly. "Testing, testing." He glanced at the notes in his shaky hand. "We have a real treat in store today. Thanks to Mary Fleet from Wheatland Bank—stand up, Mary, take a bow—" Mary rose blushingly and smiled at the audience "—we have with us a local boy—used to play golf with this whippersnapper's grandfather—who's gonna perform us a little Western music on that 'gittar.'" He smiled with satisfaction. "So let's give a big Sooner Arms welcome to Mr. Russ Coulter."

Polite applause greeted Russ as he straddled a stool and adjusted the mike. Glancing in Mary's direction, he noticed that the red-haired woman next to her had straightened up and was looking at him intently.

"I'm glad to be here today, but before I sing, I need to set you straight. I'm not a professional performer. I just grew up strummin' and hummin' some of the old cowboy tunes. I'll do my best and I hope you'll join in." He played a lead-in and began with "The Streets of Laredo."

Going through his repertoire, Russ found himself surprisingly touched by the response. An expressionless bald gentleman in a wheelchair tapped a slippered foot, one

lady raised her arthritic fingers to play an imaginary piano, and an off-key soprano unfailingly joined in the
chorus. Mary's smiles were encouraging. He relaxed and
let the music take him. For the finale, he launched into
"Home on the Range" and was gratified when everyone
chimed in.

Chauncey insisted he take a bow and sing "The Blue-
Tailed Fly" as an encore. He'd barely replaced the gui-
tar in its case when Chauncey introduced him to Woody
Higgins.

"Wait a minute." Russ grinned. "You're not—" he
racked his brain "—the Woody Higgins who used to
judge the amateur rodeos at the fairgrounds?"

"Hell, yes. That's me." Woody clapped a hand on
Russ's shoulder. "I remember you. Most damn fearless
young saddle bronc rider I ever saw. Thought you might
go professional."

"I considered it, but Dad suggested a college degree
might be more productive."

Chauncey took Russ by the elbow. "You two can talk
later. It's time for the reception." He led him to a small
group standing with Mary. "Russ, meet Rose Farnsworth—" the plump lady smiled "—and Sal Mc-
Clanahan."

The gaunt red-haired lady seized Russ's arm. "Glad to
meetcha. Damn fine singing. Woke up these fossils
around here."

"I was nervous to begin with, but I enjoyed myself after I got started." Russ looked around at the nearly empty
room. "I thought there was a reception."

Chauncey Butterworth chuckled. "Oh, there is, there
is. Just a very small one."

Sal's grip tightened on Russ's sleeve. In a hoarse
whisper she said, "Reception's just a—whaddya call

it?—euphemism. Can't be too careful around this place. Some folks don't approve." She glanced around surreptitiously and turned back to him. "We're going up to my place for a little knock."

"A knock?"

"Sure, you know. A knock." She rapped her fist on the wooden chair arm three times. "Only way a bootlegger'd open the door. Drinks're on me. Come on." Mary unfolded Sal's walker and Sal led the way down the hall to the elevator.

Laid out on the sideboard were a cut-glass plate loaded with pimento-cheese finger sandwiches, a bonbon dish of chocolate-covered almonds and a relish tray of carrot sticks and limp celery. In the kitchenette, Chauncey presided as bartender. Sal held court from her tapestry-covered wing chair, Rose and Woody settled on the stiff sofa, and Russ and Mary sat on two dining room chairs carefully positioned by the sliding glass doors leading onto the tiny balcony.

Russ felt as if he were in a museum display depicting "Living Room, circa 1950." All the place lacked was the braided velvet cord across the door. He balanced a flowered china plate of food with one hand and held his highball in the other. He'd kill for a beer, but that hadn't been an option. Chauncey arranged a tole-painted metal TV tray in front of him. "Set your food down there." Russ hadn't seen a tray like that since his Boy Scout troop's garage sale.

Rose Farnsworth smiled at Russ. "It's such a pleasure to have a young man come visit." She leaned over to pat Mary's hand. "Of course, we love seeing Mary, too. But you're a real treat."

Woody laughed. "Hell, boy, you're already a regular sex symbol around here. Kinda like that guy Fabio."

Russ took a gulp of the bourbon and seven. It tasted like carbonated cough syrup. "As John Wayne would say, Aw, shucks." He caught Mary's laughing eyes. "I reckon the ladies might be robbin' the cradle a bit, though."

Sal guffawed. "Nothin' some of us like better than a young stud."

Russ was surprised to see Mary blush. But then this kind of talk wasn't what a St. Louis deb was accustomed to. The chatter spun on around him and he occupied himself by looking at the photographs exhibited on the nearby shelf. A much younger Sal in a thirties-style dress and buckled heels. Sal and a tall man posed in front of a frame farmhouse. Sal, in full Western regalia, mounted on a big palomino.

He overheard snatches of conversation. Mary telling someone about her visit to another retirement center, Woody and Chauncey discussing the Oklahoma University football team and Sal recalling for Rose her days as a rancher's wife in the Oklahoma Panhandle near Guymon. Tough country. No wonder Sal was such a salty old gal.

Rose Farnsworth excused herself to make a phone call before supper. Sal motioned Russ to move his chair closer to her, out of earshot of the others. "I like you, young fella." She studied his face. "You remind me of your father when he was a boy. Same rascally gleam in the eye."

"You knew my father? I thought you lived in the Panhandle." He'd never heard his father mention her.

"I lived in the Panhandle from 1933 until just a year ago when I moved back. But I'm a Ewing girl originally. Visited here a lot." She placed a bony hand on his forearm. "You don't know who I am, do you?"

"No, ma'am. I'm sorry, but I don't."

"Not surprising." She looked him straight in the eye. "I'm Buck Lloyd's sister."

"Oh." Russ felt like an insect caught on flypaper. He didn't know what to say.

"I know all about the Coulters. And lemme tell you, son—" her faded blue eyes gleamed with conviction "—just because my brother chooses to be a horse's ass doesn't mean I follow suit." She lowered her voice. "It was an accident, son. An accident. Your father's a good man."

He swallowed and covered her wrinkled hand with his. "Thank you. I appreciate your saying so."

Chauncey rose. "Supper time, everyone. Best get ourselves down there. Coming, Mary? Russ?"

Russ stood, gathering up his plate and glass. Mary set her plate in the sink and then leaned over Sal's chair to offer help with the dishes.

Russ couldn't avoid noticing how the neckline of Mary's V-neck sweater parted, revealing smooth tawny skin and the swell of her small breasts above the lacy top of her ivory bra. Not a sight to turn away from easily.

When Mary straightened up, Sal stayed her, touching her arm. "Wait." Sal reached out and palmed the stone hanging at the end of Mary's necklace. "Unusual," she murmured.

"It was a gift from my mother." Mary hurried off to retrieve Sal's walker.

Russ watched. Sal, her face drained of color, stared after Mary. She placed a faltering veined hand over her heart and took several deep breaths. Then she gave a dazed shake of her frowsy red head and struggled to her feet before Russ could assist her.

"MY GOD, I'm starving!" Russ wheeled into a fast-food restaurant near the Sooner Arms. "The creamed potatoes tasted like library paste and the fish portion—hell, it was bait-size. What do you want?"

Mary, too, had found the retirement center supper less than filling. "A juicy hamburger and fries."

Russ leaned out the window to give the order. Now that the concert and dinner were over, Mary knew she had to clear the air with him. Maybe she'd do better on a full stomach. "You have to admit the pineapple upside-down cake wasn't bad."

"Easy for you to say. You got the piece with the cherry on top." He pulled up to the service window, paid and handed Mary the brown paper sack. "Give me a couple of fries to tide me over."

He munched ravenously during the short drive to Mary's condominium. Between bites he turned to her. "Can you beat that?"

"What?"

"Bodacious ol' Sal is Buck Lloyd's sister."

"Nice Sal? You're kidding!"

Russ grinned and shook his head. "Nope. She told me herself. Who'd have figured?"

Once inside the condo, Mary poured glasses of Coke to accompany the burgers, and they quickly devoured the meal. Russ patted his stomach. "That's *much* better."

Mary picked up the sponge to wipe off the countertop. "Russ, I'm glad you agreed to come today. You gave them such pleasure."

He balled up the trash and threw it away. Then he took a couple of steps toward her, spanning her waist with his hands. "You give them pleasure, Mary. Just looking at you." She felt the betrayal of her thumping heart as she looked up into his eyes. "I like looking at you, too," he whispered. "But I like this better." Before she could stop him, he pulled her body into his and kissed her deeply, sensuously. One hand cradled the back of her head and she was dimly aware of the other splayed across her lower back.

For a moment she yielded to the urgency in her own body, standing on tiptoes to taste more fully the sweetness of his mouth, soft yet insistent. Then she reached into her head for a shred of common sense. Gradually she drew away from him. "Russ, I...we need to talk."

"Mind if I shed my boots then?" He sprawled on the sofa, yanked them off and patted the place beside him. "Come here." He turned the lamp to the lowest setting.

As if drawn by an invisible lasso, she found herself curling up next to him. He propped his sock-clad feet on the coffee table and spread both arms across the back of the sofa.

Her mind raced. She had to get this over with. He was becoming uncomfortably important to her. It had to stop—here and now. She'd tried to rationalize that she was reading too much into their relationship. That his interest was casual, that she was just another in a long line of women. But she could no longer ignore the impact of his kisses. She pulled her knees up to her chest, circling her legs with her arms, her body language mirroring her tension.

She glanced sideways. He was waiting. He draped an arm over her shoulders and nestled her closer. This was dangerous. She breathed in a hint of spicy after-shave and, turning slightly, could see the faint sprinkling of freckles high on his cheeks beneath his tan. He raised his hand from her shoulder and brushed his forefinger across her cheek. How could so small a gesture send shivers of delight so deep?

Mind over body. She retreated to the corner of the sofa, clutching a throw pillow in her arms. Safety. Reason. Logic. Mantras to prepare her for what she needed to say.

The silence was unnerving. He shifted, putting one leg on the floor and bending the other up on the sofa. He looked at her. She could hear the steady hum of the traffic passing by on the street.

"You've been awfully quiet tonight," he observed.

"I know." She hugged the pillow tighter.

He stroked the wayward lock of hair falling across her cheek. "So...let's talk."

She forced out the words. "Russ, I've been doing a lot of thinking and—"

"Thinking can be detrimental to your health."

"So can *not* thinking, just drifting along."

He wound the strand of hair around his finger. "You're too serious. Try loosening up and letting the flow carry you."

Like butterfly wings, his hand kept tracing her cheek. "I just can't." She tensed. "As you've pointed out, I'm a very orderly person. I need to have life organized, to feel in control."

"And I threaten your control?" His solemn gray eyes were flecked with hazel pinpoints.

"Sometimes." She was flustered. "Maybe I'm over-reacting. I had this speech all thought out, and now—"

"What speech?" His eyes narrowed.

"The one about how I need to stop seeing so much of you and about how I'm not ready to be involved. I can't handle it right now." The words tumbled out into the silence.

"Wanna run that by me again?" Russ dropped his hand from her hair to the back of the sofa. "What's happening that's so bad?"

"Nothing yet. And it's not going to. I'm still adjusting to a new place, a new job. For whatever it's worth, just before I left St. Louis, I broke off a serious relationship. It's not a good time for me to be juggling a social life on top of everything else."

"You can't be business twenty-four hours a day."

"Maybe not, but I have so much on my mind. I don't need more assaults on my emotions."

"And that's what I do to you?" A warm gleam surfaced in his eyes.

She looked down. "Yes. Maybe I'm reading too much into things. Anyway, I'm vulnerable right now."

The gleam faded. "You think I'd hurt you?"

"It's possible. You know, love-'em-and-leave-'em Coulter. Even Janie says you've earned your reputation."

He stretched both arms over his head. "Hmm . . . my vastly overrated reputation."

She leaned forward, intent on making him understand. "Russ, I like you and I enjoy being friends. But that's all. You don't want entanglements, and I don't need any."

He rolled his eyes to the ceiling, as if considering the matter. Then, like a whiplash, he turned and took her into his arms, pinning her head with his hand and kissing her with expertise. She lost her balance and fell against him. With his other hand he pulled her toward his outstretched body. She couldn't breathe. When he found her tongue, sparks ignited in her head. Good God, she was kissing him back, reveling in the pressure of his lips, the probing of his tongue, the feel of his warm hand slithering under her sweater to caress the bare skin of her back. Control? She didn't know the meaning of the word.

He lifted his head to stare at her intently. "It's too late."

She was drowning in his loving eyes. "Too late for what?" she managed.

"Too late for 'just friends.'" And he kissed her again, this time gently, sweetly, triggering a release in her body as if someone had poured soothing oil on all the tense places. His hand rubbed small circles on her exposed flesh.

She reared up and looked at him. "Easy, Mary. I won't hurt you." He turned her slightly, all the while annointing her mouth with small, sipping kisses, until his warm hand found one small breast. He groaned softly. Against her thigh she felt his erection, distinct evidence that, indeed, they had gone beyond just friends. But even as that thought surfaced, he found her mouth and instinctively she responded. He brought out something wild in her. Intense desire beyond anything she'd ever known. With her lips she nuzzled the tan skin at the base of his throat. *This is crazy,* a distant thought kept reminding her.

Then he sat up carefully, hugging her to him, and gently but firmly pulled down the sweater that had ridden up. Still holding her by the shoulders, he drew away. "Now, what were you saying about this relationship?"

She put her hands up to her face. Her cheeks were on fire. "Okay, I concede I'm...attracted to you. Like all the other women, I guess."

He looked pained. "Maybe I deserved that, but you're not like all the other women. Frankly, I'm scared. You're not like anyone I've ever dated and we don't make any kind of sense together, but, damn it, I think we could be much more than just friends.''

Her heart pounded. Slowly she began speaking. ''Before this goes any further, let me give you the rest of my speech. Basically it's like this. I don't want to stop seeing you, but I need time and space to get used to my new surroundings and to concentrate on my search. I don't need more emotional demands.''

''In other words, you want life tucked into neat little pigeonholes.''

''Exactly.''

''Okay. Put me in the pigeonhole marked Friend. Meanwhile, little lady, I'm going to do my damnedest to lighten you up.'' He pecked her on the cheek and rose to his feet. ''Got any more soda?''

They sat at the dining room table drinking their beverages and nibbling peanuts. Russ settled back in his chair, hands laced behind his head. ''Tell me some more about this adoption business. Maybe I can help.''

She outlined briefly the steps she'd taken so far and the disappointment she faced when, time after time, her leads resulted in dead ends. Leaning across the table, she showed him the necklace her mother had given her. ''It's probably my best clue, but I can't make heads or tails of it.''

''And if you do, what might happen?'' The concern in his eyes was genuine.

''I know, I know.'' She shrugged defensively. ''It's a litany that plays in my head constantly. What if I can't find them? What if I find them and they don't want anything to do with me? What if I find them, meet them and don't like them? What if I find them and they want to be too much a part of my life? What if my mother and father feel rejected and we have a falling out? What if? What if? What if?''

''Then why pursue it?''

She rested on her elbows. ''I've told you. It's not a choice. I can't stand feeling different, rootless. As though something's missing. I need to feel complete, to feel I belong. Believe it or not, as a little girl I used to pray to my guardian angel for a miracle. Maybe it's time I made my own miracles.'' She frowned, considering. ''Russ, I know it's hard for people who've never been adopted to understand, but unless you've been there, you can't possibly know the emptiness, the sense of some...indefinable unworthiness. Even though I rationalize that my birth mother may have made a tremendous, loving sacrifice to give me up, I can't shake the suspicion that I was abandoned. I've got to find out.''

He raised sad eyes to hers and his fingers tightened around the half-empty glass. ''I *know* why I was. And it isn't pretty.''

She stared. ''Why you were what?''

The word came out like a rivet hitting metal. ''Abandoned.''

''Abandoned? What do you mean?''

His jaw worked. ''Mary, Carolyn isn't my mother.''

CHAPTER SEVEN

MARY COULDN'T THINK of a thing to say. Russ was adopted, too? No, that didn't make any sense. He was a younger, taller version of his father.

"Aw, hell!" Russ scraped back his chair and stood up. He rubbed a hand across his face, then turned the chair around and sat down again, straddling it and crossing his arms over the back.

Mary waited without speaking, watching him, his obvious anguish striking a familiar chord. Tears of recognition welled in her eyes.

"Jeez, Mary, I'm sorry. I didn't mean to blurt that out."

She moved her own chair around the table to sit at right angles to him. She laid a tentative hand on his forearm. "Russ, what do you mean Carolyn isn't your mother? You call her Mom."

He gave her a weary, lopsided grin. "She *is* my mom in every way that matters. Nobody could ask for a warmer, more wonderful parent—or for one who'd love me any more than she does. But the truth of the matter is—" he covered her hand with his own "—she's my stepmother."

"Obviously not the wicked fairy-tale type," Mary said. "I've been around the two of you long enough to see she adores you. And Brian? Janie?"

"They're my half brother and half sister. They're great, both of them." She could see him begin to relax, laying his chin on his folded arms. She removed her hand from his and sat quietly. "You know, I rarely give it any thought. They're my family. I take them for granted. But when you said no one can know the emptiness, the anger of being abandoned unless they've experienced it, my gut kicked in with all those buried feelings." He stood up and began pacing. "What a crummy thing to do to a little kid. And, jeez, to Dad. Who'd never deliberately hurt anybody." He paused at the far end of the living room, gazing out the window.

Though she longed to go to him, Mary stayed in her chair, following him with her eyes as he resumed his pacing. Softly she asked, "What happened, Russ?"

He plopped back down in his chair. "Mary." His voice was firm. "Don't be so sure you want to find your birth mother. Life isn't always happily-ever-after. You may picture your mother as some young, misunderstood victim." She could see his body tense. "But yours could be like mine." He stood again. "A slut. A selfish, two-timing slut!"

Mary rose and came around the table to stand behind him, pressing her cheek against his rigid back and embracing him, her arms circling his waist. She didn't know how long they stood like that, her body small comfort for his misery.

Finally he turned and, staring off into the distance, gathered her into him. "I only want to tell this once. They met while he was in law school at Yale. My father was taken in by her beauty, her sensuality. After Main Line Philadelphia where she grew up, she thought coming to the West would be a big adventure." Russ paused and absently trailed his fingers back and forth across Mary's neck. "It was a big adventure, all right. She hated the wind, she hated the 'hicks,' and she hated Oklahoma. Worst of all, she hated being saddled with a toddler son who wiped his muddy hands on her expensive white skirt."

Mary raised her head and placed a gentle finger on his lips. His eyes reflected the pain of the memory. "You don't have to tell me any more."

He grinned sardonically. "But you haven't heard the best part." He rubbed his hands up and down her back. "She liked men. All kinds of men. Dad never had a prayer of holding her. One day—I'd just turned three— she simply didn't come home from a shopping trip to Tulsa."

Mary's heart caught in her throat. "That's unthinkable."

"Dad was beside himself. Though I guess he wasn't all that surprised. She'd not been terribly discreet with her flings."

"Did he try to find her?"

"She sent a telegram the next day. I've read it myself. She'd met someone else. Wanted a quickie Nevada divorce. She gave him total custody of me. Said she never wanted to see either of us again."

Mary inhaled a cold shaft of air. "Russ..." Her voice quavered. "Her parents?"

"She was an only child. Both died before she met Dad." He shrugged. "So, now you know. We were abandoned." He released her and sat down.

She sank dazedly into her chair. "No wonder you're so close to Carolyn."

He smiled wistfully. "If ever there was a silver lining, it's Mom. Dad met her about a year and a half later. She's the best thing that ever happened. Moms are the people who nurse you through the flu, come to your ball games, bake the world's best sugar cookies and love you even when you trample their newly planted flower beds."

Mary experienced a sharp pang of envy. Phyllis Fleet didn't bake or garden; the help took care of those chores. Emphasis on doing the "right thing" was what Mary remembered most vividly about her childhood. Yet she'd never doubted her mother's unconditional love, and her gift of the necklace was proof, if any was needed. No point dwelling on comparisons. Phyllis and Carolyn were two very different women. As obviously had been J. T. Coulter's first wife. "You've never seen your real mother again?"

He slammed his palm flat on the table. "Never. And I never want to, either. She's *not* my real mother. Mom is." Mary heard the finality in his tone.

"It must be difficult, then, for you to understand why I'm searching for mine."

"It is. But I guess you have to do what's right for you. The mystery obviously bothers you. My situation is no mystery. Just an ugly wound that's thankfully scarred over. Yours is still open."

She lowered her eyes. "Yes."

He shifted in his chair and tilted her chin with one hand. "Let me help. Let's see if we can hoist that anchor you told me about. The one that's holding you back."

"Thank you. I . . . I think . . . maybe I'm not as independent as I thought."

He squeezed her hand and smiled. "Okay, then. Tell me in more detail what you've got to work with."

Russ listened intently as she began the recitation of registries, documents, government offices—and dead ends. She showed him her notes and told him about the necklace.

He leaned across the table, picked up the stone suspended from the silver chain around her neck and studied it thoughtfully.

RUSS GROANED at the piles of paperwork littering his desk the following Monday morning—invoices for feed, Department of Agriculture directives, an order for veterinary supplies. Then the telephone started ringing. A board member from the Oklahoma Cattlemen's Association, a livestock broker and Gil Genneret from the bank.

"Damn it, Gil, give me a break. I need to get that stock to pasture no later than February first, and I sure as hell can't buy cattle I don't have land for. Lonnie Creighton is willing to lease me eight hundred acres east of town, but I need you to work with me on this loan. Covering both the lease and the cost of calves is gonna cut it close, but I've never missed a payment with you yet." He transferred the receiver to his left ear, freeing his right hand to scrawl down the figures his banker had just given him. "Godamighty. Can't you knock off a quarter percent?"

When he heard the banker's next words, his stomach roiled. "He did *what?*" He gripped the pen so tightly his knuckles turned white. "You're telling me Buck Lloyd insinuated you should put financial pressure on me?" Russ pounded the desk with his fist. "... I know he's on your board and I don't give a damn how subtle his message was... Okay, okay. I'm trying to calm down. You seriously want me to believe you told him to go to hell?"

He got up and paced as Gil elaborated. Of course the loan officers weren't going to do anything unethical, Gil explained. He was just letting Russ know about this as a favor, the courtesy of a friend, and the rate quoted was the best he could do, for Russ or anybody else in similar circumstances.

Russ collapsed into his desk chair. "Okay, Gil. You don't leave me much choice. I'll be in soon to sign the papers.... Yeah, I understand. You're in business, too. If that's the best you can do, I'll just have to live with it. But, Gil, if I ever have reason to believe Buck Lloyd is calling the shots at Wheatland, I'm outta there."

He hung up the phone. Casey roused himself from the rug and came and laid his head in Russ's lap. "Son of a bitch, Casey! It's one thing for Buck to refuse to sell his land, but throwing his weight around at the bank? Hell's fire!" The implied threat was chillingly obvious. But Russ had never done anything except stay out of Buck's way and offer him a fair business deal. The man's veins ran pure venom. Still, it was pointless to let anger cloud more immediate issues. He'd be damned if he'd give Buck the satisfaction.

He removed Casey's head from his lap and stood up, putting the sheet of figures in a file folder. If he hired another hand, worked longer days, if the winter was mild, if... He smiled ironically. Hell of a note. The "ifs" were what made the cattle business exciting. He thrived on the uncertainties. Now was no time to turn cautious. One day, by God, he'd have enough leverage to buy that land of Buck's.

He picked up his hat, put on his jacket and leaned over to scratch Casey's ears. "Can't take you with me anymore, old boy. Wish I could." He set out for the barn to saddle up for a long ride to work off the pure cussedness generated by the phone conversation. A heavy weight of obligations bowed him down and a molten ball of anger smoldered in his gut.

He mounted Major and rode briskly through the corral and out into the pasture. The tension at the base of his neck was easing, but his insides still churned. He pulled up the collar of his sheepskin-lined coat and reined in the quarter horse. A fierce northwest wind cut across the pasture, bending the tops of the prairie grass in relentless waves. Leaden skies deadened the vegetation into dull mustards and lifeless grays and blacks.

He turned the gelding along the west fence line. When these moods came over him, he was better off spending time outdoors—alone. Thinking things through. He clucked the horse into an easy trot.

Business usually didn't get to him like this. It was a challenge, one that didn't suit men who needed greater security, predictability. He loved the variety of ranching—the pitting of man against nature, the union of man and beast. But Buck Lloyd was another matter. How could anyone let bitterness poison him like that? Damned if he knew.

He checked the gate at the southwest corner of the pasture and headed back east, the knifelike wind cutting across his left cheek. So. He might as well clear *all* the confusion sticking in his craw. There was more to it than just business, just Buck. What else?

He shoved his right hand in the deep pocket of his coat. Mary? Yeah, Mary. She kept him off balance. Pigeonholed, by God. And at his own suggestion. Was he crazy? Nobody pigeonholed him. He'd spent the greater part of his adulthood sidestepping commitment, deliberately dating women with whom he could never imagine a future. Floating along in self-protective detachment. What *was* it about Mary?

Attractive, sexy in a different kind of way. Eyes that held old secrets—and hurts. Quiet, but determined as hell. Like this adoption stuff. Nobody was going to head her off at the pass. The other night she'd laid out her paperwork in front of him—all of it neatly annotated and filed. But despite all her organization and effort, she had nothing to show for it.

That was what got him. All the logic and control she exerted over every facet of her life was failing. Was he ready to be needed? Needing imposed a heavy burden. Who'd he think he was anyway—Sir Galahad? It was a helluva lot harder to say *sayonara* if you were indispensable.

He reined the gelding back into the wind. *Sayonaras, adieus, see-ya's*—he was good at those. And that was what he should say to Mary Fleet. Instead, for two days now he'd actually been mulling over her problem. Something about that necklace nagged at him. The old Russ wouldn't have given it a thought. Easy come, easy go. He pulled down his hat brim against the wind.

Are you settin' yourself up, fella? The childhood feelings of betrayal, anger and loss that'd surfaced the other night had caught him off guard. They'd been sudden, visceral. Get too close to a woman, trust her, and you're asking for trouble. Big-time. That was the lesson he'd learned at his mother's knee. Janna Symington had reinforced it in spades. And it was a lesson that had served him well. Until now. He shifted in the saddle. If he was honest, he had to admit Carolyn balanced the equation. She was loyal, loving, trustworthy. His instinct was to trust Mary, too. She'd become important to him. But…in the same breath that she'd said she needed him, she'd suggested they cool it. What'd that mean? A hawk swooped down and lighted on a nearby fence post, its feathers ruffled by the wind. Russ spurred the horse into a canter. He'd agreed to help her. To permit her to need him.

A gust nearly blew his hat off. He clamped it back on his head as his eyes watered with wind-induced tears. No wonder he was out of sorts. On top of everything else, he'd fallen for Mary. Against every admonition piled up by years of avoiding commitment. And he was afraid—of what? Of trusting a woman again?

He slowed the horse to a walk, slipped out of the saddle and led him back to the barn. *I'll be damned. I'm still afraid of being abandoned.*

MARY WAS SWAMPED all the next week at work, so when Saturday dawned sunny and mild, she set off on a vigorous run. She loped up the long hill to the east toward the shopping center, swung past the strip shopping mall and then turned on Sunset Drive, which led down to the park. By the time she got to the bottom of the hill, she was huffing. Slowing, she became aware that she was avoiding the cracks in the pavement. The schoolyard chant echoed in her head: "Step on a crack, break your mother's back." Maybe that was her inadvertent sin—in the past she'd perhaps defied some law of the universe and put a tiny offending foot on a crack and broken her mother—her real mother—like Humpty Dumpty.

She continued down the sidewalk, irrationally but deliberately skipping over the cracks. Before she reached the park entrance, she spotted Carolyn Coulter hanging a harvest wreath on her front door. Mary jogged across the street and waved. "Carolyn! Hi."

Carolyn turned, smiling warmly. "Mary, good morning." She strolled to the curb, her burnished copper hair glowing in the sun. "I'm so glad to see you. I've been hearing good things from Chauncey Butterworth. I help take blood pressures at Sooner Arms once a month. He told me all about your seminar and Russ's musical triumph. Not that Russ would ever mention it." She gestured to the house. "Do you have time for coffee? I've made a fresh pot." Carolyn draped an arm around Mary's shoulder and gave a squeeze.

Mary smiled. "I'd love a cup."

In the kitchen Carolyn poured the coffee into two mugs and set out a plate of warm blueberry muffins.

"This looks delicious." Mary bit into a muffin. "I haven't had food like this since I left home."

Carolyn regarded Mary thoughtfully. "Do you miss home?"

Mary paused. "I miss my parents and the few friends who still live in St. Louis, but I love Ewing."

"I'm glad. Everything fine at the bank?"

"Great. I'm starting to see some return on my efforts at the retirement centers. Two new clients in the last week." Mary sipped at her coffee.

"What are your Thanksgiving plans?"

"I only have Thursday off, so I've persuaded Mom and Dad to come here."

"Have they been to see you yet?"

"No." Mary leaned forward. "They weren't excited about my moving to Ewing."

Carolyn raised her eyebrows.

"They've always been enthusiastic about my decisions. Lukewarm was the best they could muster for this one."

"Sure you aren't just imagining that?"

Mary considered. "I'm sure. Sometimes what's *not* said is as powerful as what *is*." Mary took another bite of the muffin. "These are great. Anyway, when they come, maybe they'll see how happy I am."

"I don't want to be presumptuous, Mary, but you and your parents would be welcome to join us for Thanksgiving dinner. We'd love to have you. And you could meet Brian. He'll be home for the break."

Before Mary could answer, a disheveled apparition in a formless knee-length knit T-shirt appeared in the doorway, stretching and yawning. "What time is it?" Janie, barefoot and tousled, shuffled toward them.

Carolyn caught Mary's eye and smiled. "Ten o'clock."

"Ten o'clock!" Janie wailed. "I could've slept another hour." She collapsed into a vacant kitchen chair and began peeling the wrapper from a muffin.

Carolyn cleared her throat. "Manners, Janie?"

Janie smiled apologetically. "I'm sorry. Hi, Mary. I'm a bear in the morning."

"That's putting it mildly." Carolyn handed Janie a glass of juice. "I was just asking if Mary and her family would join us for Thanksgiving dinner."

Janie straightened up, her face breaking into a sunny smile. "Great! We'll have enough people for an awesome game of touch football. Would your folks play?"

Tickled by the mental image of either of the Fleets hunkered at the line of scrimmage or going deep for a pass, Mary deferred. "You'll have to ask them."

Janie gave a whoop. "Then you'll come?"

"Only if I can bring something."

Carolyn set her mug down decisively. "It's settled, then." She faced Mary. "I'll count on you for a relish tray and a fruit salad."

"Thanks, Carolyn. It sounds like fun." The meal might provide a welcome diversion in case she still felt uncomfortable with her father.

Janie stood up, cramming the unfinished muffin in her mouth. She paused in the doorway. "Mary, it's cool that you're coming. I can't wait to tell Russ. Ha! He'll have to be on his best behavior. Meeting your parents and all." She skipped down the hall.

Mary felt the color rising to the roots of her hair.

Carolyn shrugged. "What can I say? I've *tried* to teach her manners." She toyed with her mug, turning it slowly between her fingers. "I think Russ is fond of you, Mary. Very fond."

"You do?" Mary's heartbeat accelerated.

"Yes, I do. He stopped by the other day. He said he told you about Linda."

"Linda?"

"J.T.'s first wife, Russ's mother."

"Yes, he did," Mary said quietly. "It must've been a terrible time for Russ and his father."

"It was. When I first met them, neither one of them found it easy to trust, to open up."

"That's understandable. The hurt of that kind of rejection takes a long time to heal. But, Carolyn, you made such a difference. You should've heard Russ talk about you—what a super mom you are."

"I love him a great deal. I wish you could've seen him as I first did. He wouldn't go anywhere without his Curious George stuffed animal. The first few dates J.T. and I had, we had to take Russ with us. He wouldn't let J.T. out of his sight." She chuckled. "Made for some interesting courting, I can tell you."

"Well, whatever you did, he certainly regained his self-confidence."

"And then some." Carolyn smiled and then, sobering, reached over to squeeze Mary's hand. "To my knowledge, he's never told anyone about Linda's deserting them. Never verbalized that hurt." Carolyn paused. "All joking aside, Russ's been gun-shy with the women he's dated—ever since one very bad experience in college."

"Oh?"

She looked straight at Mary. "A young woman he cared about turned down his proposal. The rejection devastated him. I think maybe you're the first woman he's trusted."

"Carolyn, I . . . I don't know what to say."

"Just say you'll be his friend. Anything beyond that is up to the two of you." She patted Mary's hand, stood up and began clearing the table.

Later, jogging home, Mary's mood felt lighter. Russ was lucky to have a mother like Carolyn. She understood people intuitively and had a knack for saying just the right thing. Mary felt drawn, not just to Russ, but to all the Coulters. Open, accepting, fun-loving people. What would her parents make of them? Of Russ? What if they read too much into the holiday gathering? Darn. She'd have to make it clear the Coulters—including Russ—were merely some Ewing friends. Or was *she* the one reading too much into it, or wishing that . . .

Russ'd never told anyone else about his mother? During the past week she hadn't been able to lay aside the memory of his gray eyes, haunted with loneliness, as he revealed the confused, hurt little boy he'd been. Nor the picture of the handsome, earnest man who'd said, "Let me help."

She quickly covered the last few blocks to her condo, unlocked the door and went directly to the kitchen for a drink. Reaching for a glass, she noticed the flashing light of her answering machine. While she fixed the ice water, she listened to the message.

Russ's deep baritone filled the room. "Mary, call me at the ranch. If you're not busy this afternoon, there's someone I want you to meet. I'll pick you up around two.'' There was a pause on the machine. ''I think I've got a lead on that necklace of yours.''

Carefully she set down the cold glass. Her hand was shaking.

CHAPTER EIGHT

"WHERE ARE WE GOING?" Mary grabbed hold of the armrest as Russ gunned the truck away from the curb.

"Here. Take a look." Russ tossed her a folded sheet of notepaper. She read the scrawled directions. East out of Ewing twenty miles, south for ten and back east to the first section line. Then north three quarters of a mile. At the bottom Russ had printed the name Clyde Peppercorn.

"Who's Clyde Peppercorn?"

"My foreman's father. He doesn't have a phone, so we'll just have to take our chances on catching him at home."

Mary had been in a state of white-hot excitement since Russ's message. When she'd called him back, he'd avoided direct answers to her questions and, maddeningly, told her to be patient, not to get her hopes up. Then when he'd been fifteen minutes late, exasperation and anticipation had pushed her to the edge.

"Can't you tell me anything at all?"

At the outskirts of town, he went through the last stoplight on yellow and accelerated into the forty-five-mile-per-hour zone. "It's a long shot, Mary. Let's just wait and see. Did you bring the necklace?"

She nodded, rubbing the stone between her thumb and first two fingers. This was the link—the disembodied voice urging her on, even when other avenues proved discouraging. The necklace was obviously unique, not some mass-produced trinket. When she touched the stone, with its patina of age, she knew, with the power of conviction, that she was not the first person to cherish it.

Odd. The more her efforts to discover her identity met obstacles, the more obsessed she became. Sometimes the urge was so strong it seemed to take on a life of its own— as if somewhere, out there, someone was beckoning her forward.

She stared out the window at the telephone poles whizzing by at regular intervals. Nonsense. Nobody was out there. She didn't believe in that paranormal stuff. She needed to stick to the here and now, the verifiable, the tangible. The circle of her thinking returned her to the necklace. *That* was tangible.

Russ drove onto a side road. "Okay. Let me tell you a little bit about Clyde. He's a full-blooded Cherokee who's lived in these parts all his life. He stays pretty close to home. I've only met him a couple of times. But Jim, his son, said it'd be all right to visit him. He's eighty and his eyesight is failing some, but Jim thought he might be able to tell us what we need to find out."

"Which is?"

"Whether those symbols are Cherokee."

"Cherokee? I don't get it."

"Consider this another lesson in your orientation to Oklahoma. Have you ever heard of Sequoyah, the Cherokee chief?"

"Yes, but..."

"He's famous, among other things, for devising an alphabet and codifying their language. There are still Cherokees around here who read, write and speak it. I think maybe those symbols on your necklace are Cherokee letters or words."

Breathing was suddenly difficult, painful, as the possibilities crowded her mind. Maybe her mother had been a Cherokee? Maybe the necklace would reveal her identity? It couldn't happen like this, so soon. It couldn't be this simple. Could it?

She drew a ragged breath. The landscape passed in a daze. Could this Clyde Peppercorn help? How fast could they get there?

"You okay?" Russ looked at her with concern.

She inhaled again, deeply. "Yeah, I think so. Wow." Russ wheeled onto a rutted dirt road winding through a grove of massive pecan trees. "I guess I'm scared."

He took her hand, the warmth of his flesh thawing the ice of hers. "I just don't want you to be disappointed."

Up ahead she saw a small frame house, its rickety front porch cluttered with two wooden rockers, an old washer, a stack of firewood and a couple of rusty barrels. A thin wisp of gray-blue smoke rose from the tin stovepipe at the back of the house. Off to one side was a dented vintage pickup surrounded by a brood of clucking hens. A pair of liver-colored coonhounds rounded the house, baying at the intrusive vehicle. Mary saw someone pull aside a curtain in one of the front windows.

"Stay here. Let me check it out." Russ reached behind the seat and withdrew a carton of cigarettes. Mary raised her eyebrows questioningly. "Thought a gift might be in order." He left the motor running and, the dogs yipping at his heels, walked up and knocked on the door. Mary's stomach churned.

Slowly the door opened a crack. She could see Russ presenting the cigarettes and talking through the screen to someone inside. It was a lengthy conversation. Was that good or bad? Were they at the right house? Was the person telling Russ to go away?

Just then Russ turned and beckoned to her. She shut off the engine and pocketed the key. Now. The time was now. Never had such a short distance seemed so far. Russ smiled encouragingly. "Mary, Mr. Peppercorn has invited us in." He held the screen door for her.

The old Cherokee's face was stoic, leathery, his body short and stocky. "Come in." His black hair was streaked with gray and held back in a ponytail; his large straight nose dominated his small mouth. His impassive black eyes assessed her. The smell of stale tobacco permeated the air.

"Mr. Peppercorn, I'm Mary Fleet. It's kind of you to let us visit."

The old man nodded his head and gestured to a sprung warped sofa. Mary sat primly on the edge. Russ settled next to her and Clyde Peppercorn took up what was clearly his accustomed place in a cracked vinyl recliner. He waited.

Russ cleared his throat. "As I told you, Jim suggested you might be able to help us."

"Might could."

"Mary has a necklace given to her by her mother. It may be useful in helping her identify some relatives. We'd like you to take a look."

Clyde Peppercorn bent forward and held out his palm. Mary inclined her neck, slipped the necklace over her head and presented it to him.

He studied it. Then grunted. Fumbling among some old magazines on the lamp table by his chair, he came up with a pair of glasses. He adjusted the lamp to the highest setting and peered through them. He turned the stone over and grunted again. Then, silently, he handed the necklace back to Mary. She sat, heart pounding.

"*Oochalata*," he said.

"Ooh-sha-lay-ta?" she repeated.

"Oochalata." His features softened with satisfaction. "Native stone. Found in eastern Oklahoma. Delaware County."

Oh, God. Mary's fingers fumbled the necklace still in her hand.

"What about the symbols or characters etched in the stone? Are they Cherokee?" Russ's question hung in the air.

Slowly the old man stood up, his obsidian eyes melting as he fixed his gaze on Mary. He walked over to her and ceremoniously placed his hands on her head. *"Jigeyu."* He removed his hands and smiled down at her. *"Jigeyu."*

"Gee-gay-ooh?" Russ echoed.

"The beloved. Beloved Woman." Clyde Peppercorn carefully sat back down in his chair.

"So it *is* Cherokee?" Mary was beside herself.

He smiled widely, and this time gaps in his teeth were visible, but his eyes were warm. "It is Cherokee. Beloved Women were important in Cherokee history." Still beaming, he folded his hands over his stomach.

Mary restrained herself from bouncing up and down on the sofa. Her eyes danced. "Would you tell me about them?"

He hummed in a monotone for several moments, eyes closed. "Before the removal to Oklahoma and the Trail of Tears," he began, "certain older women had an important position in the tribe. They were called the Beloved Women or Pretty Women. They were counselors to male leaders. They named the babies. They decided what should be done with prisoners. Very powerful." He paused, apparently exhausted by his long speech.

The heat inside the house was suffocating, but Mary scarcely noticed, so intent was she on the Cherokee's words. "This necklace. Must be important in your family," he said. "*Jigeyu*. The Beloved."

Mary didn't want to tire him further, but she had one more question. "Mr. Peppercorn, have you ever seen another necklace like this one?"

He smiled again, drawing her eyes into his. "Never."

The word hung among them in the silence. Russ got up, breaking the spell. Mary rose, too, and extended her hand to the dignified old Cherokee. "Thank you from the bottom of my heart. You've been very helpful."

Clyde Peppercorn stood then and showed them to the door. "You are part Cherokee?"

Mary flushed. "I don't know."

He changed the inflection in his voice. "You are part Cherokee. I hope you find your relatives." He opened the door to let them out, shooing the dogs away as he did so.

RUSS HELD OUT HIS HAND for the ignition key. Beside him in the passenger seat, Mary, thick lashes lowered, sat very still, studying the carved characters in the milky gray-brown agate. She was in another world.

He cleared his throat. "The key?"

She glanced up, her eyes like big shiny black marbles.

"Oops." She extracted it from her pocket and handed it to him.

He started the truck and backed carefully between the mailbox and the drainage ditch onto the rutted lane.

Her excitement was palpable, yet he sensed she needed a few moments of privacy. Out of the corner of his eye he watched her run the pad of one forefinger over the indentations in the stone. The Beloved. He could only imagine the thoughts rioting in her head. But there was a softness to the set of her mouth he hadn't seen before. Her lustrous black hair, curling slightly at her chin line, was caught in a shaft of sunlight coming through the window. Gently he reached over and cradled her reed-like neck in one hand, burying his fingers in her soft hair.

She looked up. Her smile was like daybreak after a long dark night. "Thank you, Russ. How did you ever think of it?"

He paused at the county road stop sign, dropped his hand back to the steering wheel and then drove north. "I'm embarrassed I didn't see it right away. When you told me the characters weren't Russian or something, I got to thinking. Oklahoma history was a required course in high school and we spent a lot of time on the Chero-kees, since so many live in eastern Oklahoma. Although you rarely see Cherokee written, I remembered a field trip to Tahlequah, western capital of the Cherokee Nation, where I saw letters that looked kinda like these. So I asked Jim Peppercorn who around here might know something about the Cherokee alphabet. He suggested his father."

She squirmed against the seat belt, turning toward him and touching his shoulder. "Do you know what this means? It means if my mother was a Cherokee, I can gain access to the tribal records. And if I can get at her name and family history, then I can try to locate her." Her voice rose. "It's almost too good to be true." She leaned closer and kissed his cheek. "Thank you." She bounced back around, facing the front.

"Mary, it's only a start and you may be disappointed if—"

"Don't rain on my parade, Russ. Just let me hold on to this possibility. It's my first real breakthrough." She rubbed the talisman stone a final time, and then put it around her neck again.

He sighed. He hoped to hell he hadn't complicated matters. It did seem almost too good to be true. And what if she discovered her identity? Would it disappoint her? Alter her? Would the appealing mixture of grit and vulnerability somehow be muddied by factors unknown, changing her into...into what? He'd already sensed a subtle change. Like...like there was a part of her he couldn't reach. Like there'd been a kind of withdrawal. Slight but real.

Feminine subtleties eluded him. He had other things to worry about. Cattle prices and bank loans and...Mary Fleet. Why was his stomach doing a tap dance? His noble deed was making him miserable and he didn't know why. *So, do something.*

"Mary?" Her head snapped up, her eyes coming into focus.

"What?" Her lips parted in a half smile.

"Remember when I asked you to go out dancing?"

"Uh-huh."

"Well, I reckon we've never really gone. Our first plan got sandbagged by your dad's phone call. Wanna try again?"

"Go boot-scootin', you mean?"

He relaxed and grinned. "Yeah. I was thinking maybe it'd be a good night for a celebration." He raised his eyes inquiringly.

She nodded. "I'd like that."

"Eight o'clock?"

"Eight or whenever you get there."

"Ouch, you really know how to hurt a guy." This was better. Light banter.

"Are we going to the Red Dirt Café?" The words came out of her mouth like a foreign language.

He nodded emphatically. "The Red Dirt Café." He ruffled her hair. "And much as I like that sexy black dress of yours, you might want to wear something more casual. Now don't say I didn't warn you."

SHE FELT RIDICULOUS in the cowgirl outfit, complete with slit skirt, that Gwen had talked her into buying. As if she were costumed to have her picture taken in one of those tourist-trap photography places. God only knew what the hat would look like. She glanced at the alarm clock beside her bed. Sure enough, 8:20. Late again.

She looked down at the tooled-leather boots, amazed how comfortable they were. She couldn't imagine dancing in them, though. She checked herself once more in the mirror. She didn't know whether to laugh or feel self-conscious. The turquoise blouse *was* becoming and the skirt hugged her waist to good advantage. But still... What was Roy Rogers's wife's name? Gail? Dale? Dale Evans. That was exactly who she resembled in this get-up.

She continued to stand, staring at her image, the *oochalata* necklace in her hand. Beloved Woman. Someone—her mother?—had loved her enough to pass it on as tangible proof of her Cherokee ancestry. Arrested by the reflection of her own dark eyes, she tried to visualize the young woman—lonely, frightened, maybe abandoned—whose mirror-image eyes were perhaps even now attempting to penetrate the mists of time and distance to reach Mary, to reach her baby. She squeezed the stone. Ooh-sha-lay-ta. A melodious word, like clear waters cascading over mossy rocks. She might have gone for months without recognizing the characters as Cherokee but for Russ. Russ, who didn't *have* to help her search for her birth parents, who needn't have said one word about his real mother, and who certainly didn't have to take her to meet Clyde Peppercorn.

The least she could do, by way of thanks, was endure an evening at the Red Dirt Café. In fact, she was kind of curious. And it took no effort at all to tolerate Russ—and those tantalizing eyes. She dropped the necklace over her head and tucked it inside the collar of her Western blouse. She smiled at her reflection. Turquoise *was* one of her best colors.

THE RED DIRT CAFÉ stood on top of a hill halfway between Ewing and Tulsa—out in the middle of nowhere, or so it seemed to Mary. A red neon sign at the turn-in blinked Re Dirt Café. That sign was dwarfed by the one above the entrance—a huge lighted cowboy twirling a lasso. The white lights outlining the lasso cut on and off to simulate motion. Assorted cars and pickups jammed the parking lot.

"Here we are." Russ's eyes twinkled as he escorted Mary to the fake barn door, complete with wrought-iron handle and hinges. In the smoky entrance hall a rope tacked on a weathered board spelled out in cursive, "Welcome, pardners!" In the background she could hear the pulsating beat of a country-and-western band.

Russ held Mary's hand and ran interference through a crowd of men and women outfitted like extras in a movie Western. Her hat bounced over her ears. She tilted it back on her head. They made their way to the bar where Russ ordered two longnecks and then reached over the folks sitting on the stools to retrieve the bottles.

They stood against the wall, sipping the beer and watching the gyrating, stomping dancers through a thick blue haze of cigarette smoke. The place was packed and the crowd boisterously happy. Russ's arm encircled her waist and she leaned against him. He bent over to whisper in her ear. "You look great in that outfit." He winked. "An authentic Okie." She rolled her eyes and grinned. Suddenly he straightened up, grabbed her hand and waded through the tightly clustered tables. "C'mon. I think I see a place."

An elderly couple was just vacating a small table for two tucked in a corner by the dance floor. Russ laid claim to it even before the waitress had cleared it. He sprawled in his chair. "Now then. Whaddya think?"

This was definitely another world, but at least she didn't feel self-conscious about her getup. She fit right in. "Interesting."

He laughed. "Well, it's gonna get more interesting." He stood up and extended his hand. "C'mon. Dance time."

At first she felt stiff and ridiculous, but it was hard to resist the toe-tapping rhythms and the contagious enthusiasm of the crowd. The wooden dance floor vibrated under their feet and as soon as she realized that nobody cared how inexpert she was, she felt her inhibitions slipping away. Her childhood dance training stood her in good stead and soon the line dance steps were coming to her naturally. In fact, she didn't want to sit down. It was fun!

Near the end of the evening the band segued into a slow number and Russ pulled her close. She felt his firm hand in the small of her back. He murmured, "You loosen up pretty darn well."

She traced one hand up the sleeve of his stonewashed denim shirt. "I had a good teacher." His other arm went around her and he began moving his feet in small steps. Her arms, with a will of their own, clasped him around the neck. He maneuvered her near their table, removed her hat and tossed it onto his seat. Then he buried his chin in her hair and pulled her even closer. Her face was nestled against his chest and she could smell the clean, soapy man-smell of his skin.

She relaxed, lulled by the immediacy of the music and the pleasant sensation of his hands straying lower on her back, drawing her to him as his lips brushed softly across her temple. She felt a wild surge of abandon and pressed herself closer. She experienced both a drowsy peacefulness and a powerful arousal. She could stay here all night, secure in the closeness of his long body, excited by the promise she could feel deep inside. He molded her hips to his, and his own arousal was unmistakable.

As his hands trailed up her back, he drew slightly away. She looked up. He framed her face in his hands, still moving almost imperceptibly against her, and searched her eyes longingly. "Mary Fleet, what've you done to me?" He dropped his hands, pulling her convulsively to him as his mouth, hungry and demanding, engulfed hers. Pinpricks of fire traveled all the way down to the tips of her new boots, and she forgot the music, forgot the crowd, forgot everything but the thudding of her own heart and the pleasure of his tongue seeking hers.

His mouth softened and he withdrew his lips to move them tantalizingly over her face—her eyes, the corners of her mouth, the soft spot just beneath her ear. She felt faint, yet she didn't want him to stop.

The music ended and the crowd applauded appreciatively. Mary and Russ stood staring at one another, oblivious to their surroundings, unaware of anything but the powerful unspoken feelings mirrored in their eyes.

He was the first to move. "Ready to go?"

She hesitated. She didn't trust herself. "Yes."

The frigid night air hit her in the face as they exited the dance hall. The parking lot was almost empty and the neon signs had been turned off. From the hilltop they could see for miles, the dark sky arching far above them, dotted with a dazzling display of blue-white twinkling stars. Mary succumbed to the impulse to reach her arms up to the heavens. "Look, Russ, how glorious!" She turned around and gave him a big hug. "You've given me a wonderful day—stars and hope."

Hope. That she might know, at last, the answer to the mystery of her birth. Was it as close, or as far away, as those stars? She was hardly aware of Russ's arm around her. Tomorrow... no, tomorrow was Sunday. Monday she'd send a letter to the Bureau of Indian Affairs. Or could she find an address for the Cherokee Nation? That would be quicker. Then she'd be able to...

"...your thoughts?"

Had Russ said something? "Huh?"

He looked straight ahead, his jaw clenched. "I *said*, 'A penny for your thoughts.' You're a million miles away."

"I was just thinking about today. Mr. Peppercorn. How I'm going to proceed. All the things I need to do."

He removed his arm from her shoulders. "I see."

Her mind raced. A whole string of possible leads might surface. So absorbed was she in her mental agenda that she didn't feel the slump of Russ's shoulders or see the warm glow fade from his eyes as he turned to unlock the truck.

CHAPTER NINE

AFTER A FITFUL NIGHT, Russ awoke the next morning around nine, squinting into the bright November sunlight crisscrossing his face. He pulled on jeans and a faded Western shirt, made breakfast and attempted to read the Tulsa Sunday paper. He couldn't concentrate, even on the sports page. He rubbed a hand over his sandpapery beard. The hell with it. He wouldn't shave. He folded the other sections of the paper, threw them down on the coffee table and wandered to the kitchen window. Out of the corner of his eye, he saw Casey cock his head and regard him with that what's-the-matter-now look.

God, he was restless! He didn't feel like going to town, and he sure didn't feel like lying around all day watching pro football on the tube. The outdoor thermometer visible through the window registered fifty-two degrees. Warm enough. Decisively, he grabbed a faded OSU sweatshirt and his Dallas Cowboys ball cap. He'd do the chores and then tune the ultralight engine. He closed the back door and strode to the barn.

Later, he flung the tarpaulin over the nearby fence and studied the aircraft. Not a bad job if he did say so himself. He'd ordered the construction kit a year ago and it'd taken him several months to assemble the lighter-than-air craft.

He removed the blocks from the wheels and turned the tiny plane so he could tinker with the engine more easily. His tools, glinting in the sun, lay around him as he hunkered, fiddling with a gasket. But the usual absorption in the task didn't come. Disgusted, he flung down the wrench and stood up. What the hell was the matter with him?

He put a boot on the first rung of the corral fence, climbed up and sat on the top, elbows on his knees, hands dangling between his legs. "What have you done to me, Mary Fleet?" That was the question he'd asked her last night. And her answer? An eager, pliable mouth seeking his. A warm, willing body pressing against him, driving him to distraction. And those rich coffee-brown eyes that softened something in his gut.

Right. Sure. If he didn't know better, he'd say she was nothing but a tease. There was that moment on the dance floor when the crowd had evaporated, and he and Mary had moved together in their own special world. She'd gotten him all aroused and then, just as he'd thought she, too, was caught up in the magic, she'd pulled back into a distant private place. Not Russ Coulter but Clyde Peppercorn had occupied her thoughts! Mary was like a damn covey of quail—just when he thought he had her cornered, she flew off in all directions.

He removed his ball cap and scratched his head. Hell, ever since Janna's unexpected adios, *he'd* called the shots, *he'd* kept it light, *he'd* waltzed away. Women! Damned if he could figure Mary—or himself. The wind ruffled his short sandy hair and he replaced the cap.

He jumped down from the fence and kicked the toe of one boot against the post. So many women, so little time. That *had* worked as a self-protective credo. And now? One woman. Eating at him, worming her way into his thoughts, her trim, curved body beckoning him even in memory, controlling him in ways he wouldn't have thought possible. Sabotaging his careful avoidance of commitment. A woman whose stars and hope had little to do with him.

Distractedly he bent down and began gathering up his tools. Mary Fleet. It defied logic. How in God's name had he permitted that quiet, preoccupied little dark-eyed mule to get to him like this?

Damned if he'd wallow in uncertainty. She'd have to fish or cut bait. No more of this "friends" crap. Either she was interested in him or he was wasting his time. And, as he hollowly reminded himself, there was no shortage of available women.

He replaced the tools in his toolbox and covered the airplane with the tarp. If only females were as simple to deal with as engines.

MARY FLOPPED gratefully into her desk chair and filed the Howington trust papers in her "to do" stack. It'd been a Monday morning from hell. Activating her voice mail, she leaned back, eyes closed. A reminder about a horse show committee meeting, a buy recommendation from the St. Louis trust department and then Woody Higgins's strident voice. "Can you hear me, Mary? Why the hell can't I talk to a real person? Damn fool machines. Now, listen here. I told a fib when I said I didn't have a dime to invest. Might have a little something tucked away in an old sock. I want an appointment with you to talk about my—whaddya call it—estate planning. Sal, too. If I don't hear from you, I'll figure this idiot contraption didn't work."

Mary nearly laughed out loud. The way he'd shouted, he must've thought she was not only invisible, but deaf.

She was pleased her talk at Sooner Arms had resulted in at least two prospects, and two of her favorites, at that. She returned Woody's call and also spoke with Sal. Both appointments were scheduled for Friday.

On her way home from work, she stopped by the Ewing Library and checked out several books dealing with Cherokee history and the tribal government in Tahlequah. She intended to write letters that evening inquiring about access to tribal registration and adoption records. Later, she would follow up on the significance of the necklace.

Setting the books on the checkout counter, she instinctively fondled the *oochalata* stone, its solidity reinforcing her determination. This breakthrough would *not* result in a dead end if she could help it. If anything, it had served to redouble her commitment to her search. Now was not the time for distraction. *Even Russ Coulter?* She rubbed her hand over the smooth surface of the checkout counter. Would he stay neatly pigeonholed? Did she want him to? The librarian stacked her books and shoved them over to her. Mary sighed as she gathered them up. The *oochalata* clue, the promise of a Cherokee heritage and confusing feelings about Russ—it was too much to assimilate all at once.

A LITTLE SOMETHING in an old sock? Mary grinned as she walked down the carpeted corridor between Woody's apartment and Sal's on Friday afternoon. Woody had an estate that would keep a probate judge busy for months; establishing a trust would help his heirs avoid large probate fees. She paused before Sal's door to shift gears from Woody's situation to Sal and her estate planning needs. She rapped softly.

"Come in. It's unlocked."

Mary pushed the door open. Sal sat in her wing chair, a lap desk, spread with playing cards, resting on her knees. "Can't beat ol' Sol today. Ace of spades is stuck in the pile." She gestured Mary to a seat on the sofa, scooped up the cards with her gnarled hands and set them on the lamp table. Carefully she propped the lap desk on the floor beside her chair, then looked up. "Solitaire's okay, but poker's my game. Ever play?"

"I'm sorry, no."

Sal flapped a hand. "Oh, I do love a good poker game. In my day, I could hold my own with the best of 'em."

Mary smiled. "I'm afraid I don't have a poker face."

"Bluffing comes easy to me. Good way to keep the men in line. Little dose of humility." Sal chuckled. "Can't tell you how many times my husband lost the ranch to me. He never could hold his cards long enough to stare me down. Ha!" Her eyes strayed with the reminiscence.

Mary waited as Sal positioned her hands on the chair arms and levered to her feet, pausing to steady herself. "Lemme show you what I've got." She pointed to the dining room table covered with documents and papers. Mary assisted the frail old woman across the floor and helped her settle into one of the straight-backed dining room chairs. "Maybe your bank can help me, maybe not. My trust account's been at the Panhandle Western Bank ever since my husband's death. But, honey—" she reached over and patted Mary's hand "—if I can throw some business your way, I'd like to. I've been a women's libber since before they invented the term. We gotta stick together."

They spent the next half hour hunched over the table, reviewing the trust documents and quarterly reports from the rival bank. Mary marveled at the way Sal's mind moved with far greater facility than her body. She knew to the penny where and how her assets were invested. Finally Sal set down the ballpoint pen she'd used as a pointer, raised her head and fixed Mary with an appraising stare. "Can you beat that return?"

"It would be foolish to make any promises today, but I'd like to make a copy of your latest statement and run it past our investment people. I'm optimistic that we can outperform your current earnings. Also, it might be more convenient to have your trust in a Ewing institution where you can get personal attention and service."

"I'd like to work with you, honey." Sal shoved the papers to the other side of the table. "But sentiment and money don't mix. You've gotta show me how I can get—what do you young people say?—more bang for my buck." She chortled at her own words. "Kind of a suggestive comment for an old lady to make, but that's about the only bang I get anymore."

Mary blinked. Sal must've been something in her day. Uninhibited, outspoken, earthy. "Let me see what Wheatland can do, Sal, and I'll get back to you."

"Honey, if we can do business, fine. Whatever happens, though, I hope you'll visit us at Sooner Arms. You and that young Coulter are a shot in the arm for us old folks."

"We enjoyed coming here."

Sal gazed shrewdly at Mary. "That's one fine-looking young man, Mary. I always did like that lanky, lazy cowboy type. Just when you think all they care about is cows, they fire up like a summer storm."

Mary felt a shiver run up her spine and across her shoulders. Russ had a way of taking her off guard, of pulling her into his arms at unexpected moments, that jump-started a racing in her blood too powerful to ignore. "Was your husband like that?"

"Hell, honey, they broke the mold when they made Will McClanahan. He was all man—stubborn, ornery—but with a heart of gold. He'd do anything for anybody. And fun? My, we had us a good time." She leaned forward. "And he got himself a handful with me, I can tell you. Sparks were always flying. I wouldn't trade a minute I had with him."

"You were very lucky," Mary affirmed, envying the excitement still radiating from Sal's eyes.

"Luck, my foot! I went after that man with a vengeance. He never knew what hit him. You know that old song 'A Good Man Is Hard to Find'? Honey, when you find one, you gotta nail him. Like that Russ. I saw how he looked at you. Like a young bull eyeing the herd."

Mary lowered her eyes, confusion reddening her face.

Sal poked her with a gnarled finger. "You like him, don't you? Nothing wrong with that, Mary. Nothing at all."

Mary shifted in her chair and faced the red-haired, wrinkled woman scrutinizing her. "We're very different."

"So? Opposites attract."

"But he's unorganized, spontaneous, doesn't care a thing about promptness, planning ahead. I'm punctual, orderly, businesslike." Russ's words echoed in her mind. "We don't make any sense."

"But you do like him. Am I right?"

"Yes." The one-word admission was accompanied by a tightening in her chest.

"Then you hang in there, honey. Nothing's worse than a partner who's just like you. Will and I had our share of knock-down-drag-outs, but we were never bored, I can tell you. It's just like two stones, rough and pitted and oddly shaped. The fun's in the rubbing against each other, in the friction, wearing each other down till your smooth sides fit together."

The fun's in the friction? Maybe. But she'd avoided friction all her life. Until recently. Mary stood, gathered up the quarterly report and slid it into her briefcase. She placed a hand on Sal's bony shoulder. "I've got a lot to learn from you. I appreciate your friendship and the opportunity to talk with you about your trust. I'll be in touch soon."

The old lady looked up with a smile. "Take your time." Then she reached for the chain around Mary's neck. "You're wearing that same necklace again." She held the stone between her thumb and forefinger.

Mary resisted the urge to still Sal's hand on the *oochalata* stone. "Yes."

"It's unusual. You mentioned that your mother gave it to you." Sal dropped her hand into her lap.

"That's right." Mary slipped the stone back inside her blouse.

"How nice. And your people are from . . . ?"

"St. Louis. My mother's a native Missourian."

Sal nodded. "I see. Do you know the origin of the stone?"

Mary tightened her grip on the briefcase. "I've been told it's *oochalata*. Cherokee."

"How'd your mother come by it?"

"I don't know. I don't think she really does, either." The lie seemed harmless.

Mary heard Sal murmur, "Interesting." Then the old woman picked up Mary's hand and gave it a squeeze. "If you don't mind, just let yourself out. I'll put away these papers before I lock up."

Mary returned the squeeze and left the apartment, closing the door quietly behind her.

SAL MCCLANAHAN didn't hear the soft click of the latch. She sat staring off into space, lost in thought. Inside her head she was still young, vibrant—managing the business end of a working ranch, making love in the heirloom four-poster bed while the Oklahoma wind howled around the house, riding her big palomino for miles on hot, dusty summer afternoons. Now her arthritic body kept her physically captive. But her mind still roamed. Memories of the past, images of the present competed for her attention.

She wrinkled her brow, trying to fit snatches of information together. *Oochalata?* St. Louis? She shook her head and, using the table edge for support, pulled herself to her feet. Her brain was working overtime, she told herself. Old ladies and their wishful thinking. God save her from silly senile delusions.

She moved slowly, working the puzzle around in her mind. She turned the lock and sagged momentarily against the door. Still . . .

Nonsense. She gathered her strength and walked carefully back to her chair. Besides, she'd made a promise. She always kept her promises. Couldn't abide a person who didn't keep his word. Weren't many you could trust. But this promise had always lain heavy on her heart. And it was getting heavier.

DAMN IT. He couldn't stay away. Not now that he'd made up his mind to get this thing settled. He circled the block, waiting for Mary to get home. What if she'd stopped somewhere after work? He should've called.

He circled the block again. Not home yet. The hell with it. He'd park and wait for her. He needed to get the words out before he changed his mind. He pulled in at the curb across the street from her condo, aware of the dryness in his throat.

After ten minutes, he saw her blue Regal turn the corner and nudge into a parking place down the block. He climbed out of his truck and leaned casually against the door, arms folded across his thumping chest. Mary stepped out of her car and started up the street, a briefcase in one hand. Her shiny black hair swung against her cheek and her conservative navy wool suit marked her every inch the banker. He straightened. "Hi there."

She turned in midstride, surprise reflected in her eyes. "Russ? What're you doing here?"

He sauntered over to join her. "Waiting for you." When she continued up the walk, he fell in beside her. "Thought we might grab a bite to eat."

She set down the briefcase and fished in her handbag for the door key before facing him with a humorous expression. "Let me guess. This is one of your spur-of-the-moment ideas, right?" She inserted the key, opened the door, scooped up the briefcase and stood facing him.

Had he ticked her off again? "Impulse—that's my middle name. And I'm supposed to loosen you up, remember?" He stepped closer. "Whaddya say?"

She hesitated, then smiled wearily. "Russ, not tonight. I have plans."

He walked past her into the living room. "You do. Dinner with me."

She shrugged in mock indignation, but before she could speak, he captured her in his arms and kissed first one side of her neck, then the other. As he found the soft moistness of her lips, he heard the muffled thud of her briefcase hitting the carpeted floor and felt the resistance go out of her system as her palms found a home against his chest. "I've been wanting to do that all week." He bent down again, brushing the tip of his nose gently across her forehead as he held her close. He smelled the lemony, rainwater-clean scent of her hair, satiny against his face. Sudden fear gripped his heart. Down what hazardous path was he traveling?

He felt Mary disengage herself. "Russ, I have work to do tonight."

"Can't it wait?"

"I don't think so. I'm putting out a mailing to gallery owners and artists' groups to see if anyone can help me discover the origin of my necklace." She crossed her arms. "I thought you understood things like that have to come first right now."

Russ grabbed her by the shoulders. "Mary, I came over here to say something and if I don't say it now, I may never feel this courageous again." His stomach muscles coiled as they had when he'd waited in a chute astraddle a bucking bronc. "Listen to me. I'm crazy about you. I think about you all the time. I understand you're busy, but I need to know if there's any future in this." He shrugged, rubbing his hands up and down her arms. "In us." Her eyes widened, and he dropped his hands awkwardly to his sides. "Mary, say something."

She slowly exhaled. "I don't know what to say."

He turned away, raking the fingers of one hand through his hair, and then faced her again. "Sorry, I've got all the finesse of a charging bull." He moved closer to her and gently cupped her chin in his hands, studying her startled, tentative eyes. "Mary, I haven't had much practice saying this—" he paused, struggling with his emotions "—but I think I'm falling in love with you."

He'd thought getting the words out would make him feel better; instead, he felt as if flying hooves had kicked the air out of him. He nestled her against his chest, hesitant to look into her eyes, afraid of the rejection he might see there.

"Russ?" The sound of his name was muffled. Tensely, he drew away and dared to look down at her. Her high cheekbones were flushed. She slowly lifted her eyes to his. "Love? I...I didn't have any idea...any idea that...not yet, anyway..." Her voice trailed off.

"That anybody could get to old love-'em-and-leave-'em Coulter?"

"No, I mean—" she stammered. "I meant...certainly not me, not now."

"Why not?"

A mélange of emotions played across her face. "I don't know how to answer you. I'm touched, and I can't deny the chemistry between us. The feelings I have for you are strong—" she rested a hand on his arm "—but I haven't had time to sort them out. Somehow I didn't expect this to—" she seemed to struggle for a conciliatory tone "—to...you know...move along so quickly." As she slowly withdrew her hand, he stood waiting, confusion strangling the protest rising in his throat.

She continued, gathering speed, not looking at him. "We need more time to get to know each other. I'm way too serious. You're a free spirit. I don't know whether we'd ever—you've said it yourself—make sense together. Besides, I have all these other things racing around in my mind." She picked up *Cherokee Legends* from the books stacked on the coffee table. "Like this book. Like the necklace. Even Sal McClanahan commented today how unusual it is. Surely someone must know *something* about where it came from." She put the book down and grasped his hands tightly. "Russ, be patient with me. I'm so close to some answers." Her eyes pleaded. "I'm feeling ... how can I explain it ... overwhelmed. Please don't smother me right now."

As if he'd been catapulted from a gyrating bronco onto the unyielding turf of a rodeo arena, he could taste the sawdust filling his mouth. Smothering her! That was the last thing he'd intended, but he wasn't a fool. Mary and her compulsion to compartmentalize her life! Well, he saw where her priorities lay. He strode toward the door. "I'll shove off then, so you can get started on your project."

She crossed to him, restraining him by one elbow, her eyes filling with tears. "Russ, I didn't mean—"

"Sure you did." He paused, then pecked her on the cheek. "Good luck."

He walked slowly down the steps and crossed the street. He'd finally exposed himself by telling a woman he loved her and had she swooned at his feet? Hell, no. He was "smothering her." She didn't have time for him right now. She'd turned him six ways from loose and then left him to flounder. He opened the truck door and sat down heavily. When would he learn? She'd already taken him on one roller coaster ride. Why volunteer for another?

CHAPTER TEN

ON THANKSGIVING DAY, Mary, temples throbbing with a dull headache, eased her car up to the entrance of the motel to pick up her parents. She winced as they walked through the lobby doors. Their definition of "casual dress" was pure Ladue—her mother in a fawn-colored wool skirt with a matching tunic sweater and designer scarf and her father sporting Oxford gray slacks, an argyle sweater-vest over his shirt and tie and a camel blazer. Not exactly football attire.

"Happy Thanksgiving, Mom, Dad. Watch the relish tray and salad on the back seat." As she drove, she pointed out local sites of interest—the Emerson Oil building, a restored city block devoted to antique shops, the old railroad station recently converted to an upscale restaurant.

"Mary." Her mother shifted in the front seat. "Tell me about the Coulters."

"Carolyn and J.T. are the parents. He's an oil-and-gas attorney. The older son is Russ. Brian's a law student at Kansas University and Janie's a senior in high school." She paused, tension knotting her stomach muscles. She hoped her parents would rubberneck in silence for a while. She couldn't imagine how this day would unfold. "Now we're entering the nicer residential area."

Russ had been on her mind a great deal since Friday night when he'd blindsided her with his surprising declaration. It was uncharacteristic of everything she thought she knew about him. Mulling it over since, she realized that her less-than-positive response had dealt a severe blow to his pride. Bottom line, she'd hurt him badly.

In the past few days, she'd spent many uncomfortable moments trying to assess her own feelings. Unquestionably, she did care for him. What was wrong with her? Why couldn't she juggle everything at once? Why did she have to deal with things one at a time? Logically?

By way of amends, she'd invited him over for dinner Sunday night, but he'd cooly claimed a prior engagement. She hadn't heard from him since. How on earth was she going to spend an entire day with the Coulters, her parents and Russ? She tightened her grip on the steering wheel.

"What does young Coulter do, Mary?"

Her father's question irritated her—as if he'd somehow intuited her interest in Russ and felt obliged to launch the paternal inquisition—profession, memberships, age, health, income.

"He's a rancher."

"I see."

End of conversation. Mary's stomach cramped. She nodded toward the park. "Here's where I run sometimes."

Her father leaned forward. "Are you keeping in training?"

"It's hard to find time with my work schedule."

"I'd hate to see you give it up."

"No chance of that, Dad. Running's too important to me."

She parked in front of the Coulters' large colonial-style house, the exterior bedecked with fresh Christmas greenery and bright red bows. "Here we are. The Coulters have been very welcoming to me. I know you'll enjoy them."

Mary held her breath all the way up the brick walk. Just as they climbed the porch steps, Carolyn flung open the door and stretched out her arms. "Happy Thanksgiving!" She hugged Mary and then offered both hands to Mary's mother.

Mary watched from the hallway as Carolyn ushered her parents into the living room and continued the introductions. Her own discomfort was paralyzing. She sensed someone moving up behind her from the direction of the kitchen. She turned. Russ, in jeans and a faded forest green chamois shirt, lounged against the wall, his expression neutral. "Happy Thanksgiving."

Mary's instinct was to reach out, to touch him, to draw him in. But even without the salad bowls she clutched, something in the way he held himself—distant, removed—would have checked her. "Russ..." She felt flustered. "Same to you."

He looked at her intently, then roused himself and took her by the elbow. "Como mect Brian." He propelled her into the living room and introduced her to a six-foot-tall version of J.T. with Carolyn's red hair.

She stood on the sidelines with Carolyn and her mother during the touch football game that began in the park a few minutes later. To Mary's surprise, her father acquitted himself well. Afterward, Janie, flushed from exertion, caught Mary on the way back to the house. "What's with you and Russ?"

Mary's shoulders drooped. "What do you mean?"

Janie regarded her curiously. "You're way too polite. Like you're just, you know, acquaintances or something."

"I guess I hadn't noticed."

"Hadn't noticed? Give me a break! I saw how lovey-dovey you guys were at the ranch. Anyway, Russ is mooning like a sick calf these days." She stuck both hands in her front jeans pockets.

Mary watched as the others, entering the house, laughingly rehashed the game. She stopped and faced Janie. "It's that obvious?"

"Like a big news flash."

If Janie had noticed, undoubtedly so had everyone else. And this was hardly the time or place to reconcile with Russ. "Janie, I'm sorry. I don't want to spoil the holiday for anybody."

"We'll all be fine. Except maybe you and Russ." She held the door. "Mary—" her green eyes were deadly serious "—I think for once my brother's fallen hard. Try not to hurt him. It'd prob'ly serve him right, but I love the guy."

Mary rubbed her icy hands together. "I'll try. Right now, Janie, that's all I can promise."

"That's all I'm asking." Janie stepped aside, held the door for Mary and smiled encouragingly as they joined the others in the living room.

At the dinner table later, conversation swirled around Mary. At the beginning of the meal, she'd politely inquired about Brian's law studies. Since then, she'd sat quietly, feeling more like an observer than a guest. She pleated and unpleated the napkin in her lap. She looked around the table—earnest Brian, irrepressible Janie, good-humored J.T., effusive Carolyn, her dignified father, gracious mother and...Russ. Her throat felt scratchy. *Thankful.* She should be thankful, but the words stuck. Why was she out of sync with this Norman Rockwell portrait of the family Thanksgiving gathering? Looking at Russ made her even more miserable. Seated next to his mother, eyes fixed on his plate, he ate steadily, speaking only when a question was addressed to him. Mary noticed Carolyn frequently glancing at him in puzzlement.

After the dishes were loaded in the dishwasher, J.T. and Carolyn drove her parents out to the ranch for a tour. Brian, Russ and Janie were glued to the televised pro football game. Mary left them in the den and curled up on the living room sofa with a novel Carolyn had recommended. A homey fire crackled in the fireplace and the lights of the tastefully decorated Christmas tree standing in the corner winked on and off. At dinner, Carolyn had laughingly admitted putting up the tree early helped put her in the holiday spirit. For Mary, however, it served as an ironic contrast to her own dark mood.

She'd read two whole chapters before realizing she hadn't the foggiest notion what the book was about. Resolutely she turned back to the first paragraph of Chapter One. She was halfway down the page when she became aware of a stillness in the house.

She looked up. Russ stood in the doorway, hands thrust in his back pockets, studying her. Marking her place with her forefinger, she closed the book.

"It's halftime," he said. "Janie and Brian went for a walk." He came closer, standing over her, his expression solemn.

She could hear the sonorous ticking of the grandfather clock in the entry hall, the creaks and twinges of the quiet house. "Oh?" Her voice came out a whisper.

"Actually I asked them to leave." He sat down at the far end of the sofa. "We need to talk."

Her mouth went dry. She carefully set the book on the cushion between them. "You're probably right."

He cleared his throat. "I came on too strong the other night. I assure you it won't happen again." She detected a hint of bitterness in his voice.

"Russ—" She absently tucked a tendril of hair behind her ear. "I owe you an apology, too. I was insensitive, absorbed in my own problems. It's not as if I don't care about you."

"Damned by faint praise?" He looked at her, his eyes stony gray.

"That's not what I meant." She struggled to find the words. "I simply can't cope with everything at once."

"You mean I'm just an added complication when you need to be concentrating on your search?"

"You're not a complication, but I thought we were...I don't know." She ignored his skeptical expression. "That you understood." She found herself sounding defensive. "You said you'd help."

"I thought I already had."

"Well, yes, but that's just the start." She paused to collect her thoughts. "I'm grateful for your help, I really am..."

"But?"

She smiled ruefully. "... but I've got to see this search through. I'm attracted to you, I have feelings for you—is that honest enough? But I can't think about us while I'm putting all my energy into finding out who I am." She reached out tentatively and touched the hand he'd draped along the sofa back. He didn't move.

"Mary, you can't expect to put life on hold while you follow a dream."

"I've got to."

He withdrew his hand. "Why are you letting the past get in the way of the present? Can't you live in the here and now?"

She stared into her lap. He didn't get it.

"Mary," he went on, "you have wonderful parents. You couldn't ask for nicer people than Charles and Phyllis. Let it be."

"I can't." She looked up, willing him to understand.

"Can't or won't?" He tipped her chin up with one finger. "What if the you I see right now is more than enough for me?"

"But it's not enough for me." She saw the cloud darken his eyes.

He stood up. "Mary, I'm trying very hard to understand. But I guess what you're telling me is to back off. Cool it."

She got up, too, her legs shaking, and put one palm on his chest. "Patience. That's what I'm asking. Help if you can give it. But patience . . . and time."

She met his eyes, saddened by the pain she read in their unflinching gaze. He carefully removed her hand from his chest. "I wouldn't want to *smother* you."

The front door banged shut. "Hey, you two." Janie cavorted into the room. "Oops, sorry." She retreated to the doorway. "I didn't mean to butt in."

Russ turned away, moving toward the den. "It's okay. It's time for the second-half kickoff, anyway."

Janie gave Mary a bewildered glance. Mary shrugged, sank down on the sofa and picked up the book. Opening it, she saw the words through shimmering tears. What had she done? Why was there a gaping hole in the place her heart used to be? She looked up, fighting back a flood of emotion. Her eyes came to rest on the Christmas tree. Childhood feelings swept over her. Her angel. This Christmas, at last, she might unravel the mystery of her birth. But at what cost? Russ?

RUSS LEANED INTO the refrigerator, moving beer bottles and juice cartons around to make room for the leftovers his mother had sent home with him. It'd been a difficult Thanksgiving. Mary's presence had put a severe strain on him. All he'd wanted to do was take her by the shoulders and shake some sense into her, tell her how damn much he needed her, how it didn't matter a hill of beans to him whether she'd been found under a cabbage leaf or delivered by the stork. But he wasn't going to grovel.

He slammed the refrigerator door harder than he intended, rattling the loose jars and bottles. Her parents must've thought he had all the charm of a hibernating bear prematurely awakened. The whole day had been a disaster. Even Carolyn, catching him alone in the kitchen, had thrown him a baleful look before giving him a quick, concerned hug.

Good God! He didn't need this abuse. Big brown eyes notwithstanding, Mary Fleet was a pain in the ass. He'd never had this kind of trouble before, and if this misery was what it meant to fall in love, he wanted no part of it. No, sirree! A change of scene, that was what he needed. Something to take his mind off a stubborn, exasperatingly sexy brunette. The one he "smothered." He did a quick mental review of ranch business. It was the slow season; things wouldn't be picking up until the new stock arrived in January. And he hadn't been skiing in over a year. Hell, yes, Jim and the boys could handle things for a few days.

Decision made, he went to the phone and dialed his college buddy in Oklahoma City. "Hey, Corky, long time no see.... Say, you still own that cabin at Angel Fire?... Yeah, I would. Just for two or three days.... Great. I'll swing through the city and pick up the keys on Sunday.... Thanks, fella. I owe you one." He hung up the phone, satisfied that he was back in control of his life. No more misguided sorties into emotional danger. Free and easy, from now on. That was the Coulter way.

SATURDAY MORNING Mary paused before knocking on the door of her parents' motel room. A day of Christmas shopping and museum-hopping in Tulsa, and then her parents would be flying home this evening. Sadly she felt more relief than regret.

Work yesterday had offered a welcome reprieve from her own edginess, as well as her parents' uncharacteristic superficiality and disconcerting questions. From her mother, she'd heard, "Carolyn tells me you and Russ have been seeing something of each other. Is this anything serious?" And from her father, "Have you given any thought to how soon you'll return to the St. Louis area?" Worse yet, both of them had studiously avoided any reference to the search for her birth parents. She felt like an actress in some three-character absurdist drama.

She sighed and then knocked. Her father greeted her with a perfunctory kiss on the forehead and gestured toward the king-size bed strewn with clothes. "I can't get Phyl moving this morning. She's still not packed."

Her mother shrugged. "Charles, if you're so antsy, dear, go down to the lobby, get a cup of coffee, buy a newspaper. Mary and I'll finish up here."

Mary threw her purse on the bed. "There's plenty of time. The stores don't open until ten."

Her father smiled stiffly. "I can take a hint." He scooped up the key card from the credenza. "And, Phyl, you'd better be ready or Mary and I will leave you behind."

"That man!" Her mother smiled indulgently. "If he had his way, we'd arrive at the airport a day ahead of time." She picked up a pair of shoes and wedged them into the open suitcase.

"Here, Mom, let me help."

Her mother waved her into a nearby chair. "Thanks, but I have my own idiosyncratic packing methods. Just keep me company."

Before Mary could launch a safe conversational topic, her mother, eyes focused on the suitcase, said, "I don't believe you ever answered my question about Russ Coulter."

Mary swallowed. "What question?"

Phyllis straightened up, shaking a slipper at her. "*What* question? Don't play games with me, young lady."

"Russ is a good friend."

"Are you sure that's all?"

"No. I mean—" Mary stood and walked to the window, staring out at the covered swimming pool. "I just don't know." She fingered the taut drapery cord.

"I don't want to pry, but something was going on between the two of you Thanksgiving Day."

Mary felt her mother's eyes bore into her back. "I guess everybody noticed." She turned around to face her.

"So?"

"I like him, Mom, I really do. But I don't have the time or energy for a relationship. I'm busy. A new town, a new job..."

"And your search?"

Mary sank back into the chair. The word had surfaced at last. "Yes."

Her mother made a show of folding up a bulky sweater. "Are you sure you're not deliberately putting obstacles between you and Russ?"

Was that what she was doing? Or was she just being cautious, practical, self-protective? "Hunting my birth parents has to be the priority."

"Mmm-hmm." Her mother tucked two scarves into the corners of the suitcase, closed the lid and sat down on the edge of the bed. She reached over and took one of Mary's hands in hers. "How is the search coming? I've wanted to ask, but not in front of your father."

"He's still having trouble with this, isn't he?"

"That's putting it mildly."

"When something's this important to me, it's hard not being able to talk it over with you and Daddy."

"I know. I wish things were different." Her mother squeezed her hand. "Have you discovered anything?"

"The necklace, Mom. It's the only real lead so far."

Her mother's voice fell. "Oh?"

Mary moved to sit beside her mother. "Mom, I think my birth mother was Cherokee."

"Because of the necklace?"

"Yes—I've been told it's a Cherokee piece. You didn't have this information before?"

Now it was her mother who stood and slowly walked to the window. The loud hum of a vacuum cleaner down the hall filled the silence as Mary, fingernails digging into her clenched palms, awaited her mother's response.

Finally Phyllis spoke. "Mary, I've told you all I know about your birth mother." She pulled Mary to her feet and hugged her. "But I do know you must come from good stock. They don't make daughters any better than you. Whoever she may be, I'll always be grateful to her for giving us you."

Mary felt her mother's soft cheek against her own and her eyes misted. "Thanks, Mom."

They drew apart, her mother still gently clasping her arms. "Mary, one more thing. I know this search is a priority, but you've always been single-minded to a fault and—" she lowered her voice when they heard the click of a key card engaging the door lock "—you may want to do some thinking about your other priorities. I noticed the way you looked at Russ when you thought no one saw you."

"Okay, *now* are you ready, Phyl?" Mary's father set down two take-out coffee cups. "Here, you two, drink up while I load the car."

Mary busied herself with the coffee, avoiding her mother's all-knowing eyes.

RUSS TOOK A deep breath of the thin, pure air and adjusted his goggles for the day's last ski run. This trip had been an inspired idea. Already he felt invigorated, refreshed and, best of all, free.

He shoved off, feeling the updraft hit his face, hearing the hiss of his skis as they sank into the deep powder. He flew down the slope, hunkered for the jump over a small rise, soared and landed solidly on both skis. God, it was fun. The snow-laden branches of dark green pine trees blurred, and he focused on the black trail markers, the cold chapping his exposed cheeks and jaw. Faster and faster he went, shifting his weight over his skis, leaning dangerously into the curves. As the hill leveled near the base lodge, he slowed to a stop. He put his hands on his knees and bent over, drawing deep breaths into his oxygen-deprived lungs. He grinned. A great day on the slopes! And an equally great evening lay ahead.

He shouldered his skis and stored them in the outdoor rack. Inside, the après-ski crowd was winding down. He'd have a peppermint schnapps before showering and heading out for dinner at one of the hot night spots. He found an empty stool near one end of the bar and ordered his drink. Next to him a middle-aged couple debated the merits of various ski areas and in the mirror over the bar, he caught the reflection of a group of festive college kids.

He smelled her before he saw her—the heady scent of jungle flowers, then the striking columbine-blue eyes appraising him from the fur-bordered hood framing her face. She edged up close to him. "Is this seat taken?" She gestured to the recently vacated seat beside his.

"Allow me." Russ stood and pulled out the stool.

She sat down, flashing him a dazzling smile that showed off perfect white teeth. "Snow was great, huh?"

"Can I get you a drink?" He scooted his bar stool closer to hers.

She licked her lips in contemplation. "I'll have one of what you're having." She unzipped her parka, throwing back her shoulders as she eased out of it.

Whoa! He couldn't take his eyes off her. Her silver-blond hair cascaded down her back in silky ripples. As she shrugged out of the parka sleeves, her tight-fitting turtleneck left little to the imagination. If anybody was a sure cure for the lovelorn...

He ordered her a drink and a second for himself. "I'm Russ Coulter from Ewing, Oklahoma." He extended his hand.

She smiled enticingly as she shook his hand, her carmined fingertips lingering a beat too long as she withdrew from his grasp. "Kirsten Lindblad."

"Let me guess. A Swede?"

"Oh, ja." She parodied a Scandinavian accent. "A Swede from Minn-e-sot-a." She batted her thick mascaraed lashes. "St. Paul, to be specific."

After another round of drinks and a half hour of flirtatious small talk, he'd determined she was in Angel Fire on business as a sales rep for a skiwear designer and, best of all, available for dinner. He'd hit the mother lode.

Later, sitting in a small booth in the restaurant, he pondered his luck. Her long, thick corn-silk hair fell across her shoulders. The tight-fitting, scoop-necked black evening sweater she wore revealed tantalizing cleavage. Frequently, in a catlike gesture that drew attention to her breasts, she lifted her arms to push her hair back off her face. He had trouble keeping his eyes raised and his attention directed to the conversation.

"Care for some dessert?" he asked after their entrées had been cleared from the table.

She stretched her arms over her head and contemplated. "Maybe. Yes." Under the table he felt the unmistakable caressing along his calf and up his thigh of a shoeless foot. She put both elbows on the table and leaned closer, the glow from the candle reflecting in her ice-blue eyes. "I can think of several things I might like."

He stared at her, warmth rising from his belly upward to his face as he felt her toes prodding between his legs. He shifted uncomfortably in his seat and glanced nervously around to determine if they were being observed. He felt trapped in the booth. "Why don't we think it over on the dance floor?" He stood up, shielding his involuntary arousal with his napkin.

She uncoiled from the booth and whispered breathily in his ear. "C'mon, cowboy."

The small, packed dance floor made it impossible not to hold her close. She was nearly as tall as he was. Her lush breasts thrust against his chest and her hips ground insistently against his. Her gardenia perfume rose like steam and there was no mistaking the invitation in the movements of her fingers at the nape of his neck. She was doing her damnedest to turn him on. With some success.

Yet, somewhere above it all, he couldn't relate to her, to this. She didn't fit neatly against him the way Mary did, she didn't smell fresh and clean like Mary, her movements were contrived, not natural, not innocent. Damn. What was the matter with him? All he knew was that Kirsten was suffocating him. He stopped dancing, stepped away and led her off the dance floor. "I don't know about you, but I've decided on the bread pudding with caramel sauce."

She eyed him invitingly. "I think I'll have the Bananas—Foster." She linked her arm through his and slithered into the seat beside him.

What had he gotten himself into? Hadn't this been part of his plan? To get away from Ewing and Mary, revisit familiar haunts, let some eager snow bunnies take his mind off his problems? And the statuesque ice goddess beside him filled the bill. Mary. The contrast was striking. In his wildest dreams he couldn't imagine Mary acting like Kirsten. The hell of it was, he was glad.

Beside him the blonde scooped up the last bit of ice cream and turned toward him, seductively licking the back of her spoon. He felt one breast pressing against his arm. "Now, then, Russ from Oklahoma, your place or mine?"

Nothing subtle about this lady! "Wouldn't you like an after-dinner drink?" He felt an insane desire to escape.

"My bar's well stocked. My place?" She arched an eyebrow at him.

"Well, I'm not quite sure what you have in mind..."
Yeah, sure! Was he going to back out now? This was exactly the antidote *he'd* envisioned.

"Just use your imagination. It's settled then." She wiped her mouth on her napkin and stood up, extending her hand. "My place works out anyway. I need to call my husband."

His legs refused to move. "Begging your pardon, your *husband*?"

She rubbed a soothing hand up his arm. "Don't get excited. Rolfe and I have a kind of understanding." She smiled knowingly. "Neither of us expects the other to spend long, lonely nights when we're apart. Anyway—" she bent down to nibble at the soft spot under his ear "—don't you agree this makes life much more, uh, interesting?"

"Interesting?" A lewd, grotesque image of his mother exploded in his brain, drowning him in a wave of revulsion. A surge of anger and betrayal seared his chest. With shaking hands, he carefully disengaged her clinging arms and got to his feet. In a cold, controlled voice, he continued. "No, lady, I don't think it's interesting. Kinky, maybe. Where I come from, Kirsten, we call it infidelity." He threw down a ten-dollar bill for a tip. "Find your stud somewhere else." He walked away, leaving her standing by the table.

RUSS PLOPPED DOWN into the hard seat for the day's first chairlift ride and shaded his eyes against the fresh white snow. A puny sun rose over the far peak, and gathering heavy clouds promised more snow. The fresh air felt good, clearing the fuzzy, hung over feeling in his head. Three schnapps, too much wine and the cloying promiscuousness of the predatory Valkyrie had left a foul taste in his mouth, both literally and figuratively. His stomach recoiled. Had his mother been like that? Sleek, lascivious, sexually aggressive?

He squeezed his eyes shut. Was he really much better? Avoiding involvement, going from woman to woman in an escape from commitment, never pausing long enough to establish a relationship or risk the pain of rejection.

He opened his eyes and stared, unseeing, at the chair ahead of him. He'd been looking for a good time, not a sexual adventure. A few laughs, some dance floor snuggling, maybe a little groping. He was no fool, though. The days of safe one-night stands had ended about the time he'd noticed his first zit. What kind of man must old Rolfe be? The sick bastard.

The metallic whirr and jolt of the lift attracted his attention just in time to make a smooth exit. Screaming muscles he hadn't used in a while, coupled with his headache, demanded a tamer attack on the slopes today. A safe blue run to start with. As he crisscrossed down the mountain, he couldn't get over the tawdry feeling last night's escapade had produced. Had he really spent significant portions of his adult life with that kind of creature?

He'd tossed and turned all night, his mind fixed on the clean-cut, refreshingly unsophisticated image of Mary Fleet. Her transparent dark eyes that revealed more truths than she realized bore into his soul like an accusation. If he *really* preferred flirtatious blondes, what had prompted him to tell Mary he was falling in love with her?

He pulled off the course to adjust his goggles. What indeed? The cloud mass rolled eastward, obscuring the sun. It was getting colder. He pushed off down the slope at a steady pace.

What the hell *had* prompted him? Over and over the answer came back to him, resounding in his head. The inescapable fact: he *did* love her.

So, ham bone, what're you doing here? Pride hurt? Didn't like it when she didn't immediately fall into your arms? When she told you she had a slightly different agenda? The mocking alter ego was right on. He'd run away. He'd been planning to show her. God, he disgusted himself. *Cut the "poor me" crap! What're you gonna do now?*

Good question. He worried it out in his mind as he worked his way down the trail. He loved her for the very reasons he was repelled by Kirsten—for her innocence, moral rectitude, even her determination. What it added up to was character. Plain old-fashioned character.

And for all his machismo, she was a bigger risk taker than he. Her search for her birth parents took guts. And what had he done? Given little more than lip service to helping her. If you loved somebody, you were supposed to stand by them, no matter what. His bruised pride had gotten in the way of his heart. Was it too late?

He skidded to a stop at the base of the slope. Not if he could help it. He could be on the road in half an hour. He tore off his skis and took off toward the parking lot.

No more wasting time in self-indulgence. You want something, you gotta fight for it. But how? How could he prove himself? Suddenly, he stopped in his tracks, the obviousness of the answer taking him by surprise. He sure as hell could make every effort to help her find the one thing that was most important to her—her identity.

CHAPTER ELEVEN

MARY HAD FOUND the days since Thanksgiving difficult, and this Wednesday was no exception. She'd come home from Tulsa Saturday evening exhausted. Sunday, fighting a scratchy throat, she'd sat by the phone, staring at it, willing it to ring—willing Russ to call. At work the past two days, beneath her businesslike exterior, she was aware of an ache, an emptiness. She'd operated on autopilot, drifting through routine.

She closed the thick folder on her desk and put her head down on her arms. Everywhere she looked was a strained relationship. Nearly a week had passed since she'd seen or heard from Russ. Over Thanksgiving her father had seemed particularly reserved.

She sighed. What'd she expected? Her father joyously to accept and participate in her search? Russ to defer his feelings and set aside his pride while she plowed down her own path? She straightened up, brushing her hair back. She was a rational, precise person. There was no reason to drown in an emotional whirlpool. She would work it out. Starting with the search.

Did she still want to locate her birth parents? Yes. What about her father? His feelings? He hadn't totally shut her out. In time, he'd come around. Especially when he understood that nothing could diminish her love for him. And Russ? Her eyes swam with sudden tears.

"Mary?"

She jerked upright, swiping at her eyes, as Gwen peered around the door. "How about lun—" Gwen stopped in midsentence and hurried to Mary's side. "Honey, you look awful. What's happened?"

Fanning her fingers back and forth in front of her eyes, Mary reached in her desk drawer for a tissue. "I'll...I'll be all right." She sniffled. "Just give me a minute."

Gwen laid a soft hand on her shoulder, waiting until Mary regained control. Then she circled the desk and pulled a chair close. "The adoption?" She eyed Mary empathetically. "Or Russ?"

"Am I that transparent?"

"It doesn't take a genius. Especially when I've heard you talk more about him in the past few weeks than about any other subject."

"I think I've botched everything."

"How's that?"

Mary wiped the tissue under her eyes, blotting up black streaks of eyeliner. "He's been charming and funny and supportive. But I never dreamed he'd, I mean... that...he'd say he was..."

Gwen sat up straighter. "Wait a minute. Don't tell me someone's finally gotten to Russ Coulter?" She stammered. "I...I didn't mean it like that. You're a wonderful person—"

"But I'm not a classic Coulter selection?" Mary managed a wan grin. "That's exactly what I thought, too."

"So?"

"When he told me he might be falling in love with me, I guess I...shot him down."

"Why?"

"Gwen, I'm not ready. I have this job to worry about, the search. I'm overwhelmed."

"What did he say?"

"He asked me why I can't live in the here and now. Why I'm trapped in the past. Even my own mother questioned my priorities where he's concerned."

"And . . . ?"

"I'm not sure anymore."

Gwen stood up. "Well, kiddo, it sounds to me like you better think this one through real carefully. Russ is a terrific guy. There's a lot at stake." She paused. "Tell you what. I'll run down to the deli and bring you back some lunch. Meanwhile, you might want to do some serious thinking. Okay?"

"Thanks, Gwen. Maybe you're right." Gwen shut Mary's door softly. Mary walked to the window, staring at the sheets of rain funneling down the streaked pane and blurring the red and green Christmas lights on the building opposite. How *did* she feel about Russ? What was she asking of him? Generous, impulsive Russ who'd given her those "welcome to Oklahoma" gifts. Funny, gregarious Russ, the apple of his family's eye. Committed, businesslike Russ who loved his ranch. The Russ who'd held her close, offered his support and kissed her in ways that caused tingles to radiate in private, secret places. The devil-may-care Russ who'd risked telling her he was falling in love.

Her heart knocked against her ribs, and another sob caught in her throat. Just thinking about him—about the firm line of his jaw, the cowlick of sandy hair at the crown of his head, his sexy grin, full of promise and his hard, angular body—did things to her that defied reason or logic.

Okay, smarty-pants. Quit being so stubborn. Have you, the sensible, pragmatic one, fallen in love, too? With a fingertip she traced the trail of a single raindrop down the cool glass.

He'd asked her an important question, one she kept trying to bury. Why *was* she letting the past obscure the present? No more evasions. Was it possible not only to recover her past but to embrace the here and now?

Priorities, her mother had said. Mary knew she'd been hiding from herself and been unfair to Russ in the process. He *was* a priority, maybe even *the* priority. She needed to be honest, to tell him. She'd jettison logic and deal straight out of her emotions. A thaw started somewhere deep inside, and she felt her jaw and shoulders relaxing as a warmth crept up, suffusing her face. She found herself grinning idiotically, aware of an aliveness, an expectancy that hadn't been there even seconds before. Like a kid counting the days until Christmas, she had an overpowering urge to talk to Russ, to tell him she might be falling in love, too. "Falling in love." The words knocked out all her underpinnings, all her preconceived, carefully thought-out notions. She turned from the window, picked up the phone and dialed the ranch number. No answer, not even from a machine.

After lunch and throughout the long afternoon, she kept trying, each time holding her breath in anticipation of his deep warm voice. At five o'clock she let the phone ring ten times before slowly hanging up. Her exhilaration had faded, but she couldn't feign indifference or patience. Where was he? She wanted to see him, to touch him, to tell him—now!

Should she? Before she could change her mind, she called the Coulter residence. When Carolyn answered, Mary began by thanking her for the Thanksgiving meal. Then, swallowing hard, she asked if Russ happened to be there.

"No, honey, I haven't seen him since Thursday. Have you tried the ranch?"

"Yes." Mary struggled to keep the disappointment out of her voice. "He's not there."

"That's odd." Carolyn paused. "Is there anything I can do?"

"Thanks. It's just something between him and me. I'm sorry to have bothered—"

"Just a minute, Mary." She could hear Carolyn talking to someone in the background. "Great! Sometimes I despair of family communication. Russ called yesterday and talked with Janie. She failed to pass on the message. Typical. Russ's in New Mexico skiing."

"New Mexico?" Mary could barely control her irritation. He obviously hadn't given Thanksgiving another thought. She'd nearly made a complete fool of herself.

"He didn't tell you, either?"

"No." Mary waited while Carolyn cleared her throat as if considering something. "I'm not terribly surprised."

"Does he do this sort of thing often?"

"He's impulsive by nature, but he usually doesn't flee the territory unless he's upset about something and needs to think. He's only done this once before—when Janna turned down his proposal."

"I see." Mary's voice was flat.

"Mary, stop me if this is none of my business." Carolyn hesitated. "Is everything okay between you and Russ?"

Mary brushed a hand through her hair. "Things have been a bit strained lately."

"I thought so."

"I guess our Thanksgiving charade didn't fool anyone."

Carolyn chuckled. "Let's just say neither of you will be nominated for an Oscar." Her tone grew serious.

"Mary, call it mother's intuition, but I'd be very surprised if his disappearing act didn't have something to do with you."

Mary realized she'd be very surprised if it didn't, too. But what did it mean? Was this another example of his impetuosity? Of his inability to stick with things when emotions were involved? "Maybe so, Carolyn. I'm sorry to have bothered you." She tried to collect her thoughts. "When he gets back, you might tell him I called. Goodbye now."

She cradled the receiver, questions jumbling in her head. Had he run away? Had he grown tired of her equivocation, her uncertainty? Was he seeking greener pastures? Or... had he simply gone skiing?

If she told him she loved him, how would he react? Would he even care? Was she too late? An interior voice rebuked her. *Don't you dare chicken out now. You've been cautious all your life—too cautious. For once, do something really risky. Tell him!*

She stood up, flipped off the office light and put on her coat. Maybe. Okay. She would. And let the chips fall where they may.

ONE LEG TUCKED under her, Mary sat Wednesday evening at the dining room table listening to Christmas CDs and addressing large red envelopes. She hated last minute preparations and always mailed her Christmas cards by December tenth. She pushed back her bangs and turned to the next page in her address book. She'd had to do something! Even her favorite silky nightgown and a steaming cup of English tea had done little to ease her edginess. And the cheery Yuletide lyrics—"Have yourself a merry little Christmas"—served merely to depress her.

Sighing, she picked up her pen and bent over the next envelope. Before she could inscribe a letter, a loud knocking at the door startled her. She glanced at the kitchen clock. Eleven-thirty. Who could it be at this hour? She stood up, heart pounding, nervously smoothing the soft ivory fabric. She tiptoed into the living room and cautiously peered through the miniblinds. The insistent knock was repeated. At the same moment she saw the streetlight glinting off a silver truck, she heard Russ shouting, "Mary, it's me. Let me in before I wake the neighbors."

Her throat thickened with apprehension and desire. She should be angry—after all, he'd run out on their problems—but he was here. Now. She prayed for the courage to dig away the self-protective layers and get to the bedrock of her feelings. She released the dead bolt, standing behind the door as she opened it.

He stood in the doorway, his face drawn, his arms behind his back. He leaned forward. "May I come in?"

"Please. My feet are getting cold standing here on this bare tile." Not to mention her nipples, puckering in the freezing blast from outside. Keeping his back hidden from her, he sidled into the living room as she closed and locked the door.

They stood several feet apart, motionless.

"Russ—"

"Shh." He hesitated. "Mary, I'm sorry I've been such an ass."

"You? But—"

He withdrew his hands from behind his back and held high in the air a bedraggled handful of twigs, covered with small, pale green leaves and gray-white globules hanging in bunches. "I've brought you flowers."

She stared at him, pressing a hand over her spontaneous smile. "Flowers?" she managed.

His anxious features melted into that radiant grin that always captured her heart. "They don't look like much, do they?" He appraised the sorry bouquet. "But I like them." He lowered his hand to let her examine the gift. "This, dear Mary, is the official flower of the state of Oklahoma, and I've spent the last half hour climbing a tree in the dark to get them for you."

She studied the tiny oyster-colored berries. "Why, it looks—" she raised her face to his twinkling eyes "—like mistletoe!"

He laughed aloud. "It is." Holding the bouquet over her head, he grabbed her with his free arm and pulled her so close she could feel the rapid beat of his heart just before he bent his mouth to hers. He dropped the mistletoe and swept her off the floor, kissing her in a way that left no doubt about his feelings. She felt herself swooning and, as if to save herself from drowning, reached her arms around his neck, pulling into the safe harbor of his chest. His warm mouth plied her lips, seeking her tongue. In a flash of recognition, she knew that nothing had ever felt so good, so right, as his kiss...as their bodies welded in this closed circuit of desire.

Breathlessly, she drew back to gaze into his eyes. Her body, pressed against his, slid tantalizingly down the length of him, the silkiness of her gown caressing her skin, until her feet found the mooring of the floor. Solid ground. He looked at her with such tenderness, such vulnerability, that her breath stopped in her throat. She should be annoyed with him. She should ask him where he'd been. Why he'd just dropped out of sight, expecting everyone to understand. Instead, she stood, tracing his cheeks with her fingertips as if to assure herself he was really there. She found her voice. "Russ, why did you leave without telling anybody?"

She heard him choke out the words as he reached for her again, enfolding her in his arms. "I'm sorry, Mary. I've been such a fool!" He covered her forehead, her eyelids, her neck with tiny firefly kisses. "I don't have to think about it anymore." He held her at arm's length and studied her face. "I love you."

Mary paused—one last rational thought surfacing. *Can you risk it?* Then she did a very uncharacteristic thing. She giggled, she laughed, then she twirled away, bending over holding her stomach. She tried to catch her breath. She felt like a half-inflated balloon somebody'd released—cavorting crazily around the room, air whooshing out in a sudden rush. Seeing his bewildered look, she took a running start and jumped into his arms, hugging him tight as she wound down to a muffled giggle and hiccup. Only then could she speak. "I don't know whether it makes any sense, especially after your disappearing act, but I love you, too, you crazy Okie!"

Slowly, carefully, he set her down and leaned over, staring at her incredulously. Another tiny giggle surfaced. Russ Coulter—notorious flirt and self-proclaimed heartbreaker—was at a loss for words! Finally, he closed his mouth, cleared his throat and managed to rasp out, "You do?" A broadening grin creased his face. "God, I'd have brought the mistletoe long ago if I'd known its effect." Then he did a very characteristic thing. He raised his fist, pumping it in the air, and let out a piercing "Yippee-i-oh!" guaranteed to make any cowboy proud.

Mary put her fingertips against his mouth, feeling his warm breath. "Shh. You'll wake the neighbors."

He grabbed her and whirled her around in looping circles. "I'd wake all of Ewing if I could." He gradually stopped spinning and gazed at her again with that funny, dumbfounded look. "You're not putting me on?" She was amused and touched by the uncertainty in his voice.

"Have you ever known me to be much of a kidder?"

"Well, no."

"So, let me say it one more time, loud and clear." She held both his hands in hers and accentuated each word. "I—love—you."

He shook his head as he led her to the sofa. "I can't believe it. I came here prepared to storm the battlements, only to find the drawbridge down." He sat and drew her to him, snuggling her in the curve of his arm. "What's happened? You ought to be mad at me."

She nestled in closer. "I was at first. Maybe I still am— a little. I thought you'd run away."

He tousled her hair. "I did."

She straightened up, turning to look at him. "You *did?*"

"Flat-out, fast as I could go, on the lam." He nodded emphatically.

"Why? Because I rejected you?"

"You did kinda jerk the rug from under me, didn't you?"

"I guess I did. You're the one who should be mad at *me.*"

"Maybe I needed this time away to face my fears."

"Fears?"

"Of commitment."

He massaged the base of her neck, sending shivers to the tips of her fingers. "But I'm not afraid anymore." She felt her head drawn to his lips by the pressure of his palm on her bare back. Her arms went around his shoulders as he pulled her up onto his lap. He made a deep guttural sound. "Oh, Mary." The last of his words was lost in the roar in her ears as his lips sought hers. She held on to him for all she was worth, as her lips and tongue eagerly responded to his.

Dimly aware of the Christmas carols in the background, she felt the gentle play of his fingers across her exposed skin as he ran his hands up and down her back. Deeper into the kiss, she dissolved, mindful of the singing sensations thrilling every part of her body as he moved one hand to caress her thigh. *This is what it's all about. This abandon. This feeling that nothing else in the whole world matters.*

She felt his fingers tracing her rib cage and then, lightly, palming her breast, ever so gently testing its weight and contour against his hand. Her inhalation was stuck somewhere in her chest. Would she ever breathe again? She felt his warm lips nipping at the soft skin of her neck, each tiny kiss creating a fierce longing. She ran her palms down the solid muscles of his back. She wanted to know every plane, every surface of his body.

He drew away, his fingers fumbling with the pearl button at her neckline. The fabric whispered as he tenderly exposed her breasts. He looked down and then smiled back into her eyes. "I wanted to see." Mesmerized by the emotion in his gaze, she checked the instinctive protest that an instant before had risen to her lips. She returned his loving look.

Then slowly, deliberately he gathered the material and carefully rebuttoned the gown and cradled her against his chest. "That's enough for one night." She frowned with disappointment. He tweaked her nose. "You're a good girl, remember?"

She settled back against him. She remembered—with more than a trace of regret.

They sat quietly for a time, his chin resting on her hair, content in the magic of the moment. Finally he lifted her from his lap and set her down next to him. "It's time we talked, don't you think?"

She nodded.

"I didn't expect and don't deserve such a warm greeting after disappearing like that. What happened?"

She twirled a lock of dark curl around her index finger before answering. "I've been too logical." She caught the hint of a grin out of the corner of her eye. "I mean, I came to Ewing with my goal and my plan, and nothing, not even you, was going to stand in my way. Finding my birth parents will always be important to me. But something you said drew me up short."

"What was that?"

"You asked me why I couldn't live in the present. Why the past, especially an unknown past, had to govern everything." Her hand fell into her lap. "All I've been thinking about is me. Not you, not Mom and Dad, not anybody. Just me, my needs."

He tilted her chin up. "Were you doing such a good job of that?"

A rueful smile accompanied her words. "No. Because, tonight, right here and now, I need *you.*" The risk of admitting her vulnerability was like watching a storm on the horizon that could blow either way.

He kissed the top of her head. "And what about me? I ran away when everything didn't go my way. When I realized love wouldn't always be smooth—that commitment might involve hardship. Helluva guy you've got here."

She chuckled. "You're right. It *is* a helluva guy I've got here."

The smile faded from his face and his eyes grew serious. "I asked you to sacrifice a dream, maybe not in so many words, but the implication was there. I was wrong."

When she reached up to quiet him, he took her hand in his. "No, let me finish. I was wrong. I only gave lip service to your need to find your birth parents. Because of my own past, my real mother, I couldn't understand why you'd want to risk what you've already got. But I've been thinking. For you to be fulfilled, you probably do need more than me, more than Charles and Phyllis. You need an answer to the question that, for whatever reason, has haunted you all these years." He raised her hand to his lips. "You don't have to do this by yourself. I won't run away again." He chucked her under the chin. "It's you and me, babe, all the way."

She hugged him. "I love you," she breathed into his neck, cuddling contentedly against him.

After an interval she straightened up, her eyes clouding. "Right now I need all the help I can get."

"Oh?"

She stood up and gestured toward the table. "That came in the mail today." She picked up the document. "It's from the Cherokee Nation. Another dead end."

He grabbed the paper from her hand.

She listened, shoulders drooping, as he read. "'Certificates of Degree of Indian Blood—CDIB—are issued only through the natural parents. In cases of adoption, quantum of Indian blood must be proven through the *biological parents* to the enrolled ancestor. A copy of the Final Decree of Adoption must accompany the application for CDIB, as well as the state certified, full image photocopy of the birth record.'" He studied the words. "I don't get it. You're not trying to get a CDIB."

"No, but it means there's no way I can access tribal records without knowing my natural parents."

"Why, it's a damn chicken-and-egg situation."

"Yes, and I'm the shell caught in the middle."

He hugged her to him. "So one door is shut. We'll just have to look for the open window."

She laid her head against his shoulder.

He continued. "Together."

Fittingly, from the stereo speakers, she heard the ancient, soothing refrain, "Sleep in heavenly peace, sleep in heavenly peace."

PALE WINTER SUN streamed in Mary's bedroom window the next morning. Still half adrift on an airy billow of sleep, she slowly opened her eyes and smiled contentedly. Russ loved her! She loved him! Suddenly she sat straight up in bed. Sun? Horrified, she turned to the clock radio. She'd failed to set the alarm. She'd be late for work.

She took a quick shower and threw on the first blouse and suit she encountered in her closet. Then she blow-dried her hair, dabbed on some makeup and bolted from the house. Driving to work, she found her spirits soaring despite the last frantic minutes of preparation. She waved at schoolchildren waiting for the bus, she hummed "Rudolph" along with the radio, she smiled at evidence of the Christmas season—cheery wreaths on doors, yard decorations, the nativity scene set up outside the Lutheran church. Christmas with Russ. She giggled. Mistletoe. He'd brought not a puny sprig, but a whole bouquet. Kisses. Lots and lots of kisses. She felt giddy. She didn't care if she was late to work, if her desk was a mess, if her schedule got screwed up. She was in love—with Ewing, with Russ, with life!

He'd promised to help with her search, a real promise this time. They'd agreed to keep trying to track down information about the necklace, and she'd decided on a trip to Denver. Now that she knew her mother was possibly Native American, it might be easier for the doctor or somebody at the hospital to remember and give her some information.

Inside the bank, as she passed the loan department, Gwen arched her eyebrows and smiled. "Well, good morning, Miss Mary."

Mary grinned and shrugged her shoulders. "I know, I know, I'm late."

"You sure are." Gwen laughed. "I'm glad. It shows you're human, just like the rest of us."

Mary hugged herself as she walked down the hall to her office. *I'm human. Just like the rest. Not perfect, at all. Human.* It had a nice ring to it.

RUSS SWIVELED in his chair and propped his feet on the desk as his foreman, Jim Peppercorn, rambled on with an account of the maintenance work the hands had undertaken in his absence. Russ let the monotone wash over him. His mind was elsewhere. He'd known everything with Mary would be all right when she'd laughed at the mistletoe. But in his wildest dreams he hadn't been prepared for the extent of her turnaround. He sighed contentedly, lost in the remembered sensations of the soft gown riding up her smooth skin.

"...changed the oil...checked the earthen dam on number three...mended holes in the west fence... somebody's cut..."

Suddenly alert, Russ dropped his feet to the floor with a resounding thud and leaned over the desk. "Wait a minute. Run that by me again, about the fence."

"Well, boss, this is the third time this fall we've had to mend fence along the property line where our land butts up against Lloyd's. Same general area every time. And it don't seem like no coincidence. Somebody's been using wire cutters."

"Why in hell'd somebody do that?" He didn't like the sound of it. Something screwy was going on.

"Hard to say. Hunters. Kids thinkin' it'd be funny to let steers loose. Plain damn vandalism." Jim ran his fingers over the crease in the hat he turned slowly in his lap.

"Appreciate your tending to it, Jim. Anything else?"

"That's it." Jim stood, shifting from one foot to the other.

"Fine. I'm driving over to Lonnie Creighton's this morning to finalize lease terms for that eight hundred acres." After Jim left, Russ picked up his sheepskin-lined coat, slammed on a range-scarred cowboy hat and headed for the door. The ringing of the phone stopped him. He picked up the receiver. Hearing Mary's soft, warm voice unknotted some of the tension produced by Jim's report. He cocked the hat back on his head.

As she told him, laughing, about waking up late, he sat on the edge of the desk, giving in to the memory of one small, pert breast nesting in his palm, of the warmth and passion of her soft, generous lips. He realized she'd finished her story.

"Yes, I'm still here." He sat up straighter and lowered his voice seductively. "I was just remembering last night and what a trembling Mary Fleet feels like in my arms." He paused, hearing a quick rush of breath before she spoke again.

"Russ, I don't even feel like me. I'm sappy and disorganized and I laugh at nothing. It seems like Christmas already." She giggled. "I think people at the bank are noticing."

"See what love can do? Ms. Efficiency has a weakness after all."

"For you." The phone line sang in the silence.

"I love you, Mary."

"Russ, I'm sitting here blushing. I don't blush at my office."

"You do now."

He could hardly hear her. "I know. I like it." Again the companionable silence. "I *did* have a reason for calling you," she finally began. "I—"

He interrupted. "Besides just wanting to hear my sexy voice? When you were a kid, I'll bet your mother told you it wasn't proper to call boys without a good reason."

She laughed. "How'd you know? But I *do* have a good reason. We have an invitation."

"Oh?"

"Sal McClanahan called. On behalf of our friends there, she invited us to the Sooner Arms Christmas Open House Sunday afternoon."

"Are they having another 'reception'?" He wasn't sure he could handle a second dose of Chauncey Butterworth's highballs.

"No, this is a big do for all the residents and their guests. Tea and punch, maybe a few Christmas cookies. You game?"

He chuckled. "You bet. I like those folks. Woody and Chauncey are salt of the earth, and what's not to like about Sal? You're on."

Her voice turned tentative. "Would you like to come over for dinner tonight? I don't think I can wait till Sunday to see you."

"I love it when you talk that way. Seven o'clock?"

"Fine."

"And, Mary, wear something sexy. I love you."

LATE THAT EVENING Russ quietly eased the truck away from the curb in front of Mary's condo and accelerated down the dark street. Whew! It'd been all he could do to control himself. The sensations were as vivid as if she was in the truck with him. He still tasted the cinnamony velvet of her lips, still smelled the sandalwood fragrance of the soft place under her chin. Heard the whoosh of the satiny chemise slipping to the floor, saw the tawny ripeness of her breasts, taut brown nipples teasing the skin of his chest. And then there was the muffled cry just as he'd started to shuck off his jeans. She'd reached up to stay him, framing his face in her hands and managing to whisper, "Russ?" Through misty eyes, she implored his understanding.

He'd sat up, gently cradling her to him as he stroked her hair, willing away the torrent of desire that threatened to undo him. "It's okay. It's okay," he'd soothed. "There will be a right time."

At the highway intersection, he paused for the red light that swayed in the gusty wind. There *would* be a time. And damn soon if he wasn't going to spend an eternity of sleepless nights.

The light changed and he hurtled along the deserted road to the ranch. Some knight in shining armor! He could barely control himself around her—and he couldn't think of a damn way to help her find her holy grail. Denver seemed like a million-to-one shot, and the Cherokee tribal records left them hardly anything to go on. Earlier in the evening she'd shown him a letter from the Southwestern Trails Gallery. He tried to recall the exact words. "Without seeing your necklace, it is difficult to say, but it could be one of a kind, perhaps a family heirloom that might once have belonged to a Beloved Woman." Even at that, there must be thousands of Cherokee families.

Still, the necklace had to be the key. It was the only solid piece of evidence they had if, in fact, it was her birth mother who'd passed it on. "Could be one of a kind."

He squinted at the road, flipped on his brights. An elusive, nagging scrap of memory, like a tick, kept digging into his consciousness. The necklace. Something about the necklace.

Was it the words? Beloved or beloved woman? Would such an heirloom be passed down through the eldest daughter? Or would a man give it to his wife? Did each family have its own distinctive talisman? There, at least, was a route to explore.

One of a kind. Hold on. Who was it? Somebody. Then it hit him. Sal. At her apartment the day of the cocktail reception. She'd noticed the necklace around Mary's neck. The image of Sal's pale, shaken face etched itself in his brain. Maybe Sal had seen another like it—wait, Mary had mentioned to him that Sal had asked her about the necklace. The day Mary'd gone to her apartment on bank business. That made two times. The old gal apparently had more than a passing interest in the *oochalata* piece. Why?

A cold tremor passed through his body. What if Sal knew something? He snorted. The sheer coincidence of it was nonsensical. Crazy!

Yet an eerie certainty seized him, clamping his breath to the back of his throat. No idle adage—truth often *was* stranger than fiction. The wildness of his hypothesis and its implications left his mouth dry. If he was right, this truth would be not only strange, but potentially dangerous.

When he turned in at the ranch driveway, he'd already made his decision. No reason yet to involve Mary, to build up her hopes without real basis. Especially not if the idea forming in his brain had even an ounce of evidence to support it.

He'd handle it himself. Tomorrow he would pay a call on Sal McClanahan.

CHAPTER TWELVE

RUSS HEAVED A SIGH as he stood outside Sal's apartment the next morning. He'd lain awake for over an hour the night before constructing the line of questioning he intended to pursue. Then he'd lain awake another hour visualizing Mary. As requested, last night she'd definitely worn something sexy. The black sweater matched the sheen of her hair, the red of the lacy chemise reflected her blush of excitement when she'd moved her body suggestively against his. She'd been all satin and softness under his hands, feeding his senses with an abandon that belied her normal control. Tenderness and fire.

He squared his shoulders and rapped on the door. Perhaps he should've called, but he hadn't wanted to alert Sal to his purpose.

"Who is it?" He could barely hear her.

"Russ Coulter."

He sensed rather than saw her appraisal through the peephole before he heard the rasp of a chain lock being disengaged. Then she opened the door, her red head cocked like an expectant bird eyeing a worm. She arched her brows, a smile hovering. "A gentleman caller?"

He winked. "And an admirer, I might add."

She put a hand on his sleeve. "Well, come on in. I'm not so old that I don't enjoy the attention of a handsome young man." She ushered him across the room. He sat in a low rocker, his legs uncomfortably bent, while she took her accustomed wing chair. Holding his cowboy hat in his lap, he felt about nine years old. The morning sun streamed into the room, already too warm from the wall heater humming in the corner. He wished he'd removed his leather jacket.

She crossed her wrists in her lap and waited for him to speak.

"Since I was in the building, I thought I'd drop by and say hello. I brought Woody an article from the latest Oklahoma tourism magazine. All about the old rodeo days." At least that part was the truth.

"That'll keep him busy for a week. He'll show it to anybody who'll give him the time of day. Memories. That's about the only thing that keeps some of these old geezers going. Me? I'm not about to sit around every day reliving the past." She gestured to the end table next to her chair. "I've got books to read, CNN to watch, letters to write."

She leaned forward and poked an index finger in his direction. "Today I'm writing my congressmen. Damn fools keep tinkering with term limits. Hell, we already have term limits. It's called vote the bastards out." She sat back, smiling with satisfaction.

"You've got a point. I take it you don't have much use for politicians?"

"Never known an honest one in my life. Snakes, all of 'em."

Russ laughed. "Give 'em hell, Sal."

"You bet I will. They oughta let women have a whack at running the country."

"I'll wager there'd be no nonsense if you were in charge."

"You got that right." She nodded sagely. "That little Mary, she'd run a tight ship, too. I've been mighty impressed with her business sense." She fixed her pale blue eyes on him. "How about you? Are you kinda impressed with her, too?"

Russ shifted in the torturous rocker, stretching his legs out in front of him. She'd given him an opening. "You don't miss much, do you?"

She chortled. "You'd be a fool not to go after her. Pretty, sensible. Bright, too."

"Well, to tell you the truth, I *am* going after her." Sal shot him an I-told-you-so look. "In fact, I suspect you could give me some advice."

Sal glanced at him inquisitively. "Something us old folks are darned good at. Advice."

"Christmas is coming and I want to get just the right gift for Mary."

"An engagement ring would do."

"You cut right to the chase, don't you?" He set his hat on the floor and folded up his legs again, leaning forward. "I'm not quite ready for that—yet. But—" his throat had suddenly dried up "—I thought maybe a bracelet to match her necklace would be nice."

Sal's eyes narrowed ever so slightly. Russ continued to watch her. "I don't know where to find one, though. I thought maybe you could help."

"Why me?"

"Because you admired the necklace. Maybe you know where it came from?"

Too late Sal looked away and then turned back. "What necklace?"

"The *oochalata* necklace Mary wears, the one with the Cherokee inscription." He struggled to keep his tone neutral.

Sal appeared startled. "Cherokee inscription?"

"Yes. I thought since you'd been around these parts a long time, you could help me locate a matching bracelet."

She closed her eyes as if meditating on a serious matter. He waited, feeling beads of perspiration gathering on his forehead. Slowly she opened her eyes and pierced him with a steely gaze. "I don't think I can help you."

"Sal, you're a straight shooter, an honest woman." He bored in with a point-blank question. "Have you ever seen a necklace like that?"

She stared back, and her spine seemed to stiffen. "Once."

"Where?"

"Someone I knew a long time ago had one."

The room heater clicked off and the silence hung like a curtain between them. "Your niece?"

Her eyes wavered, but she didn't turn away. A look of recognition passed between them, so powerful Russ felt his stomach implode. In a soft but resolute voice she answered. "Maybe."

Later, walking to his truck in the Sooner Arms parking lot, he recalled that look. It was as if she'd wanted to tell him something, but couldn't. As if they'd negotiated an unspoken pact, understood but never to be discussed. Cagily, she hadn't corroborated the assumption implicit in his question, but she hadn't denied it, either. She was a shrewd old gal. He'd hate to play poker with her!

He climbed in the truck, slamming the door behind him. Now what? A certainty grew like sour yeast inside him. He'd check out some more details, but if what he suspected turned out to be true, he would feel neither satisfaction nor triumph.

He needed more facts. He picked up the car phone and dialed his father's office, hoping J.T. would be free for lunch.

RUSS HANDED THE worn plastic menu to the waitress. "Chicken-fried steak special and a glass of milk. What about you, Dad?"

His father shrugged. "Make it two specials, but coffee for me, please." He dropped his voice to a stage whisper. "Don't tell your mother. She gets on my case when I have what she calls a cholesterol food-fest. But, damn, I love cream gravy."

Russ winked. "My lips are sealed."

The waitress set down their drinks. The older man took a swig of his coffee and eyed his son over the rim of his cup. "Glad I could make lunch on such short notice. What's up?"

"I need to fill you in about the Creighton pasture lease and the terms of the note I signed at the bank." Russ paused, hoping his explanation wouldn't reveal his nervousness about the financial limb he'd climbed out on.

"Shoot, son."

His father pulled a silver ballpoint pen from his shirt pocket and scrawled figures on a paper napkin as Russ went over the details of acreage, cost of feeder calves, debt servicing and interest rates. Just when he'd finished his explanation, the waitress set down two steaming platters heaped with chicken-fried steak, limp green beans and mashed potatoes covered with cream gravy.

"Isn't that beautiful?" His father beamed as he scooped up the first forkful.

"Sure fills up the empty places." Russ attacked the crisp round steak.

"You're taking a risk with this cattle venture, son, but—" his father stabbed the air with his fork "—if anybody can make it work, you can."

"I figure at some point I have to make a move if I want to expand the business."

"Gil must have confidence in you, too, or he'd never have worked out that kind of deal."

Russ sopped up some gravy with his roll. "I'll feel a lot better when we sell off the first batch of steers and make a payment to the bank." He hesitated, trying to find a way to shift into the topic uppermost in his mind. "I sure wish Buck Lloyd wasn't such a tough character. I want to buy that land."

"You know what kind of chance you have there. Slim to none."

"I'm still gonna try to wear him down. How long can he continue punishing Coulters for something that happened nearly thirty years ago?"

"As long as he holds me responsible for his daughter's death. You haven't noticed him softening recently, have you?"

"Not if my last encounter with him is any indication." Russ shoved his plate to one side. "Was his daughter as unpleasant as he is?"

His father signaled the waitress for a coffee refill and then folded his arms on the edge of the table. "Ellie wasn't unpleasant at all. Quite the contrary. In high school, she was the golden girl—striking looks, a terrific sense of humor. And, for most of us, unattainable. She usually dated guys from Tulsa. But she was a great friend." He rotated the coffee mug slowly between his fingers.

"You know, I still can't figure out what happened to her. How somebody could change so drastically." A shadow fell across his face. "I didn't see that much of her in college, but when I did, she was the same old Ellie— fun and gorgeous. I never knew exactly where she went after she graduated from O.U. Worked out West somewhere, I think. But when she came back, man! She was different." He fumbled for the words. "Like she was detached, uninvolved. Sad. Sad in a way that goes beyond a temporary mood."

"Didn't you say alcohol was a problem?"

"Alcohol, drugs. Hard to say. She just didn't seem to care anymore. It was like she needed to deaden herself just to go on."

"What exactly happened that night?"

His father's eyes filmed. "Some of the parties back in those days were pretty wild. I had my hands full that evening, and Ellie had really tied one on. She stood on the diving board, dancing and pouring a pitcher of margaritas into the pool. When I tried to get her off the board, she pushed me in. Finally with the help of her friend Pam Kendall, I got her into the master bedroom and we suggested she sleep it off. We covered her with the spread and left her dozing on the bed." He looked away, vacantly. Then he turned back and solemnly faced his son. "That was the last time I ever saw Ellie Lloyd." He seemed lost in the recollection. "She was an experienced and fearless horsewoman. In her stupor she must've wandered out to the barn and put a bridle on the stallion. She took off bareback." He shook his head. "What a tragic waste!"

He sat quietly, then drained his coffee and set down the mug. "This is a depressing conversation, son. Why the sudden interest?"

Russ bought time, refolding the paper napkin before setting it on the table. "Just thinking about Buck. I'd hate to be that bitter about anything." He looked up. "How long had Ellie been away before she returned to Ewing?"

His father pursed his lips. "Let's see. She graduated in May of 1967. And she was here in Ewing when I came home from law school that next spring break. I remember because Buck had a big party for the young set—trying to lighten Ellie's depression, get her in circulation, I guess. That would've been March of '68. But she hadn't been home at Christmas. So I guess she came back in February or early March." He frowned. "What's gotten you off on this subject?"

Russ squirmed inside. He wasn't comfortable being this evasive with his father. He answered in a deliberately offhand tone. "Oh, I recently met Sal Mc-Clanahan, Buck's sister. She doesn't seem anything like Buck."

"That's an understatement. I've known her since I was a kid. Old Sal's never had a mean bone in her body—lots of opinionated bones, but not a mean one."

"I know."

His father picked up the check and stood. "Lunch is on me today. By the way, how's Mary?"

Russ gave him a wide smile. "She's great!"

J.T. clapped an arm around Russ's shoulders as they walked toward the cashier. "Don't want to make too big a deal of this, son, but your mother and I like her, too."

Russ felt torn between the warmth of his father's approval and the task he had before him—because its outcome might shatter Mary's dream.

THAT AFTERNOON, after calling the ranch and checking in with Jim Peppercorn, Russ stopped at the Ewing Public Library. His nagging suspicion had to be addressed, the sooner the better. He hoped to God he was wrong.

He approached the reference desk.

The librarian waited expectantly. "What can I do for you?"

"Do you have back issues of the *Ewing Herald*?"

"On microfilm. What do you need?"

"Let's start with the issues from July 5 to July 15, 1968."

The librarian turned away. "I'll be right back."

He shifted his weight from one foot to the other, hoping he'd find his answers quickly. She returned, holding a small box. "Follow me." She led him to one of the carrels in a far corner of the library. "Know how to work the projector?"

"I think so. Thanks." He began threading the reel. What did Mary envision her search would uncover? A loving welcome from a teary mom, herself tortured by the loss of her infant? A made-to-order set of half brothers and sisters? Merely an answer to the mystery of her birth and genetic background? *Or,* he wondered, frowning slightly as he turned the crank and advanced the pages of type, *heartbreak?*

July 5, 1968. An account of the Independence Day celebration, complete with a full-page photographic spread. A news story concerning the escalation of hostilities in Vietnam. A rundown on the upcoming major league all-star game. Nothing. He scrolled to July 6, passing directly to the obituary page. There it was, the funeral parlor notice. "Lloyd, Eleanor Grace, age 22. Born April 6, 1946, died July 5, 1968. Arrangements pending with Miller-Gates Funeral Home."

The stark words, so matter-of-fact, carried with them none of the pain and tragedy of her last hours. But the "age 22" wrenched his gut.

Grimly, he flashed through the blurred newsprint until he came to the third page of the July 7 issue. A haunting photograph of a lovely laughing girl, bouffant pageboy framing her heart-shaped face, gazed at some invisible person beyond camera range. Beneath the picture was the headline, Daughter of Local Oil Magnate Killed, followed by the subhead, Freak Accident Claims Ellie Lloyd.

Russ rubbed his forehead, tension building in his muscles. He scanned the excruciating details of the late-night horseback ride and several quotations from prominent Ewing residents. Then he found what he sought. "Miss Lloyd was vice president of her social sorority, served on the Student Union Program Committee and the Homecoming Events Committee and was crowned Track Queen in her senior year. A 1967 cum laude graduate of the University of Oklahoma, Miss Lloyd worked out of state following her commencement until returning to Ewing in March of this year to join her father's business."

Russ ticked the months off on his fingers. May, June, July...December, January. Nine months. Then January 10 to March. Six weeks. If it weren't for the *oochalata* necklace and Sal's oracular look, he'd dismiss this whole crazy notion. What an utterly inconceivable coincidence! Yet the sheer improbability lent a weird kind of credence to his speculations.

Dazedly, he skimmed the next few issues of the newspapers. One later article, an account of the funeral, followed on July 8, then nothing.

Slowly he replaced the reel in the box, turning the possibilities over in his head. Should he tell Mary his hypothesis? Find some way to verify it first? Check with Sal? Confront Buck?

He sat, head in his hands, aware of the library stillness, punctuated occasionally by the ratcheting of a nearby microfilm reader. God, he didn't want Mary hurt. If he was wrong, it served no purpose to tell her. If he was right and she went racing off to see Buck, she could end up devastated. Somehow, he knew intuitively that right now Sal had gone as far as she could with him—as if she'd pointed him in the right direction and had therefore ceded responsibility to him.

Maybe the best thing for the moment was to let Mary continue believing her mother was Cherokee. She'd waited twenty-eight years; a few more weeks wouldn't hurt. That would buy him time to decide on a course of action.

He stood and shoved the wooden chair beneath the desk, his mind racing. He couldn't shake the conviction that Buck was the answer. God help her. That heartless son of a bitch! He ground his teeth furiously and stalked out of the library.

EVEN BERTHA MAYHALL pried open her pursed lips to join in the communal carol-singing, enthusiastically led by a loud, if not harmonious, Chauncey Butterworth, dressed in a velour Santa suit. Bent over the piano, a florid, silver-haired gentleman accompanied the chorus with the flourishes of a Liberace. Behind her, Mary could hear Woody mumbling along, getting about every fourth word of the lyrics.

She glanced over at Russ, seated on the love seat beside Rose Farnsworth, the two of them warbling delightedly—"…Hark, the herald angels sing, Glo-ree-ee to the newborn king." Mary smiled. Russ liked women—young women, old women, all women—but he'd picked *her.* He'd skied right off the slopes, driven eleven hours cross-country and burst into her condominium with that ridiculous mistletoe. She'd consulted the encyclopedia—it really *was* the Oklahoma state flower!

He caught her eye and winked. Beside her, she felt the jab of Sal McClanahan's elbow. She leaned over to catch Sal's raspy whisper. "Don't you let that one get away, Mary." She nodded toward Russ. "That's prime man-flesh."

Mary felt her cheeks redden. Were her feelings that obvious? She concentrated on the piano player, but his extravagant arpeggios threatened to convulse her. Blessedly, he swung into "We Wish You a Merry Christmas" and the musical portion of the program concluded.

Mary and Russ admired the twenty-foot tree, decorated in burgundy and gold, then nibbled on bell-shaped sugar cookies and red-and-green tea sandwiches and dutifully paid court to their special friends. Finally Russ maneuvered Mary into the front hallway. "Had enough?"

She smiled. "Eager to leave?"

He clamped a possessive arm around her waist. "Eager to have you all to myself. Besides, I'm suffocating on eau de cologne."

They made their farewells, studiously ignoring the knowing looks being exchanged as the senior citizens bestowed their unspoken approval upon the "young people."

Russ held Mary's coat. "There's a little daylight left. Would you like to see the new pastureland I've leased?"

"I'd love to."

The interior of the truck was cold and Mary huddled against Russ to ward off the chill. He pulled her close, buckling the middle seat belt around her. As they rode toward the edge of town, the heater kicked in, filling the cab with warm, musty air. Russ had tuned in Randy Travis on the radio and something plaintive and sincere in the lyrics moved her profoundly.

In the fading afternoon sun, the barren gray-brown hills were mosaic formations of light and shifting shade. Barns and trees cast long shadows as the winter sun etched its descent through wisps of magenta clouds. On the roof of an isolated ranch house nestled against a mauve-brown hill, twinkly white Christmas lights spelled out Peace on Earth. Mary hugged herself. Out her window, the open grasslands, rimmed by scrubby cedars and blackjack oaks, made her want to fling her arms wide and race like the wind toward the horizon.

Russ slowed the truck and put his arm around her, snuggling her closer. "You're mighty quiet."

She smiled up at him. "Make that content."

As they topped a low hill, Russ turned onto a rutted dirt road and stopped the truck in front of a cattle gate. He switched off the ignition and pointed with his left hand. "Everything to the east of us between here and the pond is the land I've leased."

She glanced at him. His eyes had narrowed and he studied the terrain as if seeing something way out there—beyond the moment. Finally he spoke. "Would you be terribly disappointed if you learned something unpleasant about your past? Even tragic?"

She looked up, startled by the seriousness of his tone. "What makes you ask something like that?"

He continued gazing toward the distant pond. "I don't want you hurt." The set of his jaw underlined the emotion behind his concern.

She laid a hand on his knee. "I think I'm prepared for that possibility."

"Really prepared?"

"Russ, you're the one always telling me to lighten up. Remember, there's just as much chance that things will work out well. It's not like you to be a pessimist."

He sighed and covered her hand with his own cold one.

She shivered slightly. He turned abruptly to face her. "Are you chilly?"

"A little. Maybe it's this solemn discussion. It's giving me the creeps."

He started the motor and adjusted the heater control. "Sorry. It's nearly dark. Let's head back."

Russ rummaged in the glove compartment and pulled out a cassette tape and rammed it in the slot. Mellow Christmas music, a guitar and harp, filled the air. Mary closed her eyes and leaned her head back. "Nice," she murmured.

"I love Christmas," Russ said quietly. "I don't really remember holidays before Dad married Carolyn. Maybe I was too young. But I always associate Christmas with her."

"How's that?"

"Oh, I dunno. She made a big deal out of all the preparations and we had traditions from the very start."

"For instance?"

"Gingerbread boys. We always made gingerbread boys on a Sunday afternoon before Christmas. The NFL game on TV would be blaring in the background, and Brian and I would be hard at work planting red-hots and raisins in the dough. Then we'd slop colored icing over our creations. They didn't look a thing like the picture in the cookbook, but we didn't care. Then some evening when the family was all at home, we'd pop corn, drink hot cider and decorate the tree together."

Mary opened her eyes to look at him. A small smile played around his mouth. "What about you?" he asked. "What're your family traditions?"

She thought for a long while. "This is going to sound petty, but what we did felt more like habit than tradition."

"What do you mean?"

She searched her memory. "We went to certain events every year, like the Christmas tea dance at the country club and the neighborhood fancy-dress open house. The florist always decorated the house and tree. Oh, everything looked lovely, I guess, but a gingerbread boy with three eyes wouldn't have been welcome." She was silent a moment before continuing. "Even the treetop ornament I loved—my guardian angel—was replaced one year by a crystal star. It was when Mother threw her away that I realized her rich satin gown was only cheap taffeta and her golden hair just spun synthetic. I'd always thought she was so beautiful. That she watched over me. So much for Christmas illusions."

He responded to the wistfulness in her voice. "But your parents...?"

"Well, yes, they were wonderful. Except for a brother or sister—" she smiled ruefully "—I always got exactly what I asked for and much more—all wrapped in designer gift paper with large fancy bows. And Christmas morning was a ritual, the three of us taking turns opening our gifts, that is, if Dad wasn't at the hospital..." Her voice trailed off.

She felt his hand on her shoulder. "But?"

"It wasn't joyous or...spontaneous. I don't remember any noise. You know, like you see on television. Kids shrieking and jumping up and down, adults laughing and exchanging hugs. The floor littered with ribbons and paper." She paused. "I think we're a sedate, almost solemn family."

"God, the Coulters must scare the hell out of you. We're nothing if not rough-and-tumble."

"No." Her voice was emphatic. "I like it. That's what I missed. No brother, no sister, no big dog knocking ornaments off the tree with his tail."

Russ laughed. "How'd you know? That's exactly what Casey used to do."

She felt a lump rising in her throat, both for all she'd missed and for the truth fighting its way to the surface. "There was another reason Christmas was hard."

The truck neared the first stoplight. "What was that?"

She cleared her throat nervously. "At Christmastime, I always wondered where my real mother was. If she missed me. If she was sad, too, when she looked at her tree. If she prayed *her* angel had answers. Christmas and my birthday. Those were times when I couldn't stop wondering about why...why someone didn't want me."

"Oh, Mary." Russ drew her close and turned into the empty parking lot of a medical clinic. Mary felt his arms engulfing her as he held her to his chest. "Somebody may have wanted you very much. There're lots of reasons why she would..."

"I know, I know." Mary snuffled against his coat. "And Mom and Dad are wonderful people." She swiped at her tears as she raised her head. "I'm a grown-up. I understand the way it is. But sometimes when I hear a certain carol or see a manger scene, the sad little-girl feelings wash all over me again."

Russ kissed the top of her head and then framed her face in his hands. In the light from the overhead street lamp, she could see the earnestness, the caring in his eyes. "I love you, and I want you to have the best Christmas ever." He gently pulled her face closer to his and placed his warm, tender, yielding lips on hers. His kiss was poignant—and soothing. Slowly, he pulled back, still caressing her face in his hands. "And we're going to start by creating traditions of our own."

Mary smiled through her tears. Traditions, commitment, security. "I'd like that."

He gathered her into the sanctuary of his embrace. "It's settled then. Christmas is just over two weeks away, so let's start at the ranch Wednesday night, just the two of us, with popcorn, hot cider and tree trimming." She trembled, a rush of heady anticipation overwhelming any lingering regrets.

CHAPTER THIRTEEN

DURING HER LUNCH hour Monday, Mary trailed through a downtown gift shop, inhaling the spicy fragrance of holiday potpourri. A Regina music box rendition of "O Come All Ye Faithful" played through the sound system as she studied the elaborately decorated theme trees—Victorian, country, Southwestern and traditional. She fingered the tree ornaments—a shiny tin angel, a tree-bark Santa face, a delicately tatted star. She wanted to find just the right one to give Russ Wednesday night.

She smiled wistfully. For all the joy associated with Christmas, for many it was also a bittersweet time. Russ was the first person in whom she'd confided her ambivalence about the season. She paused in front of the Southwestern tree. It reminded her of Russ and the rustic, masculine decor of the ranch house. Starting a holiday tradition, he'd said. She liked the idea. Maybe this Christmas really would be different—better.

She studied the decorations. As if it were meant to be, there, hanging directly at eye level, was an intricately painted, wooden ornament—a red-clad Santa wearing a cowboy hat and sitting astride a bucking bronco. Perfect! She carefully unhooked it from the branch and carried it to the cash register.

RUSS HAD MADE his decision. He'd have to proceed cautiously, orchestrating every step. And, no matter how much he might be goaded, he couldn't lose his cool.

Early Tuesday morning, he went to Buck Lloyd's office, this time equipped with a sack lunch and a bestselling Western novel. Again, the receptionist greeted him with all the enthusiasm of someone having a tax return audited. "You're wasting your time, you know." She smiled smugly. "I've been instructed to tell you Mr. Lloyd has nothing to say to you."

Russ leaned on the counter and folded his hands. "That's pretty one-sided, doncha think? Downright unneighborly. 'Cause I have some mighty important things to say to him."

She glared. "He won't see you. Period. End of discussion."

"Well, then." He straightened up and removed his cowboy hat. "Here we go again. I can be very patient, and when you mention to Buck that I have a vested interest in events occurring in January of 1968, he just may develop a sudden...interest in seeing me." He took off his jacket, hung it on the coatrack, settled into the leather sofa and opened his book.

At lunchtime, under the scathing looks of the watchdog receptionist, he extracted from his sack two ham-and-cheese sandwiches, a bag of chips and a banana, spreading them out on the coffee table.

"You can't eat in here," she barked. "This is a place of business."

"Watch me," Russ said as he took a large bite of the first sandwich. He held up the banana and mumbled through a full mouth, "Hungry? I'll share."

He smiled to himself as he watched her close her appointment book and march from the room. He chewed contentedly and continued reading.

During the afternoon, a steady stream of businesspeople succeeded in getting past the desk. Each time one was admitted to the sanctum sanctorum, the receptionist pursed her lips in satisfaction and glanced over to see if Russ had noticed this most recent snub.

At five o'clock when she'd tidied her desk, she stood and accosted him. "You'll have to leave now, Mr. Coulter. We're closed."

Russ checked his watch. "That so? Well, you go on. Don't mind me. I'll just sit here and wait on old Buck."

The receptionist's face reddened. "I've tolerated you all day. And, believe me, it's been a trial. Do I have to call security?"

Russ spread his hands placatingly. "Hey, I'm easy. No bother at all. Calling security might be a bit extreme. What are you going to tell them? That Mr. Lloyd won't see a fellow rancher?"

"Mr. Coulter, I—"

Russ got up, stretching to his full six feet two inches. "It's simple, ma'am. Before you go, just step into Buck's office and ask him if he wouldn't like to chat about his January 1968 acquisition." He shrugged elaborately. "I'll wait."

For a moment the woman seemed torn; then she picked up her coat and purse and headed down the interior hallway toward the suite of offices. Russ wiped his damp palms on his pants, hoping his bluff would succeed.

Shortly, the receptionist reappeared. She tilted her chin defiantly. "Mr. Lloyd will see you now." She gestured. "The corner office."

He couldn't resist. As she put on her coat and walked toward the exit, he smiled. "Have a nice day, ma'am." For an answer, he heard the decisive slam of the door. The smile faded. He quickly reviewed his plan, took a deep breath and walked toward Buck's office.

He hesitated in the doorway. The drapes had been drawn and the only illumination came from the brass reading lamp on one side of the massive mahogany desk. African game heads—zebra, gazelle and rhino—stared down from every wall. A huge bearskin covered the carpet in front of the desk. If the cumulative effect was intended to be intimidating, Russ was convinced.

He walked into the office, squinting to adjust his pupils to the dimness. He heard the tinkle of ice from the corner before he saw Buck standing at the bar, his broad back to the door. A highball in his hand, the older man pivoted slowly. He studied Russ and then, without a word, crossed to the desk, set the drink down and leaned against the front edge, arms folded across his beefy chest, eyes hooded. Poised like two wrestlers, each awaited the other's first move.

Russ opened. "Changed your mind about selling me your land?"

"In a pig's eye."

"Well, Buck, the way I see it, there's no reason to hold me responsible for what you think my dad did to you." Russ noted Buck's eyes narrowing. "Besides I'm offering you a fair price."

"And I told you to get out of my office."

"But here I am." Russ held up his palms. "Now why do you suppose that is?" Buck pinned him with a malevolent stare. "Could January 10, 1968, have anything to do with it?"

Buck turned on his heel and went around behind the desk. "I don't know what the hell you're talking about."

Russ approached the desk. "Oh, I think maybe you do." Russ could feel sweat gathering in his armpits. "You see I have some interest in the, er, *property* you acquired on that date, and I'd like to protect my investment." He paused. "Seems the best way to do that might be to become business partners."

"Goddamn it, boy, are you trying to extort something from me?" Buck leaned heavily on the desk, his eyes never leaving Russ's.

Russ tried a smile he hoped looked innocent. "No way. Why should you think that? Got something to hide?" He stared intently at Buck, looking for the telltale swallow, the tightening of the jaw, the fleeting blink of an eye.

"Damnation, if you aren't just like that puny-assed father of yours. Hell, no, I haven't got a thing to hide and certainly not from a pissant like you."

Russ, too, leaned on the desk. "I'm sure glad to hear that Buck, because if you *did* have something to hide concerning that 1968 transaction, I'd be all over your ass like a buzzard on dead armadillo meat."

Buck held Russ's gaze while he extracted a cigar from his shirt pocket and made a show of lighting it. Then he sank into his leather chair, tilted back, hefted his feet onto the desk and blew a big smoke ring. "Son, I had no idea you'd go to such lengths to get my land. Hell, you're already using my sister and now this veiled threat of blackmail. But what can you expect from a Coulter?" He shook his head at the sadness of it all.

Then he continued, his voice menacing. "You're playing with fire, boy." For emphasis, he drew in on the cigar; the glowing tip sent a clear signal. "No sale, no deal, no nothing. Now get the hell out of my office."

He abruptly put his feet down and shifted forward, jabbing the smoldering cigar in Russ's direction. "And if you know what's good for you—and anyone you care about—*don't come back.*"

Russ had his answer. "I guess you're telling me I'm not welcome. That's a shame." He glanced toward the corner bar. "Sorry I couldn't stay for that drink." He raised his hat in mock salute and ambled out of the room in his best John Wayne gait.

At the elevator, he savagely punched the Down button, barely controlling the rage that engulfed him. It'd taken every bit of self-control not to jam that cigar down Buck Lloyd's throat. Obviously the only reason Buck had seen him was because of the mention of January 1968. Despite Buck's outward show of composure, there'd been no mistaking the momentary flash of recognition and panic in his eyes *or* the threats. Russ'd gotten the message loud and clear—give up your investigation, or else.

The elevator doors opened, and Russ was grateful to see he was the sole occupant. The downward lurch threw his stomach into his throat—he didn't know when he'd been so outright furious. The elevator jolted to a stop and Russ hurried through the lobby and out the revolving doors into the cold icy air. He turned up the collar of his jacket, pulled down his hat and walked to his truck.

It was small satisfaction to have his suspicions verified. Now what? He still didn't have absolute proof that Ellie was Mary's mother. And even if he did, would it be wise to tell Mary? Especially under the circumstances. At best she'd be heartbroken over her mother's death; at worst she faced total rejection from Buck. But overshadowing all of that was the very real danger she might be in if Buck made good on his implied threats.

Russ climbed in the truck and shut the door so force-fully the windows rattled. How had he gotten them into this mess? He'd promised to help Mary, yet what he'd discovered had the potential to harm her. Did he have to tell her? he asked himself. On the other hand, how could she trust him if he didn't?

STRAINS OF AN Anne Murray Christmas CD overrode the wind screaming around the ranch house and provided accompaniment for the crackling fire. The aroma of buttery popcorn and the taste of the spicy hot cider Mary was sipping completed her sense of holiday content-ment. She snuggled beside Russ on the deep leather couch, basking in the reflected glow of the Christmas tree lights they'd wound around the seven-foot-tall Scotch pine.

"Looks good, huh?" Russ, legs propped on the cof-fee table, hands behind his head, surveyed their handi-work.

"One of the best ever." Mary couldn't remember a time she'd felt so happy. How could her parents have opted for a decorator tree and missed all this fun?

"You're sure, now, that the wooden soldier is in the right place? I can move the toy train." He cocked an eyebrow at her, a smile hovering around his lips.

"I'm sure. It's perfect. Except for one thing." She set down her mug and went to the coat closet, returning with a small package. "Here."

He looked up expectantly. "For me?"

"For you and our tree." She sat down, pulling her legs under her and turning so she could watch him open the present.

He broke the red satin ribbon, removed the paper and then laughed when he saw the cowboy Santa. "This is great. It's me, all right. Thank you." He cupped the back of her head and leaned forward to kiss her lightly. "Let's hang it up." He led her to the fragrant tree. "All right, Miss Perfectionist, where shall we put it?" Russ held the ornament high. "How about here?"

"No one will see it up there." She moved a silver ball to another branch. "Give it to me." He proffered the ornament. She took it and bent the hook over the branch. "Now it's at eye level and everyone can see. Perfect." She applauded.

He captured her hands between his and grinned down at her. "Thank you. Our tree may not be color-coordinated, but it's full of memories." He turned her toward the tree. "Every one of these ornaments has a story. My grandparents knew just which ones they inherited from their families, which ones Dad and his brother made, which ones were gifts. Now I have my very own."

For a brief moment the pine shimmered as Mary gazed at it through misty eyes. "I never knew a tree could be so special."

Russ kept his arm around her shoulder. "What do you mean?"

She struggled for the right words. "There's so much love, such tradition there. In your holiday memories. In family stories." She looked up at his pensive face. "It's a rich legacy, Russ."

He reached out and traced the design on one glittery ball. Although the paint had chipped away in places, Mary made out the words, "To Pawpaw from Rusty, Xmas 1974."

"Rusty?"

Recollecting himself, he hugged her to him. "Promise not to tell? Nana and Pawpaw—my grandparents—always called me that."

"I'll bet you were a cute little boy."

He groaned. "Enough. We're *not* going to pull out family pictures tonight. Besides, I have a little something to help you get into the Christmas spirit."

He disappeared down the hallway. Mary settled back on the sofa, holding the warm mug in her hands, draining the last few sips.

"Mine isn't wrapped, though." He placed several videocassettes in her lap and stood watching her.

"What...?"

"You said Christmas at your house was too solemn, not noisy enough. These ought to help. I've spent several nights taping them." He picked up the first one. "Here we have *Miracle on 34th Street* and *It Happened One Christmas*. Then—" he reached for another "—we have *The Grinch Who Stole Christmas*, *Frosty the Snowman* and *The Best Christmas Pageant Ever*. Next—"

"You're making me laugh." Mary felt the bubble of joy bursting forth. "How about *A Christmas Carol?*"

He grinned, picked up the fourth cassette and shook it in her face. "Right here with *Holiday Inn*. No more quiet, solemn Christmases for you."

She swept aside the tapes and threw herself into his arms. "Do you have to work at it or do you just naturally know how to please me?"

He held her tightly and murmured into the curve of her neck. "Naturally. It just comes naturally. Like this." As his fingers stroked through her hair, he found her lips, gently parting them with his, and then as the pressure grew more insistent, he sought her tongue. She circled his neck with both hands and stood on tiptoe to hug him even tighter. She felt one of his hands drop to the small of her back, the thrusting of their tongues replicating the pressure of his arousal against her. Breathless she pulled her mouth away so she could look into his eyes, transparent and honest in their longing. She felt a stirring so sharp, yet so incredibly soothing, that it took her by surprise. She tenderly caressed the angles of his cheeks, feeling beneath the pads of her fingers the fine sandpapery texture of his clean-shaven skin. Each tiny sensation shot from her fingertips to a wanton secret place.

As she traced his lips, she became aware of his steady gaze, of his quick breathing. Her subtle, gentle gestures, the stillness of his body, the flickering firelight were erotic in ways she'd never dreamed.

She lowered her hands to his chest, feeling his heartbeat against her right palm. To be joined just so—heart of my heart. She wrapped her arms under his, laying her cheek against his chest, holding him close, feeling the solidity of his body, sensing the straining of his control. Finally she stood back, lifting her face. "I love you."

In the background the CD player clicked off. The only sounds were the snapping of logs shifting into the ashes of the fireplace and the wind moaning through the trees. "Oh, Mary—" The words seemed torn from somewhere deep. "I love you, too." He reached one arm around her back and cradled her legs with the other, scooping her up so they were nearly eye to eye. He paused, his expression questioning.

"Love me. Please." She buried her head in his shoulder. She felt her breasts press against his shirt as he carried her down the hallway and into the bedroom. She couldn't have said when she'd reached the decision to make love with Russ, but it had come as naturally as spring follows winter.

Moonlight cast a faint glow over the pine floor and casual Navajo rugs. In the center of the room was a high burled-oak bed covered with a comforter in an Aztec pattern. Russ curled her even closer to him. "Are you sure?"

She heard the tentativeness in his voice. She raised her head and looked into his eyes, a devilish grin breaking across her face. "Don't you think it's time I stopped being quite such a 'good girl'?"

"God, yes," he breathed against her cheek as he set her feet down on the floor, nuzzling her neck. A tremor shuddered through her as he lifted the red Christmas sweater over her head.

He'd just started skimming his hands over her chemise when a metallic clatter outside stopped him. "What the hell?" he mumbled as he stepped to the window and drew back the drapes. Nearby trees swayed in the onslaught of the December wind and metal chairs rattled against the brick retaining wall of the patio. In the dark, he made out a metal object, lying on its side. "The barbecue grill blew over." He started to close the drapes, then froze. "Oh, shit!" He raced past Mary, flipped on the bedside lamp and grabbed the phone. "911? This is the Coulter ranch. Our west pasture's on fire!"

Mary stared out the window at a thin line of orange at the top of the rise. In the background she heard Russ giving directions to the dispatcher. Even as he spoke, the tongue of flame spread, fiery billows swelling, fed by gusts of the strong northwest wind.

Russ dashed down the hall to the closet, yanked out a coat and hat and tore open the door. "Stay here, Mary!"

Fumbling with her sweater, she snatched up her own coat and followed him into the night. "I'm going with you! I can help."

"I haven't got time to argue." He took her by the elbow and ran for the pickup. "Damn it to hell. This is all I need."

OVER THE KEENING of the wind, Mary heard the wail of sirens approaching from all directions. "Volunteer fire department," Russ muttered as the truck bounced crazily over cattle guards, rocks and fallen timber. "Are they coming?"

Mary braced herself with one hand against the dash and twisted around to look at the assortment of vehicles—a pumper truck, a tanker, several utility vehicles and a brush buggy. "Yes, they're following you." Turning back to the front, she felt a surge of panic. In that brief instant, the fire line in front of them had jumped and the south edge had taken on a life of its own.

Russ braked to a stop and yelled as he jumped from the cab. "Get the hell out of here." He ran toward the first vehicle and signaled it to stop. The driver threw him boots, a fire fighter's coat and a fire helmet. Good God! Russ was one of the volunteer firemen. Behind him the others were spreading out and gesturing to one another as they prepared their line of defense.

She slid into the driver's seat, palms moist on the steering wheel. Her breath came in gasps. The entire pasture was ablaze. She backed up and turned the truck around. Russ could tell her to stay away, but there had to be *something* she could do to help. The firemen were in for a long night. Food, coffee, water. She could at least do that! She gunned the engine and jounced back toward the ranch house, its windows eerily reflecting a crimson that had nothing to do with Christmas.

As she dug through the pantry for thermoses, covered pitchers, paper cups, she prayed silently. "Keep him safe. Please keep him safe." As if to taunt her, the wind picked up the unlatched storm door and banged it against the jamb. It took an eternity for the coffee to brew, but by then she'd made several dozen sandwiches, filled three pitchers with instant lemonade and located a cooler, which she crammed with ice and bottled water.

With the supplies loaded in the bed of the pickup, she started back toward the pasture. Fear clawed at her as she spotted tiny dark figures silhouetted against the yellow-red monster howling and lapping up the dry brush in its path. She could make out one vehicle digging a trench line. It was followed by a tanker truck spreading water over the adjacent vegetation. Apparently they were trying to make a fire break. Other vehicles had circled to the south and were doing the same thing. She parked the truck and waited, her mouth tasting metallic, her stomach cramping.

A pickup sped toward her, stopping driver's window to driver's window. "Lady, you need to stay back."

"I've got food and drink for the firemen."

"You'd best set up by the barn. Another company's arriving soon to help out. I'll tell the boys where you are so they can find you if they get a break." He pulled away, did a 180 and sped back toward the conflagration.

Mary drove toward the barn, found a level area outside the corral and parked the truck so the bed faced the fire. She hopped up into the back, arranging the food and drinks for easy accessibility, and then stood on top of the cooler, doing her damnedest to see what was going on, which one of those men was Russ. The west pasture.

Where they'd ridden horses, where he'd pointed out Buck's fifteen hundred acres, where she'd first seen his love of the land, first heard the excitement in his voice when he'd talked about ranching.

Her legs were numb with cold by the time the first of the fire fighters arrived. Face rimed with soot and body reeking of smoke, he gulped the water greedily. "Thanks, ma'am."

"How's it going?"

"All's we can do is try to contain it. That wind's a bitch." He took off his helmet and wiped his sleeve across his forehead. "It's gonna be an all-nighter. I'll spread the word you're here." He replaced the helmet and started off.

"Wait. Have you seen Russ Coulter?"

The man held up one arm and pointed toward the group at the south end of the pasture. "Over there, I think."

Mary squinted, but couldn't make out anything but the trencher doggedly etching a tiny seam in the earth. She hugged herself, jumping up and down to keep warm, and tried unsuccessfully to keep worry at bay.

As THE FIRST streaks of light crested the eastern horizon, Mary finished washing the last pitcher. Her eyes burned and her legs were rubbery. She'd been up all night. She looked out the kitchen window at the blackened, barren pastureland where occasional wafts of smoke still rose from isolated patches. The devastation was thorough. Burned cedars speared the sky like grotesque witches' fingers. The last few firemen were coiling hoses and preparing to leave. At last she saw Russ shake out of his heavy fire fighter's coat. Slowly he removed his helmet, gloves and boots and handed them to one of the men in the tanker truck. As the last vehicle pulled away, he spoke briefly with his ranch hands, then trudged toward the house.

Her throat was clogged with emotion. He looked exhausted, beaten. But he was safe, thank God. When he opened the door, heedless of the grime streaking his skin, she ran to him, holding him tight, murmuring endearments between the kisses she planted on his sooty face. He stood motionless, just holding her. She could feel the tension draining from his body, sense the resignation and pain in his silence. She raised her head. "I'm so sorry, Russ."

He stepped away, eyes hollow and streaked with red. "Nobody was hurt. It's over now." He raked one hand through his hair. "It might've been worse. We could've had cattle on that pasture." He slumped into a kitchen chair.

She set a cup of coffee and a sandwich in front of him. "Get some food in your stomach, take a shower and then lie down for a while. You're worn out."

He took a bite of the sandwich. "Yeah. Guess that's a good idea." He sounded whipped. He looked up at her, his face doleful. "You've gotta be tired, too."

"A little. I've let the bank know I won't be in today."

"You go on in and stretch out. I'll join you later." With a sad smile and a shake of his head, he added, "But I don't think we'll take up where we left off."

REVIVED BY THE SHOWER, Russ pulled a white T-shirt over his clean jeans and padded on bare feet into the bedroom. Mary lay on her side, one hand curled under her chin, legs pulled up to her chest. Her black hair fell away from one rosy cheek and thick sable lashes veiled her eyes. Her chest rose and fell rhythmically. Russ sat gently on the edge of the bed and tenderly traced the curve of her shoulder with a finger.

Now what? The danger he'd hoped to keep at bay was licking at their heels just as surely as the fire had devoured the pasture. He'd deal with that mess and his anger later. Right now he had only one concern. Keeping Mary safe. He sighed, looking down at her. He had to protect her, divert her into another avenue of her search. Better still, get her to abandon it.

There was no escaping his dilemma. He'd made a solemn promise to help her, one he'd had every intention of honoring. A promise he'd now have to break. She'd be safe, but what price would he pay? What would he lose? He stood up. Her trust, he was afraid.

There was no way he could tell her what they'd discovered tonight. The origin of the fire was a stack of kerosene-soaked logs right at the edge of Buck's property, where the fence had been cut. His father had warned him, but Buck was even more ruthless than he'd imagined. He'd made good his threat, all right. Buck's words twisted in Russ's stomach like a hot poker: "You're playing with fire, boy."

CHAPTER FOURTEEN

MARY PULLED THE blanket up around her shoulders and snuggled into its fleecy warmth, a smile curling her lips. Awakening involved too big an effort, especially when the dream of floating along wrapped in Russ's arms was so pleasant. She twitched her nose. She smelled bacon. She cracked open one eye. Her gritty lashes wouldn't cooperate. She sat up slowly, brushing the hair out of her face. In that instant, she remembered. The fire!

She threw back the covers and fumbled for her shoes. Images of burning cinders, screaming sirens, sheets of orange flame and howling wind flashed tumultuously through her head. Panic surfaced before she remembered Russ was all right. Where was he?

She nearly tripped over the supine Casey, who rose clumsily to his feet and followed her into the kitchen, where Russ stood at the range frying bacon. He turned, smiling crookedly. "How about some coffee?"

When she sat down at the kitchen table, he handed her a steaming mug. "What time is it?" Her brain refused to focus.

"Just past noon." He removed six strips of bacon from the skillet and plopped four eggs into the sizzling fat.

"You okay?"

He shrugged. "Tired. Upset. But all in one piece. You?"

"Fine. I just can't seem to wake up." She sipped from her mug. Casey settled by her side, resting his nose on her feet.

Russ reached over and gently drew a finger across her cheek. "You've got a sleep mark." She looked up into his eyes. He tried a smile that didn't quite work and then returned his attention to the breakfast. She'd never seen him so quiet, so contemplative, as if he'd aged ten years overnight. He flipped the eggs onto two plates, arranged the bacon strips and toast and sat down across the table. "Some night."

"Did you get any rest?" she asked.

"About three hours. I woke around eleven and couldn't get back to sleep."

The eggs and bacon filled the gaping hole in her stomach. She hadn't realized how hungry she was. Then she remembered she hadn't eaten since their popcorn the night before. It seemed ages since they'd decorated the tree, since he'd kissed her, since... She blushed. Nothing had ever felt as good as his arms when he'd carried her to the bedroom. His fingers playing over the sheer fabric covering her breasts... Had she really abandoned herself so completely?

The fire was a disaster for Russ—but for her, had it been a curse or a blessing?

"...Mary?"

"Oh, sorry. What were you saying?"

He sat, staring at his plate, swirling a piece of toast around and around in the runny yolk. He cleared his throat, then raised his eyes. "The fire made me realize I care too much about you to let you get hurt." He set his fork down. "If anything had happened to you, I don't know what I'd have done."

"I'm okay, Russ. It's all over."

"No, it's not."

"Come on, Russ. Grass fires happen all the time. I was never in any danger. Why are you being like this?"

"This wasn't just any grass fire. When I spoke with Buck this week, he indirectly threatened me and, more importantly, anyone I care about. That would definitely include you."

"Why would he do such a thing?"

"I have some thoughts, but I'm not saying anything until I find out for sure. Meanwhile I don't want you in the middle—of this or anything else that could hurt you." He watched her, his mouth a grim line. "Mary, I want you to give up your search."

Of all the things she'd expected him to say, this was the last. Anger and confusion swept over her. "I...I beg your pardon?" She could feel the color draining from her face. "What possible connection could there be between this fire, Buck Lloyd and my search?"

"Probably none, but the fire made me realize that I will go to any lengths to protect you from harm. I can't ignore Buck's threats." He sat forward, his expression full of supplication and conviction. "Please, Mary, give it up. The outcome of your search could hurt you, too. We have each other. That's all we need."

"All *you* need, maybe." She couldn't believe it. She picked up her plate and walked to the counter, emotions churning. Casey made a low, growling sound. With a clatter, she set down the dish, then turned to Russ, heat searing her face. "You smug, patronizing—" she sputtered "—I thought you understood. Give it up? Because of a range fire?" Her voice rose. "I don't need your protection, thank you very much. I'm perfectly capable of weathering more hurt. What happened to your promise to help?" She rolled her eyes at the ceiling. "God, I believed you!'' She stormed over to the table and jabbed him in the arm. "What do you take me for? Your problems with Buck Lloyd are just that—*your* problems.''

Slowly he got to his feet, towering over her, his eyes the color of quarried granite. Casey stood guard at his side. Moving closer, Russ put a hand on her shoulder. "Please, Mary. I love you.'' His voice echoed in the quiet kitchen. "I couldn't stand it if you got hurt. Do it for me.''

She brushed his arm away. "Not until you give me some better reason than your feud with Buck Lloyd. Take me home, please.''

"Are you going ahead with your search?''

She shot him a scathing look. "I'm leaving for Denver in the morning, remember? Do you have any other stupid questions?''

He leaned on the kitchen table. Then, as if collecting himself, he straightened, fixing his eyes on hers. "Well, I guess that's that.'' He walked toward the hall, trailed by a dejected-looking Casey. "I'll get your coat.''

Mary's hands shook as she picked up her mug and returned it to the sink. With his track record, what had ever made her think he could be trusted to follow through on a promise?

HE CURSED under his breath as he pulled away from the curb after taking her home. All the way into town, she sat mute, arms folded across her chest. The one time he'd tried to reopen the subject, she had turned and deliberately stared out the passenger window, ignoring him. When they reached the condo, she had jumped from the truck and raced up the walk before he could react.

Damn! He'd known his argument wouldn't work. She was too stubborn, too persistent, too obsessed with finding her birth parents. He loved her. He didn't want to see her hurt, not if he could help it. If Buck had set the fire, it was Russ he was after, not Mary—at least not yet. He still didn't have proof that Buck was Mary's grandfather, and until he did, he'd have to try to keep Mary out of harm's way. The trip to Denver would help temporarily... unless she learned something while she was there.

Buck wasn't given to idle threats. Now that Russ had tipped him off about January 10, 1968, it wouldn't take him long to put two and two together. If Russ was going to have even a hope of protecting Mary, he had to act quickly.

He drove around aimlessly, considering the possibilities. Was fatigue muddying his thinking? He stopped at a café for a cup of coffee to clear his head. Finally he settled on two courses of action, both risky. But he didn't have many choices.

He parked in front of the Sooner Arms at 2:25 p.m. Nap time? He'd have to chance it. The deserted lobby and living room felt tomblike. Grimly, Russ strode down the hall toward Sal's apartment. Fortunately, she was awake and willing to ask him in. He carried a straight chair from the dining room table and sat opposite her.

"This is a surprise." She massaged her gnarled hands. "What brings you out on a beautiful Thursday afternoon?"

"I'd like to say this is a social call, but it isn't."

Her lids lowered a fraction and her hands stilled in her lap. "Do we have some business, then, that I don't know about?"

He forced down the knot in his throat. "I'd say we do. Some unfinished business. About Mary."

Her tight lips relaxed into a weak smile. "Oh, you've found a bracelet?"

"No, but I think I've found something else." He bent toward her, speaking earnestly. "I need your help. It's important, Sal."

She sat motionless, her back straight, her eyes fixed on him. Finally she gave a slight nod of her head.

"You didn't deny your niece might have had a necklace like Mary's." He spurred on into the *big* question. "Sal, is there any possibility Mary's necklace once belonged to Ellie?" Russ waited, moist palms gripping his knees, his eyes never leaving Sal's face. On the balcony melodic wind chimes tinkled incongruously.

Sal sat Sphinxlike, her eyes gradually misting with unshed tears. She played with the cuff of her sweater, then rolled her watch around on her thin wrist. Finally, with a slight quaver, she spoke. "Why is it important to you?"

There was no turning back. "For two reasons. Number one, I love Mary." He noted a satisfied gleam in her eyes. "And number two—" he rubbed his hands up and down his thighs "—if Ellie had a necklace like Mary's, I have reason to suspect Mary may be Ellie's daughter. And if I'm right, Mary could be in danger."

Sal gripped the arms of her chair and cocked her head. "Danger?"

"Your brother knows of my interest in events occurring on January 10, 1968. And last night we had a suspicious range fire at my place."

Sal's nails bit into the upholstery fabric, but she didn't speak.

"Can you confirm or deny my hypothesis?"

He could barely hear her response. "Yes."

He leaned forward eagerly. "And?"

"I can, but I won't." Then she did a singular thing. She locked her eyes with his and smiled with all the shrewdness of an accomplished riverboat gambler.

"WE ARE CRUISING at an altitude of 32,000 feet. Our estimated time of arrival in Denver is 9:45 a.m., Mountain Standard Time. Weather on the ground is cloudy, temperature twenty-nine degrees." Mary shifted in her seat and stared out the window into the billowy clouds. She'd always been a tense flyer, but this time her mission, more than the flight, was responsible for the taut muscles in her stomach.

She was well aware that the trip might accomplish nothing.

But, silly as it sounded, she had to see the hospital, the place where she was born, the place where her mother had reached that irrevocable decision. Under the guise of a gynecological problem, she'd made an appointment for this afternoon with Dr. Altmuller. Until she saw him face-to-face, she wouldn't feel she'd tried everything. She rubbed her temples where a dull throb had set up a tattoo. The last thirty-six hours had been chaotic—the fire, Russ's betrayal, the rush to get packed and now the trip. She smiled sardonically at her reflection in the plane window. *Where's your objectivity, your logic, now?*

She had prided herself on being a good judge of character and making decisions based on thorough, proven data. How had she been so terribly wrong about Russ? Beyond just *wrong,* how had she permitted herself to fall for his line? She shuddered. God, she'd nearly gone to bed with him! She'd totally taken leave of her senses! No, she was well out of it. She grudgingly admitted his role in helping with the *oochalata* necklace, but that was it. Period. End of story.

The plane lurched and she felt her stomach—and an involuntary sob—rise with it. She fumbled in her purse for a tissue. Damn, she wasn't going to cry. He wasn't worth it. She dabbed at her eyes and blew her nose. She'd believed him when he'd said he loved her. And she'd meant it when she told him she loved him. How could it turn to ashes so quickly? Ashes. That damn fire. Something happened to him overnight. How could he pull such an abrupt about-face? She sighed. She knew herself well enough to know she wouldn't be satisfied, wouldn't be able to put Russ Coulter to rest until she understood how he could so quickly and radically have gone back on a promise.

"Return your tray tables to their upright position..." the garbled voice of the steward intruded. "We should arrive at the gate five minutes early." At least something was going right.

SATURDAY EVENING Russ sat stiffly in a slate blue leather wing chair staring at the gas logs blazing in the faux marble fireplace. It was too painful to look up at the large oil portrait hanging above—the first thing he'd seen when he'd entered the Fleets' Ladue living room. Mary as a young woman, her glossy black bob framing her heart-shaped face, the high cheekbones setting off those luminous dark brown eyes, her smooth skin highlighted by the artist. But it was the smile that wrenched his heart—that same wondrous smile she'd given him the day they'd visited Clyde Peppercorn. It was all he could do to respond politely to Phyllis's suggestion that they have some coffee while they waited for Mary's father to arrive home from hospital rounds.

What he was about to do could cost him everything. Yet not to do it was even riskier. He stood as Phyllis entered the room, bearing a serving tray. She set it down on the gateleg table and poured him a cup before serving herself and sitting opposite him. Everything—the high ceilings with the delicate moldings, the thick Persian rug beneath his feet, the exquisite white-flocked Christmas tree bedecked with shimmering gold and silver baubles—conveyed tasteful luxury. Nothing—not the leather-bound books in the walnut glass-paneled bookcase, the porcelain Nativity figurines in the corner cabinet nor the red bayberry candles in shiny brass candlesticks on the mantel—was out of place.

Phyllis sipped from the china cup, replacing it in the saucer before she spoke. "I can't tell you how surprised and delighted I was when you called. What brings you to St. Louis?"

"Actually you do or, more precisely, Mary does. As I told you on the phone yesterday, I'd hoped to be able to spend a little time with you and your husband tonight."

Phyllis smiled as if she hid a delightful secret. "Charles should be home any time now."

Good God! He reviewed his last words. The implication hit him. They probably inferred he was the dutiful suitor here to ask for their daughter's hand. If only... He scrambled for a rejoinder. "If you don't mind, I'll wait until he's here to explain my purpose in coming."

Phyllis asked about his family and he elaborated on that topic until Dr. Fleet arrived. He kissed his wife's cheek, folded his suit coat over the back of the other wing chair and sat down. He, too, seemed happily expectant. There was no point in delaying the inevitable. Russ cleared his throat. "It was good of you to make time for me on such short notice. As you may have guessed, I'm more than just fond of Mary." He winced as Phyllis brightened and moved to the edge of her chair. "But I'm very concerned for her welfare right now and I'm here to...solicit your cooperation." Phyllis's hand went automatically to her throat and Charles edged forward, concern tightening his features.

"What do you mean?" Phyllis managed.

Russ marshalled the thoughts he'd mentally rehearsed in preparation for this encounter. "As you're aware, Mary is determined to follow every possible avenue in trying to locate her birth parents."

Charles removed his glasses and rubbed his nose between thumb and index finger. "That again," he muttered.

Russ continued. "I'm aware this is a painful subject for the two of you. Mary's told me how you feel. But because of the way things have developed, I have some concern for her safety. I must emphasize that what I'm going to tell you is mere supposition at this point. For this reason, I haven't said anything to Mary. But if what I suspect is true, she needs to proceed very carefully." He launched into his story about the necklace, Ellie Lloyd, Buck's implied threats and the fire. Phyllis occasionally interjected a question. Charles, however, sat staring straight ahead, the muscles of his jaw working.

When Russ finished, there was total silence. Phyllis looked at her husband helplessly and Russ read fear in her eyes. Finally, Charles put his glasses back on, then turned to Russ. "You're right. It's a disturbing story. But what do you expect us to do about it?"

"Give me some ammunition. Either to convince Mary to give up the search or to determine if my fears have any validity. While there's always the chance I won't have to use anything you tell me, I don't think we can bank on that. Bottom line, I'm asking you to trust me."

"Why should we?" Charles asked.

"Because I love your daughter and will do anything in my power to help her and keep her from harm."

"Charles?" Phyllis's voice was tentative.

"I can't imagine what you want *me* to do." Charles frowned at his wife and shrugged in exasperation.

Phyllis stood and walked slowly over to her husband's chair. She knelt at his side, covered his hand with both of hers and gazed at him. "He's talking about our precious Mary. And, hard as it is, Charles—" tears filled her eyes "—it's time. Tell him."

Russ waited, his heart pounding, as the two exchanged a telling glance. Then, almost imperceptibly, Charles's shoulders slumped. He patted his wife's hand. "You've never asked this of me before." He faced Russ again as his wife returned to her chair. "I'm going to tell you a story I hope Mary never has to hear. I'll have to trust your judgment about whether you need to use it." He reached up to loosen his tie, then began talking.

Fifteen painful minutes later, he finished. "Now do you see why we've prayed Mary could be content without ever looking for her parents?"

"Yes, sir, I do. I promise you that I won't say anything unless it's absolutely necessary. And in that event, I hope you'll be in a position to tell her yourself." Russ got to his feet and extended his hand to Mary's father.

He grasped Russ's hand firmly. "Take care of her, son," he said huskily.

Phyllis touched Russ's arm and found his eyes. "Thank you for caring."

"That's the easy part," Russ replied. He picked up his coat and started for the door. "Oh—" he turned "—one last thing. What was the name of the law firm you dealt with in Tulsa?"

"Steadman, Jackson and Freedlander," Charles answered.

"Thanks. Well, good night, then. I'll be in touch." Russ took one last look at the vibrant portrait over the fireplace.

THE DRIVE HOME the next day afforded Russ plenty of time to mull over the implications of the Fleets's story—and to appreciate the importance of confidentiality. Mary's adoption had been unorthodox, all right, and the Fleets's concern was both potent and justified.

He hadn't known what to expect, but the truth exceeded anything he'd imagined. Charles Fleet had choked out the words: "We were paid to take Mary."

Russ's face must've registered shock because Phyllis had interrupted in an anguished voice. "It wasn't like that! It isn't what you're thinking."

Charles had continued, his voice cracking. "But, in the beginning, Phyl, it would appear to an outsider like a business transaction, pure and simple."

Phyllis's next words had been nearly inaudible. "But we always loved her, right from the very beginning. She must never think otherwise."

Miles went by. Russ was vaguely aware of going up and down the long hills of central Missouri as his mind churned with the disturbing implications. It looked bad that they had taken the money, but once he'd heard their reasons, he could easily understand their desperation at the time. He could also understand that they'd never wanted Mary to think they'd been bribed or hadn't wanted her.

More compelling was their persistent and very real fear. How could they ever be certain that a person desperate enough to pay a significant sum to place a baby and ensure their silence wasn't still a menace? How, indeed?

The more he thought about it, the more convinced he became that they'd been right to err on the side of caution.

As soon as he arrived at the ranch, he phoned his father at the office. "Dad, I need a favor and I need it fast."

"What's up?"

"Who does Buck Lloyd's personal legal work?"

He heard the hesitation in his father's voice. "Son, is it about the land? It's not that important. Leave well enough alone."

"Dad, that's not my reason for asking. You'll have to trust me on this. I need to know, and I'll find out one way or another, so I'd appreciate your saving me some time and effort."

His father sighed. "Callender and Peters handles his oil-and-gas business, but his personal stuff is handled in Tulsa." He paused and Russ's grip tightened on the telephone. "Steadman, Jackson and Freedlander."

CHAPTER FIFTEEN

MARY WENT TO her office early on Monday. She'd gotten in from Denver late the night before and dreaded facing the work piled up from the two days she'd missed. As she sat at her desk with a cup of tea, listening to her voice mail, one message in particular caught her attention. Sal McClanahan wanted to set up an appointment at her earliest convenience. Mary crossed her fingers. Maybe Sal had decided to transfer her trust account. On the computer, she pulled up Friday's closing stock prices and made a few notes.

"Hi, Mary. Welcome home." A beaming Gwen stood in the doorway with a sack in her hand. "I thought you might come in early. I picked up my breakfast at the drive-through, hoping we'd have a few minutes before the day gets started."

Mary motioned to a chair. "Sit down. I'm glad to see you."

Gwen unfolded a napkin and extracted a biscuit sandwich from her sack. "Have you eaten? I'll share."

"Thanks, but I've had breakfast."

"Okay, then. How was your trip? I'm dying to hear." She ate as Mary began to fill her in.

"I'm afraid I didn't learn much." She tried to keep the disappointment out of her voice. "Dr. Altmuller was cordial but very professional. He explained the law to me and pointed out that it would be unethical for him to provide me with any information."

"That's it? All that way for nothing?"

"Not quite. He did give me one lead." Gwen, her mouth full, gestured for Mary to continue. "He supplied me with the address of a rooming house near the hospital where outpatients, including some expectant mothers, used to stay back in the sixties and seventies."

"And?" Gwen's eyes widened in encouragement.

"I went there. It was a rambling old Victorian house that's seen better days, but something about it seemed . . . sort of familiar, even though I've never been to Denver since I was born. Isn't that crazy? I even broke out in goose bumps when I rang the bell." Mary shook her head as if to dismiss the eerie sensation. "A woman in her forties opened the door. She told me that the house no longer served as tourist accommodations. I was about to leave, but decided to ask if she knew anyone who'd been involved with the property in the sixties. I guess by then she'd warmed to me because she invited me in and told me her invalid mother, who'd been the proprietor until 1975, still lived there. Although the mother was crippled with arthritis, there was nothing wrong with her memory." Mary paused.

"Jeez, Mary, go on. I'm dying of suspense. What'd she say?"

"Nothing at first. She explained they'd had thousands of guests through the years and remembering one would be nearly impossible. I thought I'd reached another impasse."

"But?"

"But when I mentioned January 10, 1968, she seemed startled. Then she asked her daughter to dig out the registration book for that year."

"She remembered?"

Mary's shoulders sagged. "Not as much as I would've liked. She had no memory of a Native American woman being there. But she had a clear recollection of a young woman who gave birth to a daughter on January 10, 1968, because that was her own son's twenty-first birthday."

"Could she give you a name?"

"She looked at the registrations and said she thought the young woman's name was Emily Larsen and that she was accompanied by an older woman named Sarah Merriman. That was all she could come up with. But now, at least, I can go back and contact all the registries, look in Colorado phone directories, send out a new message on the Internet."

Gwen wiped the crumbs from her mouth. "That's exciting. What does Russ think of all this?"

Mary brought her tea unsteadily to her mouth. "Russ doesn't know."

"Well, you're certainly going to tell him, aren't you?"

"No, Gwen, I'm not. He's out of the picture."

"Mary, he's crazy about you!"

"In that case, he has a funny way of showing it. He broke a promise. For no good reason. One day he was gung ho to help, the next day he asked me to call off the search."

"That doesn't sound like him. What happened?"

"I haven't got a clue, except for the fire."

"You mean the range fire? I read about it in the paper. What's that got to do with anything?"

"Beats me. But it was after the fire that he reneged on his promise. He claimed he was terrified I'd be hurt by the fire—or by some discovery I might make about my birth parents. He wanted to protect me, he said. Pretty weak reasoning, if you ask me.''

Gwen sat quietly for a minute, then began speaking slowly. ''Russ can be impetuous in small matters, but I've never known him to be anything but steady as a rock about important things. If Russ wants to spare you pain or disappointment, he probably has a reason. It doesn't mean he doesn't care for you. Quite the opposite.''

''Even if that's true, Gwen, he made a firm promise to help with the search. Then, just like that, he broke his word. I can't admire a man, much less love him, when his promise means so little.'' What was it about that damn fire that'd changed him? No matter how hard she tried to put Russ out of her mind, that one persistent question kept nagging at her.

Gwen rose, crumpled her bag and tossed it in the wastebasket. ''I've got to get to my desk.'' She hesitated at the door. ''But, Mary, don't give up on Russ. They don't make 'em much better. There's *got* to be an explanation. Give him the benefit of the doubt. Please.''

Benefit of the doubt? No way. She'd had quite enough of the man's totally unreliable nature. He couldn't even be punctual. Why had she ever thought he'd be trustworthy—someone she could count on?

''JIM, SORRY I left you in the lurch the past two days. My business in St. Louis wouldn't wait.'' Russ drew the cinch tighter on Major, then swung into the saddle.

His foreman, already mounted on a pinto mare, shrugged as he guided the horse beyond the corral and kicked her into a trot. ''No problem, boss.''

Russ caught up to him. ''Now that the fire's totally out, I need to see the extent of the damage. We've got calves due to be shipped here the first week in January.

We've gotta figure how long it'll take this grass to come back and how to pasture not only the existing herd but these new ones."

"We're gonna have to do some shuffling. Hell of an inconvenience, ain't it?"

"That's for damn sure. At least we didn't end up with a stampede or barbecued beef."

Jim chuckled. "Boys did a good job of tending to the hot spots and getting fence repairs underway."

"Fire chief tell you the fire was set deliberately?"

Russ's jaw tightened. "Yeah. Who do you suppose?"

Jim spat a stream of tobacco juice toward the ground. "First, I thought maybe Buck had set it. He's a tough old bastard, but it's hard to believe he'd burn a man's pasture."

Russ didn't trust himself to answer. Not so hard to believe if a man had seen Buck's glowing cigar, heard his threat.

Jim rode on a few paces before continuing. "Sheriff called while you were gone."

"Oh?"

"He's nailed some kids."

"Kids?"

"Yeah. You know those cuts in the fence? Sheriff claims there's a bunch of wild kids in town who sneak onto the land regularly, find a gully hidden from the road and have 'em a hell of a drinkin' party. Must've been celebrating the holidays early."

"The fire?"

"It was colder than a well digger's ass Wednesday night. Kids built 'em a bonfire and when the wind came up, it got out of hand. Sheriff found a bunch of empty beer cans on Buck's land near the fence runnin' along the section road."

Russ felt his chest constrict. Had he been wrong? Jumped to a conclusion? If he *was* wrong, he'd broken his promise to Mary for nothing. Risked everything—because of what? The answer struck him with the force of a head blow. Impetuosity, that was what. Even so, he couldn't underestimate Buck's threat. He was a rattlesnake coiled to strike.

Russ spurred his horse to a gallop and inhaled the cold rushing air. Whether she knew it or not, Mary still needed him. He might have made one mistake, but he wasn't going to make another. She was worth fighting for.

MARY OPENED HER briefcase and spread the trust agreement papers out on Sal's dining room table. When she'd returned Sal's call yesterday, she'd been elated to discover she'd won over another Sooner Arms customer. Mary turned to her and smiled. "I think we're about ready." She stood up, walking toward Sal's chair. "Let me help you."

Seeming spryer than usual, Sal moved smartly across the carpet to the dining room chair. Mary gathered up the first set of papers. "This is a listing of all the bank's trust services, personnel, phone numbers."

Sal plucked her reading glasses from a sweater pocket and peered at the print. "Where's your name? Hell, the bank doesn't even have my account representative on their fancy list."

Mary chuckled. Sal didn't miss a thing. "I'm new. They'll be reprinting this at the first of the year."

Sal sniffed. "They better."

When Mary handed her the trust contract with the bank, Sal asked her to read it aloud. Mary started through the document's legalese. All the time she was reading, she felt Sal's eyes studying her with an unusual intensity. Finally, Mary finished the concluding paragraph. "Any questions?"

Sal waved a hand in dismissal. "I trust you, honey. I didn't hear anything I can't live with. What's next?"

"Do you want to assign a trustee other than the bank? Previously you used only the bank."

"What for?"

Mary outlined the advantages of having a family member or trusted friend involved as a system of checks and balances on the bank. "Makes sense," Sal muttered. She straightened up. "Yes. I think I do."

Mary reached for the relevant paper. "What name?"

"Harrison Lloyd." Mary began to write. "No, wait a minute. Can you put in a nickname, too?" Mary nodded. "Okay, then, make it Harrison 'Buck' Lloyd."

It was hard to conceal her dismay. Conceivably she'd have to do business with that mean-spirited, vindictive man. "Buck Lloyd?"

"You know Buck?"

"I met him once," Mary managed to squeeze out.

"He's an old reprobate, but I never had any children, you know. He's all I've got." Sal paused. "I think." Again Mary felt the piercing blue eyes studying her.

Mary busied herself with the papers, checking to be sure she had the dates and all inserted material in order. Finally she looked up. "I've asked the business manager here to witness your signature. That way you won't have to make a special trip to the bank. But there's no hurry. Whenever you're ready."

"I'm ready. No point wishy-washing around."

"Where's your phone? I told her I'd give her a ring when it was time."

Sal pointed to the adjoining bedroom. "In there. On my desk."

Mary stepped into the bedroom. As she waited for the receptionist to connect her with the business manager, she looked at the wall behind the desk. It was covered with framed family photographs. A thin, freckled girl in a middy blouse, hands folded in her lap, feet tucked under the chair. A young man in thirties-style knickers standing beside a roadster. Buck? A wedding portrait of Sal and a tall rake of a man. An older Sal standing with her arm around a lovely young woman with a bouffant sixties-style hairdo, big eyes and a heart-shaped face.

Mary started to look at the next photo, but something about the two women arrested her attention. Something about the younger woman with Sal. "... What did you say? Yes, I'll be happy to hold." The hairs on the back of Mary's neck began to prickle and for some unaccountable reason the blood rushed from her head. The hand holding the phone felt clammy. For a moment the room spun around her. *The young woman.* Mary leaned closer, studying the eyes, the shape of the face and, with a jolt, she identified the sensation she was experiencing. For years she'd sought her likeness in a mirror. Now it was staring at her from this picture frame.

She heard a tinny voice in her ear. "... Yes, we're ready.... As soon as you can." In a daze, Mary let the phone slip back into place.

She couldn't face Sal, not right now. She was suffocating. Trembling, she walked to the door. "Mrs. Jensen will be right up. Would you excuse me? I need to use the bathroom."

"Help yourself, honey."

Mary found the light switch, closed the door and turned on the faucet. She dabbed cold water on the back of her neck, her temples, her wrists. What she was thinking was crazy. It couldn't be. It was too coincidental, too terrifying in its immediacy. She sank onto the closed lid of the commode and leaned over, holding her head in her icy hands.

Denver. An older woman and a young girl. A young woman who looked like a paler image of herself. What had Sal said? Buck was all she had? Could it possibly be? The woman in the photograph. Ellie Lloyd? She inhaled. The necklace. Sal's curiosity. She'd noticed it twice. But the inscription was Cherokee. So her mother was Cherokee. Her mind was playing tricks. Wishful thinking. But why had her parents been so opposed to her moving to Ewing? She needed time, air, space to think this through. She stood shakily, flushing the toilet to cover the noise of the stifled sob that rose in her throat. But when her hand gripped the cold doorknob, she stopped in her tracks. Oh, God. Emily Larsen, Ellie Lloyd. E. L. And the older woman's name? She racked her brain. Sarah Merriman! Nausea clawed at the base of her throat. She swallowed twice, inhaled deeply and turned the knob.

She heard the knock on the door as she emerged from the bathroom. She admitted the efficient-looking Mrs. Jensen. "Hello, Betty," Sal said. "Let's get this business tended to."

Mary watched, her heart pounding, as Sal attached her shaky signature to the necessary documents. Then Betty Jensen signed, patted Sal on the shoulder and left the apartment. It hadn't taken three minutes. Mary's mouth was clogged with cobwebs.

Sal turned to her, beaming. "That's done. Can't tell you how glad I am to be doing business with you, honey. Trust a woman every time, I always say."

Mary pasted an obligatory smile across her face and uttered something perfunctory.

"You okay?" Sal laid a bony hand on Mary's forearm. "You look like you've seen a ghost."

Mary stirred. "Maybe I have." And before she had time to reconsider, the words poured like a torrent through a fissure in a dam. "Were you in Denver on January 10, 1968?"

CHAPTER SIXTEEN

SAL WILLED HER EYES to remain open, her hands still. She could feel the erratic rhythm of her heartbeat. A haze blurred her vision for a moment before the images snapped back into focus. The sudden dread that had initially seized her now relaxed. The unraveling had begun. And high time. But she'd have to be very careful, play her cards just right. Across the table, the young woman sat, motionless and pale with shock.

Sal roused herself. "What makes you ask a thing like that?"

Mary answered dazedly. "I . . . I thought . . . no, I was entirely out of line. But the photograph . . . over the desk . . ." Her voice trailed off, her head bowed from her neck like a broken lily.

"You mean the photograph of my niece and me?"

Mary's head whipped up. "Your . . . your niece?"

Sal answered firmly, determined to follow this to the end. "Yes, my niece. Ellie Lloyd." Could Mary be Ellie's daughter? She'd harbored the hope ever since she'd seen the *oochalata* necklace, like the one Ellie had worn around her neck that whole fall and winter. And there was no mistaking the similarity in facial structure, although Mary's cheekbones were more pronounced and her coloring much darker. Then there were Russ's questions. He, too, suspected.

Mary licked her lips and spoke tremulously. "Denver? Were you there with your niece in 1968?" Sal noted the desperation in Mary's eyes.

"Why is it so important to you?"

"Because—" Mary's voice faltered "—because I think Ellie might be my mother."

Sal exhaled. There it was! She leaned on the table and slowly raised herself erect. "If you can be patient for a day or two, honey, I may be able to give you some information." Mary looked up, hope warring with dread in her expression. "In the meantime, I must ask you a favor."

Mary swallowed. "Anything."

"This isn't going to be an easy time for either of us. I trust you won't discuss this matter with anyone else until I get back to you." Sal placed a gentle, withered hand on Mary's sleek black hair.

MARY LAY ON HER SOFA, the afghan drawn up over her shoulders. She couldn't stop shivering. Her stomach felt queasy. She'd left Sal's apartment in a swirl of confusion, not trusting herself to go back to the office. Her face would've been a dead giveaway to the emotional storm inside and she was afraid she'd burst into tears right there in the middle of the trust department. Instead, she'd raced home, composed herself long enough to call the office and say she'd wrap up Sal's paperwork at home, then collapsed on the sofa, her head full of specters. Especially one.

The young woman haunted her—the same deep-set eyes, the full lips, the pointed chin. But it was more than that. It was the sense of immediate connection—of peering into one's own soul. Mary brushed away the tears trickling down her cheek. There was something so irrational, so improbable, so otherworldly about the experience; yet in an instant she'd known beyond the shadow of any doubt—she was looking at her mother. Ellie Lloyd, whose tragic story kept rolling in her mind like some grotesque film noir. How intense her emotional pain must've been to drive her to the desperate behavior Russ had described! Could Sal offer explanations? Motivations? Waiting was an agony beyond enduring.

She had steeled herself for disappointment in this search, but she hadn't prepared herself for the awful, gut-wrenching projection she knew she'd undergo—the sense of reliving, step by awful step, the last year of Ellie's life. Like being in her mother's skin.

She rolled over on her side, clutching the afghan. The preposterous, absurd coincidence of it all! Ewing, the Coulters, Sal—it made a kind of crazy sense, yet it defied all the laws of probability. So much for her reliance on logic!

She deliberately slowed her breathing. She needed to calm down, try to figure out exactly what this discovery meant—this discovery, which awaited only the formality of Sal's confirmation and explanation. Sal. She'd be Mary's great-aunt. And . . . the full implication hit her— Buck Lloyd was her grandfather! She closed her eyes, the trite admonition ringing in her head: Be careful what you wish for; it might come true.

WEDNESDAY, AS DUSK closed around the ranch house, Russ, rooted in front of the unlighted Christmas tree, toyed with the cowboy ornament. Had it been just a week ago that he and Mary had stood here starting a tradition? He dropped his hand from the ornament and turned away from the tree. Some tradition! It had lasted all of six or eight hours. The house seemed empty, all its warmth, even its rich storehouse of memories sucked out and extinguished by the fire. What holiday mockery! He'd been a meddling fool. Always so sure what was right for everybody. Rushing off to tilt at windmills.

Assuming Buck's guilt for the fire. Confronting Sal. Dashing off to St. Louis. Had he accomplished anything at all or merely opened a Pandora's box? Did it even matter? Mary wasn't returning his phone calls. He'd sent her a huge white poinsettia this morning, hoping that gesture would at least spur a thank-you. Nothing.

Everywhere he looked was a reminder of her. The guitar in the corner, the painting of the Indian girl bathing and, worst of all, the Christmas tree itself. He flopped down on the sofa and closed his eyes. The very thing he'd feared most had happened. Abandonment. She'd left him. Just like that. He'd thought it had hurt when his mother left. Hell, that didn't begin to count. He'd been better off without her. But Mary? God, it was like someone had carved out a section of his gut.

How had this miserable state come to pass? He'd jumped to a wrong conclusion about the fire. Yet was he wrong about Buck's potential for retaliation? As long as he lived, he wouldn't forget Buck's malevolent sneer behind that fat cigar. Abandonment was a hell of a price to pay for Mary's safety, but there was no point in lying around feeling sorry for himself. He sat up and rubbed a hand through his hair. Because he knew he'd do the same thing all over again if it meant protecting the woman he loved. But damn, it hurt!

THAT SAME EVENING a taxi pulled into the circle drive in front of a large Tudor-style mansion. Up and down the street, houses dazzled the onlooker with brilliant displays of Christmas lights. By contrast, this house sat in semidarkness, only one dim light visible through the di-amond-shaped panes in the front door. The driver jumped out, removed a walker from the trunk and rushed around to the passenger side. He opened the rear door, set up the walker and escorted Sal McClanahan, bun-dled in a fur coat and wearing a dated felt hat, from the cab and up the two steps. He waited while she rang the bell. "You be back here in fifteen minutes."

"Yes, ma'am."

Sal heard muffled footsteps, then the porch light flashed on and the door creaked open. Buck Lloyd stood framed in the doorway staring incredulously at her. "Sal, what in blue blazes are you doin' here?"

"Visiting you, you damn fool. And speaking of blue blazes, what do you know about that fire at the Coulter ranch?

Buck's mouth gaped, then he recovered himself. "Not a damn thing. I may play hardball, but I wouldn't ruin a man's land."

Sal shrugged in begrudging acceptance. "You gonna invite me in or not?"

Buck put a beefy hand under Sal's elbow and helped her into the living room. "Lemme take your coat and hat. Would you like a glass of wine?"

Sal shooed him away and sat in a straight-backed chair. "I'm not staying that long." She glanced around the dark-paneled room, hung with heavy maroon velvet drapes and furnished with massive mahogany antiques. "Hell, Buck, I don't see how you can live in this mau-soleum." She sniffed. "It smells like mothballs and dead roses."

Buck went to the sideboard to pour himself a snifter of brandy. "Is that what you came for? To insult me?" He carried his glass to the armchair across from her and sat down.

"Nope. I came to talk about her." She pointed to the gilt-framed oil painting of the bust and head of a creamy-skinned auburn-haired girl about twelve years old. "She was lovely, wasn't she?"

"Damn right. Not a day passes I don't miss her. Twenty-eight years. It's been a long time." He swished the brandy in his glass and inhaled the bouquet.

"Time enough for you to forgive?"

He snorted. "Forgive? Who? J. T. Coulter?"

She waited, watching him relentlessly.

"Why should I forgive him? Damned irresponsible punk. And now—" he rolled his eyes skyward "—I have to contend with his jackass son. Snooping around, dropping innuendoes, trying to blackmail me—"

"Russ? Blackmailing you?" The skepticism was obvious in Sal's voice.

"Hell, yes. He's got his eyes on my fifteen hundred acres. And he'll do anything to get it. Just like a damn Coulter." He took a healthy swig of the brandy. "Had the gall to ask me about 'property' I acquired on January 10, 1968."

"What did you say?"

"Told him he and anybody he cared about would be in a sorry mess if they thought they could blackmail Buck Lloyd with some idiotic fairy tale."

"Buck—" Sal's voice was like gravel rattling in a pan "—Ellie was not a fairy tale."

Buck rose from his chair. "Now see, here, Sal. You may be older'n me, but I don't need you meddling in my business." He jabbed a forefinger in the air for emphasis. "Stay out of this."

Sal replied calmly. "Sit down, little brother, and let me fill you in on the facts of life."

"Oh, great. Here we go." But he sat back down. "All right, damn it. Have your say."

"Thank you. I fully intend to. For starters, Ellie *is* my business. She was my niece. And if there's any guilt to be dished out for her death, it's yours."

"Just a damn minute." Buck's face turned purple. "I didn't ply her with liquor and send her out to ride some wild stallion at night."

"No, you didn't. And neither did J. T. Coulter. But you did destroy her just as surely as if you'd knocked her off that horse yourself." She raised her hand to forestall Buck's interruption. "You're going to hear me out, Buck, once and for all. We can either get it over with, or it can take all night. Your call."

"Damnation, woman!"

"Very well, I'll proceed. *Who* couldn't accept the fact that your model daughter was pregnant out of wedlock? That the young man was, for some reason, unsuitable? *Who* insisted on an abortion, even though your daughter begged and pleaded with you? *Who* had to punish his own daughter unmercifully so that the Lloyd family name—" she spat the term out as a mocking epithet "—wouldn't be compromised? It's only by the grace of God that she finally persuaded you to let her have the child and give it up for adoption. But even then, you extracted your pound of flesh, making her promise she'd never try to locate the child. Some father you were."

Buck smoldered. "Are you satisfied?"

Sal shook her head. "Not by a long shot. J. T. Coulter had nothing to do with any of that. After having her baby, your daughter came home a broken, depressed young woman. You'd taken from her everything she loved—the young man, whoever he was, and a precious infant daughter. No wonder she drank. No wonder she was reckless. What did she have to live for? So if you want to point fingers, turn them at yourself.''

"*Now* are you finished?''

"Just one more thing. I promised you at the time you sent Ellie to stay with us during her pregnancy that I'd never reveal her secret. Well, that's one promise I'm going to break.''

He gripped both sides of the chair as if to keep from assaulting his own sister. "The hell you say!''

"Yes, the hell I say. You can remain a bitter, lonely, vindictive sorry son of a bitch, but I am going to claim my great-niece.''

He leapt to his feet, eyes blazing. "What're you saying?''

Masking the effort it took, she rose and stared into the embers of his eyes. "I am going to tell Mary Fleet that she is Ellie's daughter and—''

"Mary Fleet! Who the hell—''

"—enjoy whatever time I have remaining. I've never in my life broken my word...until now.'' She couldn't hide a smug grin. "But every rule is meant to be broken.''

"Goddamn it, who is Mary Fleet?''

"It's time for me to go, Buck.'' She started slowly toward the door, pushing her walker ahead of her. "Mary Fleet works at the bank. Young Coulter is in love with her. And most important of all, she's your only grandchild.'' She turned and drew herself up to her full height. "You leave her alone and you leave the Coulters alone or I'll expose you for the selfish opportunist you are. Better still, you might try the forgiveness I mentioned earlier in this conversation. Starting with yourself. Think about atoning for all those miserable years. Consider welcoming your granddaughter. And if you can't accept this decision I've made, I'll say it just once—you're no brother of mine.''

She left Buck fuming at the door. She looked around for the taxi driver and saw him hurrying toward her. "Sorry to keep you waiting, young man. My business here is finished." She hooked her arm through the cabbie's, feeling better than she had in years. Sometimes it took a frontal assault to crack the opponent's armor.

WHEN SHE ARRIVED back at her apartment, Sal poured herself a generous glass of sherry and sat down at the telephone. First she called Mary, whose lovely, breathless voice filled the void in her heart created by Buck's selfishness and weakness of character. "Honey, I told you I might have some information to help you. Perhaps you'd be available tomorrow evening about seven? Good. I'll look forward to seeing you then. Goodbye.''

And now for Russ. Bless his heart. How he loved her Mary! "Russ, is that you? This is Sal McClanahan. Could you drop by my apartment about seven tomorrow evening? I have a story I think will interest you.''

She heard the anguish in his voice. "Is it about Mary?''

"Yes, dear. She's going to be here, too. Perhaps you'll come together?''

He hesitated. "I don't think so, Sal. She's not very happy with me right now. In fact, she may not want me there at all.''

"But I want you here. Excuse me for butting in, but is there a little friction between the two of you?''

"I wish it *were* just a little." His voice echoed hollowly over the line.

"We'll see what we can do about that. Like I told Mary, any relationship worth its salt has its frictions. You gotta wear down those rough places before you can get to the smooth parts." She chuckled. "Even then, an occasional chafing can clear the air."

"Thanks, Sal. I'll be there."

"Good night." She hung up the phone and sat staring at the photograph of her and Ellie. Aware that she was speaking aloud—and not giving a damn—she addressed the smiling face of the young woman. "Ellie, it's going to be all right. I just feel it in my bones. And you'd be so proud of your Mary. Buck can be a lonely, bitter old man if *he* wants, but I'm gonna have a family!"

CHAPTER SEVENTEEN

OBLIVIOUS TO HER surroundings, Mary walked numbly down the hall toward Sal's apartment. "Now I'll know, now I'll know," an internal voice whispered. Not until she was nearly at Sal's door did she notice Russ, his hand poised to knock. Her fingers went instinctively to her necklace.

She hadn't seen him since the morning after the fire and certainly didn't want to see him now. What was he doing here, anyway? Russ Coulter and that damn poinsettia of his! It had arrived yesterday—a feeble attempt at apology? True-blue, through-thick-and-thin, stand-by-your-woman Russ. "Give up your search," he'd said. Gorge rose in her throat. Just then he saw her. "Hello, Mary," he said quietly.

Her voice quavered. "Why, may I ask, are you here?"

He flinched, his eyes traveling from her feet up to her eyes. "Sal asked me to come."

"Sal asked—"

Before she could finish, the door opened, and Sal, frowsy red hair a halo about her weathered face, beckoned them in. "Good evening, you two. Glad to see you're punctual."

Mary shot Russ a withering stare. This must be a first for him! She took a chair as far removed as possible from Russ's position on the sofa. Sal presided from her usual wing chair. Mary and Russ waited silently, tension crackling between them.

Mary swallowed. "Sal, before you begin, I'd like to ask what Russ is doing here. I'm uncomfortable with the situation."

Russ fidgeted on the sofa. "If I need to leave—"

"Nonsense. You're part of this and you need to hear what I have to say." She turned to Mary. "If it wasn't for Russ, I wouldn't have put things together so quickly."

"But how is he involved with—"

"Be patient." Sal paused to collect her thoughts. "I've come to a decision, perhaps long overdue. Years ago I made a promise, which at the time seemed the only course of action. So often I've wished my word undone, but I don't hold with going back on a promise. However, in light of recent events, I've decided that sometimes greater harm can be done by keeping your word than by breaking it. Mary, you asked me a question Tuesday. I'm going to answer it." Mary sucked in her breath. "From all I can figure, I believe Ellie was your mother. The main evidence is the necklace."

"The necklace?"

"When Buck sent Ellie out to the Panhandle to live with Will and me while she was pregnant, she wore a necklace just like yours the whole time. She wouldn't tell us where it came from. After she had her baby, I never saw it again."

Mary lowered her head and clutched the *oochalata* stone. "My mother—my adoptive mother—gave this to me recently. She said it'd been sent with the final adoption papers."

"Both the necklace and the fact that something about you seemed so familiar puzzled me. But it wasn't until

Tuesday when you saw the picture that the similarity jumped out at me.''

"Picture?" Russ looked baffled.

"A picture of Ellie and me—'' Sal jerked her head toward the bedroom ''—over my desk in there.''

"Why..." Mary couldn't quite get the words out, "Why... did she give me up?''

Sal took a tissue out of her pocket and clenched it in her hand. "She didn't want to, Mary. I think she'd have given anything to be able to keep you.''

"Then... ?''

"My brother can be very intimidating. When Ellie graduated and came back to Ewing, she couldn't hide her pregnancy from Buck. They'd always been close, and more so after her mother died when she was nine. It nearly killed him when he discovered his beloved daughter was pregnant.''

"But what about my father? Why didn't she just get married?''

Sal considered. "I never knew who the father was. Ellie refused to discuss him, but I've always suspected Buck knew and was violently opposed to the option of marriage. So opposed in fact that he insisted on an abortion. He'd even made an appointment.''

Mary bit her lip. Russ sat still as a statue, staring at Sal. "But... I'm here.''

"Ellie inherited some of Buck's stubbornness herself. She was determined to do anything—anything at all—to complete the pregnancy. Finally Buck forced a concession from her. He would permit her to go through with the birth, provided—'' Sal ticked off the list on her fingers ''—that Ellie come to live with us and have the baby out of state, that she make no attempt to communicate with the father, that she permit Buck to handle all the adoption arrangements and, finally, that she never make any attempt to locate the child. And, of course, I was sworn to secrecy."

Russ stood up, as if looking frantically for a place to move, an action to take. "That's barbaric." He strode to the balcony doors and then back to his seat, crumpling into the cushions.

Sal dabbed an eye with the tissue. "If Ellie ever received any calls or mail from the father, Buck kept it from her."

"Do you . . . do you think she was . . . raped or something?" Mary managed to ask.

"Quite the contrary. From everything I could deduce, she cared very deeply for the man involved."

"Sal," Russ ventured, "what do you think explains the change in her behavior when she returned to Ewing after the birth?"

"Postpartum depression was surely a factor. So was living in the oppressive atmosphere of Buck's house, resenting him every day. And, of course, despondency over the loss of her baby. Later on—was it May or June?—she grew more severely depressed. And in those days, people just didn't consider counseling like they do now."

Tears streamed down Mary's face. "That's . . . horrible." Her throat clotted with emotion. "She must've been so vulnerable . . . so alone . . ."

Sal blew her nose. "And so strong and brave. Come here, honey." Mary, blinded by tears, groped her way to Sal's chair and knelt beside her. Sal smoothed the hair back from Mary's forehead. "If I've ever known anything, Mary, I know Ellie loved you with her whole heart." She put her head in Sal's lap and the old woman continued to run her fingers through Mary's hair.

Several minutes passed. Finally, Mary raised her head, wiping her cheeks with the backs of her hands. Sal offered her a tissue. Mary rocked back and sat on the floor. She stared into Russ's reddened eyes. Something Sal had said earlier... She didn't understand.

"Sal, what did you mean when you said if it wasn't for Russ..."

"You owe this young man a debt of gratitude. He's the one who really got me to thinking about the necklace, who planted the idea that you could be Ellie's child."

"Wait a minute." She turned back to Sal. "What do you mean?" she asked again.

"Russ noticed I was curious about the necklace and I think he did a little digging on his own. Am I right?"

Russ looked miserable—and guilty. "Yes."

Mary stood, facing him. "And when was all of this?"

"After I returned from skiing. I got to thinking—"

"You got to thinking? Thanks for sharing the benefit of your wisdom with me. *I'm* only the one involved here. You offered to help me. Behind my back, I guess."

"Mary, I—"

She threw up her hands. "Did you think I couldn't handle it? Did you think I needed your manly protection? All the while I was fumbling around, planning a trip to Denver, you were withholding information from me?"

He rose to his feet and gazed forlornly at her. "I thought I was helping."

Mary scowled. "Some help! Keeping me in the dark!"

Sal cleared her throat. "Honey, Russ meant well."

Mary struggled to stop herself from lashing out. Finally she muttered, "We all know where good intentions lead." She sank into her chair, emotionally drained.

"I think I'd better leave," Russ said, picking up his hat and jacket. "But before I go—" he eyed Sal "—do you think there's a chance Buck may still try to deny all of this?"

"Yes. He's worked too hard for too long at hiding this family secret. It's almost an obsession with him."

"Do you think he'd counterattack in some way?"

"I wouldn't rule anything out." Sal directed her next remark to Mary. "You must leave Buck to me."

"But...I need to see him, find out what he knows—"

"Not now." Sal's emphasis had the force of a command. "It's going to take some time. I'll handle Buck. Agreed?"

Russ shrugged in acquiescence and Mary reluctantly nodded. "But I'm not going to wait very long."

"Before I leave, Sal, I want to tell you how much I appreciate the courage you've shown in helping Mary. And Mary—" She saw the hurt in his eyes. "There's something else you need to know. And it'll make you mad. But it's important. I've been to see your parents and—"

She sat up straight. "You *what?*"

"—before you do anything else, you have to talk with them."

"What right do you have to give me orders?"

"Mary, please."

"Listen, honey," Sal said.

"Promise me you'll talk with them before you ever approach Buck." His voice grew even more serious. "You love them. They're part of this, too. Please."

Mary looked up, her rebellion wilting under the pleading she read in his eyes and heard in his voice. "Okay."

"Thank you. And for whatever it's worth, I'm sorry I've upset you. I only did what I did because I love you."

The door shut softly behind him. Mary glanced over at Sal, who was smiling fondly at her. "You're a spitfire, honey. Just be sure all that spit and fire is directed at the right target." She chuckled. "Somehow, niece, I hope you'll figure out that Russ Coulter isn't it."

BY THE TIME Russ arrived back at the ranch, he'd switched radio stations at least a dozen times, raised a sore where he'd chewed the inside of his cheek, and ground his teeth so tightly his jaw ached. But he couldn't blame Mary one bit. He'd had it coming. What was that old saying? Fools rush in... Well, she was getting her answers now. God, he wished he'd been wrong—that the ending could have been the happily-ever-after kind. Sal, of course, was one silver lining. Buck? He wouldn't put anything past him. And regardless of how Buck reacted, there was the undeniable fact that a Coulter was in love with his granddaughter. Russ grimaced. He supposed his feelings didn't make much difference if Mary was finished with him.

He parked the truck and stomped into the house. Tossing his hat on the kitchen counter, he stooped down to greet Casey. "Damn it, pal, I haven't come this far to give up. How the hell am I supposed to win her back?" He felt the collie's rough tongue lick his face. "I'm afraid I'm plumb out of ideas." He straightened up. At least he could alert the Fleets.

He walked into his office, consulted the number scrawled on his desk calendar and picked up the phone. He'd rather have burning matches inserted under his nails. "Hello? Mrs. Fleet? Russ Coulter.... Well, I've been better." He hesitated. "Look, I'm afraid this whole thing's blown up sooner than I expected. Buck Lloyd's sister, Sal McClanahan, has confirmed my suspicions.... Yes, Mary knows." He shut his eyes as he heard the catch in Phyllis Fleet's voice and sensed the effort it took to control herself.

"Still in danger?" He couldn't equivocate. "I think she could be, although she's promised Mrs. McClanahan she won't try to see Buck yet. But, frankly, I think you need to tell Mary your story before she sees Buck. He's not above putting a very unpleasant slant on the facts. I've urged Mary to call you, but I think you need to talk with her sooner rather than later.... Saturday?" He let out a sigh of relief. "I know it won't be easy for either of you, but I'm glad you can come so soon. And, Mrs. Fleet, I— I hope it turns out all right for you—for all of you. Goodbye."

Now what? Damn it, he loved Mary. She couldn't just waltz out of his life like... like... his mother had. Then he'd been too young, too helpless. But now, by God, he was *not* helpless. There must be something he could do. He slumped in his desk chair, elbows on the armrests, his chin on his steepled fingers. *Think, man, think!*

Finally he roused himself, picked up the phone again and called home. "Mom? Did Brian get back from law school last night for the Christmas break? ... Yeah, put him on." Russ drummed his fingers on the desk, adrenaline starting to flow again. It had to work. "Brian? How'd your exams go? Great. Say, I need a favor. Could you give Jim a hand Sunday and Monday? I'm gonna be out of town.... Yeah, it's important. I'll fill you in before I leave. Thanks, buddy."

As he hung up, his stomach growled. Jeez, he'd missed lunch altogether. He was hungry as a bear. But for the first time in a week, he could see a glimmer of hope. He had one last card to play.

AT SAL MCCLANAHAN'S suggestion, on Friday evening her group of Sooner Arms friends gathered at one table for dinner. "...so somehow we've got to get them back together." Sal punctuated her remarks with jabs of her dinner fork.

Chauncey arched his eyebrows and slurped a spoonful of soup. "Not speaking, you think?"

"Not now."

"Hell of a note," Woody interjected. "Damn fine bronc rider, that Coulter."

"And Mary's such a sweet little thing," Rose Farnsworth added.

Bertha Mayhall harumphed. "She's not all 'sweet little thing.' She's got grit, that one."

"So what're we going to do?" Chauncey set his spoon down and shoved his plate back.

"Can't be too damn obvious," Woody said.

"Another party perhaps?" Rose offered.

"Maybe at my place?" Chauncey suggested. "Might look too fishy if you had it, Sal. We'll say it's our little Christmas party."

Sal smiled with satisfaction. "That's a marvelous idea, Chauncey. Tell you what. Woody, would you be willing to pick up Mary?"

He grinned. "Think she'd come with an old feller?"

"She will if you invite her."

Rose looked expectantly at Sal. "Maybe if Woody picks her up, it'll be too dark for him to drive her back, and—"

"—Russ'd have to help me out and take her home?" Woody finished.

Sal smiled triumphantly and turned to Chauncey. "Why don't you call Russ?"

"Fine." He glowed with anticipation.

"When's this happening?" Bertha asked.

"Christmas Eve?" Sal looked around at the others.

"Don't have nothin' else to do," Woody said.

"Fine. Tuesday then." Sal turned to the other women. "Bertha, can you bring crackers and cheese? Rose, tea cookies? I'll fix the vegetables and dip."

They all nodded and began eating again. All except for Chauncey. "One other thing." He wiggled his eyebrows in Groucho Marx fashion. "I'll supply the ingredients for my famous highballs."

SATURDAY AFTERNOON Mary worked on the Christmas cards she still hadn't finished addressing. Never in her life had she failed to mail in a timely fashion, but today it was nearly impossible to dredge up holiday cheer. Instead, she felt as if she were a ball of yarn suddenly thrown to yowling alley cats. Pulled this way by all her obligations, tangled by the emotions coursing through her, tossed about by Russ's cavalier treatment of her feelings. And now, she was being clawed at by dread at her parents' imminent arrival.

She'd called home this morning, as she'd promised Russ and Sal she would do. Helga had answered the phone. Inexplicably, her parents were already on their way to Ewing. They would arrive midafternoon, Helga had said. This whole adoption story was going to spill out. The necklace. Did her mother regret giving it to her? How would her father react now that she'd discovered the truth about her birth mother? Worse yet, how would her discovery affect her relationship with her parents? Why had Russ gone to St. Louis, anyway? And what was it they knew? The questions pecked at her relentlessly.

She scooped up the cards and envelopes. December 21st. They'd never arrive on time. She replaced them in the box, capped her pen and closed her address book. Then the phone rang. When she answered, her heart sank. It was Janie. She didn't need this. "Hi, yourself."

"Mary, what's up?"

"What do you mean?"

"You know, Russ."

"Russ?"

Janie sighed. "Yeah, Russ. Like he's the biggest sourpuss that ever came along. He could play the leading role in *Frankenstein* without makeup." She paused, and when Mary didn't answer, she rushed on. "I even remember when he used to smile."

Mary forced herself to speak. "Your brother is . . . no longer my concern."

"Well, I've got a bulletin for you. You're sure still his concern. He's a mess. I've never seen him like this."

"Janie, I'm sorry. I really am."

"Well, jeez, it's probably none of my business. I wasn't going to call, but then, heck, I figured what harm could it do."

"No harm done, Janie. You're a caring young woman. I wish I'd had a sister like you. Russ and Brian are very lucky."

"Thanks. I guess I'll see ya around. Hope so, anyway. Bye."

Mary sighed. There was a time she'd indulged the hope that Brian and Janie would be her family, too. A real brother and sister. She felt the now-familiar surge of disappointment and regret.

What baffled her most was why Russ had broken his promise. She'd believed him, trusted him. And then the fire. And now this latest betrayal—all the information he'd kept from her. He'd taken her for a fool. How could she have misjudged him so completely?

She glanced at the clock. Three. Midafternoon. Even a run was out of the question. She had to sit here, like some death row inmate awaiting the hour of execution. What could she say to her parents? How could she reassure them of her gratitude? Her appreciation? And, most of all, her love?

She registered, with a sickening lurch of her stomach, the sound of a car stopping in front of her condominium. They were here. When her parents walked through the door, Mary was stunned to notice that her mother's hair was slightly mussed and her tan shoes didn't match her gray wool slacks. Her father's hands were icy as he framed her face to kiss her on the forehead. "Mary." That was all he said. Just her name.

"Mother, Dad. I tried to call you this morning, but you'd already left. What's going on?"

Her mother looked at her father. Her father looked at her mother. Wasn't anybody going to say anything? Finally her mother spoke. "Could you put on a pot of coffee, Mary? We'll take off our coats, freshen up a bit and then we need to talk."

"Okay." Mary moved robotlike toward the kitchen, pulled out the canister, scooped some coffee into the filter basket and filled the pot with water. Her father had disappeared into the bathroom and she could see her mother combing her hair in front of the mirror in the bedroom. She flicked the On switch and concentrated on the gurgle-hiss of the automatic coffeemaker.

Her parents emerged together. "Sit down, honey." Her father gestured to the sofa. At least the "honey" was a good sign. "Let's talk."

"Why did you come here?"

"Russ Coulter called us," her mother said.

Mary pursed her lips. "I wish he'd let me handle this myself."

"He's concerned for you," Phyllis added.

"I'm not a child. Everyone's treating me like I'll break apart at the slightest blow." She made an effort to stifle her indignation. "Did Russ tell you I've located my birth mother?"

Her father sat hunched over, hands clasped between his knees. For a moment no one spoke. Then he straightened up and met her eyes, the light glinting off his glasses. "Yes."

"Did he tell you she's dead?"

"That, too," her father said.

"Mother, Daddy, please believe that even if she'd been alive, it wouldn't have made any difference in how I feel about you. I've always loved you and I always will."

Her mother looked with alarm at her husband. "Charles, I..."

Her father removed his glasses, anguish written in his eyes. "Mary, we love you, too. And we do understand. However, there's something—" he hesitated "—that we need to tell you. Something I'm afraid..." He glanced at his wife.

"Go on, Charles. We've got to do it."

"Something that might change your opinion about us, might change your feelings." He pulled out a handkerchief, wiped his eyes and put his glasses back on. "Oh, God. This is so difficult."

"Daddy, just tell me! Nothing could be that bad."

"Mary, we had information that could have helped your search. Like the names and locations of the attorneys involved in your adoption. We didn't give it to you."

"Why not?"

"We were terrified when you moved to Oklahoma. You were getting too close. You see, years ago, we'd entered into an agreement with an unknown party represented by a Tulsa law firm. That agreement prevented us from ever assisting you in locating your birth parents." He struggled to go on. "But beyond that, we were afraid how you'd feel about us if you knew the whole story."

"What whole story?"

Her mother shifted in her chair. "The story of how we came to adopt you." Her eyes filled and her voice trembled. "Let me try to set it up for you. Your father—" she nodded at Charles who was clenching his knees "—was in his first year of residency when I had a miscarriage with complications that resulted in my hysterectomy. I was sick at heart to think I could never have a child."

"Worse than that. Your mother was clinically depressed. And I was on call most of the time."

"We'd been relying on my job and Charles's father's financial help just to scrape by. But within six weeks of my surgery, I lost my job and your grandfather died suddenly."

Her father took up the story. "When I went home to deal with his affairs, I discovered he'd fallen hopelessly into debt trying to get me through medical school. I couldn't see any way out except to drop out of the residency program and enlist in the army or become a general practitioner."

"Your father accepted the inevitable, but I was devastated for him. He'd had his heart set on being an obstetrician. But what choice did we have?"

A sob lodged in Mary's throat for the young couple whose shimmering dreams had been so abruptly shattered.

Her mother leaned over and tentatively touched Mary on the shoulder. "Do you believe in miracles, Mary?"

"I used to."

"One happened to us. A friend your father had met in medical school knew about my hysterectomy. He called from the University of Colorado Medical Center where he was an obstetrical resident. He made us an unbelievable offer. He knew of an infant girl who could be privately adopted. However, there were some unusual strings attached."

With an effort of will, Mary restrained the sob threatening to tear loose. Her father continued. "And this is the hard part. We could adopt the baby—an answer to our prayers—if we agreed to certain conditions. We were never to reveal any information by which we or the child—you—" he smiled wistfully at Mary "—could ever identify or locate the mother. In exchange for this promise, the other party was willing, over a period of time, to provide funds sufficient to see me through my residency and to establish my medical practice. We'd have our baby and no financial worries. In one fell swoop, all our problems had miraculously been solved."

"Except for one thing," Phyllis murmured.

Mary was choking at the magnitude of Buck Lloyd's cruelty. "What?"

Again Charles took off his glasses and wiped at his eyes. "Except that if you ever found out, you'd think we were paid to take you. That money was the main motivation."

"Daddy, I—"

"Let me finish. The first time we held you in our arms, we loved you. You were ours. A blessing we couldn't have imagined. But we were consumed by guilt. We hated using that money. It was tainted. Yet we didn't have much choice." He replaced his glasses. "We vowed that as soon as the practice turned the corner, we'd repay every penny, with interest."

"And we did." Her mother was looking proudly at her father. "Every cent." She smiled at Mary. "And then you were truly and forever ours."

Mary moved to the sofa and sat beside her father, who was slumped in exhaustion. "Daddy, is this why you've been so...distant?"

Charles Fleet stared at a spot on the floor. Finally he nodded, then began to speak in a gravelly voice. "I was afraid. The more I thought about it, the more I realized someone willing to pay that kind of money for our promise must have had a compelling reason to hide the facts. Someone like that was capable of ruthlessness. And then when you—" his voice broke "—told us you were going to search... Oh, hell. I didn't know what to do."

"Dad—"

"No. I'm almost done." He took a deep breath. "Worst of all was the guilt—what would you think of me if you ever found out the truth about the adoption? Mary, you're my little girl." Weeping, he buried his head in his hands, his shoulders heaving.

Mary gathered her once-invincible father in her arms. He seemed suddenly small, vulnerable. "Daddy, listen to me. All my life you've never done anything but demonstrate your love—time and time again." She rubbed her hands consolingly over his back. "It's finished now. You don't have to be afraid any longer. I have only one mother and one father, and you're both right here in this room." She straightened up, one arm still around her father, and reached out to include her mother in the hug. "I love you both so much!"

After a few moments, Phyllis drew back from the embrace, wiping her eyes. "Ooh, I've been so worried since I gave you the necklace. I didn't know the truth would feel so good." She hugged her daughter again. "Maybe we need that caffeine now."

Over the coffee Mary told her parents the entire story of Ellie's pregnancy and untimely death and Buck's vindictiveness. She couldn't help effervescing about Sal and her role in standing up to her brother. When she finished, her father sat quietly for a moment. Then he spoke. "Mary, I want you to be careful with Buck. He's not a man to stir up."

"What makes you say that?"

"Russ."

"Russ? What's he got to do with it."

"The only reason he came to St. Louis was to solicit our help. He was afraid for you. He thought you were in danger."

"In danger? That's ridiculous!"

"I don't think so. Russ had reason to believe Buck was trying to stop the two of you from pursuing the search."

"What do you mean?"

"Russ had been to see Buck, and without mentioning you specifically, sounded him out about January 10, 1968. Buck threatened him and anyone he cared about."

Mary stared at her father, openmouthed. "He went to see Buck—about *me?*"

"Russ felt he needed proof. Buck's exact words were 'You're playing with fire.'"

"Wait a minute, you don't mean—"

"Yes. He assumed Buck set the pasture fire as a warning. Russ was trying to do everything in his power to protect you."

"Everything except tell me."

Her mother set her coffee cup down and held both of Mary's hands. "Don't be too hard on him, honey."

"He's a damn fine young man, Mary," her father said.

Her mother tightened her grasp. "And he loves you very much. That's not a thing to be treated lightly. Sometimes it comes around only once."

Mary nodded dumbly, trying to swallow the sob that had mysteriously reappeared at the back of her throat. She felt overwhelmed—by relief, by her parents' love and by... something still missing. *Russ?*

CHAPTER EIGHTEEN

THE STADIUM, home of the University of Oklahoma Sooners, dominated the north campus as Russ drove into Norman late Sunday morning. The adjacent shopping area was virtually deserted except for a few local residents and several exchange students with no place to go for the Christmas break. The swags of greenery and red plastic bells suspended from the light posts looked oddly superfluous.

For once, it was easy to find a parking place near the Student Union. Russ stepped out of the truck and zipped up his jacket. A strong north wind tore at the flags positioned around the stadium, and blustery clouds raced across the leaden skies. A few tattered posters announcing campus holiday events clung to the outdoor bulletin board. Russ ascended the steps, went inside and consulted the directory for the location of the alumni office. His footsteps echoed through the empty corridors.

As soon as the idea had come to him, he'd known there would be obstacles. It was hard to conduct research at a university closed for the Christmas break. Yet he was too restless to wait. Finally he'd phoned Kevin Sampson, a law partner of his father's and a past president of the O.U. Alumni Association. Mr. Sampson had made several calls and learned the Alumni Director would be in the office today clearing up some paperwork. It was a place to start.

Russ rapped on the locked door of the office. He heard a file drawer close, and soon after, a pleasant-faced man opened the door and extended his hand. "Russ Coulter? I'm John Travis."

Russ breathed a sigh of relief. "Glad to meet you. Thank you for agreeing to see me."

The gentleman ushered Russ into the office and sat down across the desk from him. "How can I help?"

"I'd like to start with old yearbooks. Especially for the year 1967. Then I may have some further questions."

The man wheeled his chair to the bookcase behind his desk, leaned over and from a bottom shelf extracted a copy of the 1967 *Sooner*. "You can sit in there." He gestured to a conference table in an adjoining room. "Just let me know what else you need."

Russ rubbed his hand over the hard surface of the yearbook, praying that somehow the clues he needed could be found within its pages. He'd made a mess of helping Mary uncover the story of her birth mother. He couldn't go back and do that part any differently. The past was behind him. Now she knew half the story. And she was angry with him, maybe past the point of reconciliation. Yet he was not bowing out until he tried everything.

Her words "I love you, you crazy Okie" played over and over in his mind. He would cling to this shred of hope. As long as it took. He'd try to provide her what she most wanted—her identity, all of it. She knew about her mother. Perhaps he could prove his love by giving her the gift of her father.

SINCE GWEN'S CAR was in the shop, Mary had agreed to bring her home from Sunday evening's bank Christmas party. She felt lousy, primarily because of last night's wretched sleep. She'd tossed and turned, coming instantly awake when remembered bits and pieces of the conversations with Sal and her parents became part of her dreams. The story was too much to absorb all at once. She walked an emotional tightrope—relief and affirmation on one side, grief and anger on the other. She needed time to process it all. Yet the daily routine, with all its distractions, propelled her relentlessly on.

"You've been awfully quiet," Gwen ventured from the passenger seat. "Even for you. Something going on?"

Something? Try everything. "I'm okay."

"Right. That's why you look like your dog just died."

"Thanks," Mary said sarcastically, then, in a more tentative voice, "It shows?"

"In glorious, living color. Want to talk about whatever it is?" Gwen waited as Mary drove in silence.

She was tempted. There was something confessional about being cooped up in a car on a dark night.

"Is it Russ?" Gwen asked.

"Partly."

"The search?"

How much could she tell Gwen? There was still Ellie's reputation to consider and, of course, Buck's reaction. Yet she desperately needed to talk. "Gwen, much as I'd like to, I can't tell you everything. Please don't press."

"Mary, you're my friend. I care about you."

Mary pulled into Gwen's driveway and turned off the lights. "I know that. I'm just so confused right now. I've learned who my birth mother is."

Gwen laid a gloved hand on Mary's arm. "Oh?"

"She's dead."

"Mary, I'm so sorry." Mary sensed Gwen's eyes on her. "How do you feel about that?"

Hearing the sympathy in her friend's voice, Mary squared around to look at her. "Honestly? It's not the scenario I'd hoped for. I kept telling myself that the ending might be unpleasant, but deep down I believed otherwise."

"Who was she?"

"That's part of what I can't say right now. But—" she smiled wistfully "—what I did learn about her is both very sad and very comforting."

"I'm glad... about the comforting part," Gwen said softly. "And Russ?"

Mary turned away, staring out the driver's side window. "You already know about his broken promise. But, beyond that, he's hopelessly interfered in my business." An edge of resentment crept into her voice.

"Why do you suppose that is?" Gwen asked in the tone of a schoolteacher who expects a particular answer.

"I don't know."

"I think you do. It isn't like Russ to concern himself in some woman's affairs unless—"

"I know, I know. Unless he has a reason."

"Are you deliberately being dense or do you just refuse to admit it?"

"What?"

"That the man's crazy in love with you! And if I don't miss my guess, you're in love with him."

Mary rubbed her temples. "I assume you have some advice for me," she muttered.

"I sure do. Mary, give yourself a break and cut Russ some slack. Try putting yourself in his shoes! It can't hurt." She leaned over to squeeze Mary's hand. "Good night. Think about what I said, okay?" She climbed out of the car and ran toward the house.

Mary backed out into the street and drove slowly toward home. They'd all lectured her. First Sal, then Janie, and of course, her parents. And now Gwen. Was she the only one who thought Russ had been an overbearing, insensitive meddler? *Really? Is that what you think?* She pounded a fist on the steering wheel. *Okay, okay. I admit it.* Try as she might, she'd been unable to forget the expression on his face when he'd left Sal's apartment Thursday—or the words he'd uttered. "I only did what I did because I love you."

She turned onto the wide boulevard. Gwen had asked her to walk in Russ's shoes. In fairness, she supposed she should try. She couldn't put him behind her until she made some effort to understand his maddening actions. The fire—that had started it all. If, in fact, Russ thought Buck had set the fire, she supposed he *could* conclude she might be in danger. And, unlike her, he'd already suspected Buck's motive in wanting to circumvent their search efforts. Yet, why couldn't he have just told her that? That was what really bothered her. *Okay, but what if he was wrong? Or what if you'd dashed off to cross-examine Buck yourself?*

She parked the car in front of her condominium, but sat in the dark a moment longer. What about the trip to St. Louis? Why would he rush up there? Confront people he hardly knew? The answer was inescapable. He'd only go if he was truly desperate. Desperate for what? She couldn't evade the truth. Desperate to protect her. And why would he need to protect her? Because... because... he loved her?

But she'd always been her own woman—self-sufficient, independent. She didn't need a protector. Was that what really galled her? Hating to admit her own vulnerability? Her need for someone else?

She removed the key from the ignition and put her fingers around the door handle. Then with sudden, searing insight the conclusion to this exercise in logic hit her. The flip side of independence was...loneliness. A whole yawning lifetime of it.

She opened the car door. She'd have to do more soul-searching. Maybe she didn't have all the answers, after all.

RUSS COULDN'T BELIEVE his good luck. Virginia Lamar, the housemother of Ellie Lloyd's sorority, was not only still alive, but living in Norman with her son and his family. Without revealing too much, Russ had carefully explained to the son his reason for needing to visit Mrs. Lamar. Monday morning he waited nervously in the Lamar living room while the daughter-in-law finished helping her mother-in-law dress. What if Mrs. Lamar couldn't remember? Just then he heard the distinctive *tap-tapeta-tap* of a cane. He stood. A heavyset woman, wreathed in wrinkles, her hair as soft and white as the underside of a bird's wing, entered the room. Like a partridge settling on a nest, she eased herself into a chair. She cocked her head, intelligent blue eyes studying him. "I'm Virginia Lamar. You needed to see me?"

"How do you do? I'm Russ Coulter. I'd like to ask you a few questions about a young woman who would've been in the sorority while you were housemother."

"I'll do my best. Some of the girls I remember as if it were yesterday. Others I can't recollect at all."

"The one I'm interested in is Ellie Lloyd. She graduated in 1967." He held his breath.

"Ellie? Who could forget her?" Then the spontaneous smile faded and her eyes grew troubled. "What a tragic thing her death was. Such a lively, lovely girl."

He exhaled. One hurdle cleared, and now for the big one. "I noticed something in the yearbook. I hope you can help me. The candid on the sorority page shows Ellie at a table in the dining room being served by a good-looking dark-haired houseboy. Here let me show you." From his pocket he pulled a copy of the yearbook page. "Do you recognize him?"

She took the paper and pored over the photograph. Then she handed it back to him. "Yes. He'd be hard to forget. Matthew Reeder. He was quite a track star."

"This next question is difficult to ask." He cleared his throat. "Would there be any possibility that he was romantically involved with Ellie Lloyd?"

She looked startled. "It was against sorority policy for the girls to date houseboys."

"With all due respect, Mrs. Lamar, that doesn't answer my question."

She stared down at her lap for several seconds, then raised her eyes. "I don't suppose after all these years it makes any difference. I think there was a distinct possibility. The attraction between them was hard to miss. If I remember correctly, Ellie had broken off another relationship before Christmas. So it must've been second semester when I began to worry about Matthew and her. I kept wondering if I should address my concerns with them. But then, they were both graduating, so I hoped the problem would take care of itself."

Russ rose and took the old woman's hand in his. "I appreciate your time, Mrs. Lamar. You've been very helpful."

John Travis had supplied another lead by suggesting Russ contact Wilbur Strain, Reeder's former track coach and retired O.U. athletic director. Unfortunately, Strain's housekeeper informed him that Strain was flying out that afternoon with an Orange Bowl-bound alumni group. Speeding north on Interstate 35 toward Oklahoma City and Will Rogers World Airport, Russ realized he needed a miracle—like a delayed flight or a parking place right in front. Otherwise he would miss Strain, whose plane for Miami was scheduled for departure in twenty-five minutes. He sped down the terminal entrance roadway, wheeled onto the upper deck and reaffirmed his belief in Santa Claus. An empty metered parking place! He even had the right change. He ran into the airport, checked the gate numbers and took off at a dead run, dodging passengers laden with Christmas packages, as he made his way toward Concourse B, Gate 10.

Damn. The passengers were lined up ready for boarding and he could hear the muffled words "... and those needing special assistance." He muscled up to the counter and gasped, "Please page Wilbur Strain. It's an emergency." The ticket agent started to protest, but when she looked at him, she evidently changed her mind. "Passenger Strain, please report to the gate agent." Russ turned, and a chorus of hallelujahs filled his head. Coming toward him was a spry gentleman in his sixties, with a bewildered expression on his face. Before he reached the counter, Russ intercepted him and quickly explained what he needed to know.

"Matt Reeder? Hell, yes. Hard to forget. One of the finest. A real tribute to his Indian heritage. It was a privilege to be his track coach. You don't get many athletes of his caliber. Should've run in the '68 Olympics. What about him?"

"Would you know if he had a particular girlfriend his senior year?"

The older man glanced anxiously toward the flight gate, then turned back, lost in thought. "It's hard to say.

I remember he seemed happier, more lighthearted that spring. He set some records that season. He *was* dating someone, but . . . Sorry I can't be more specific. Now, if you'll excuse me—" and he walked off.

Russ tried not to let disappointment overwhelm him. Just then, Wilbur Strain stopped in his tracks. "Attractive. Yeah, very attractive." He snapped his fingers. "What was her name?" He shrugged. "Can't recall. Only thing I can tell you is that she was Track Queen." He loped down the jetway before he could see the sun break across Russ's face or watch him pull out his credit card and step to a nearby bank of telephones.

HIGHWAY 51 took Russ into Tahlequah and the heart of the Cherokee Nation. He located a small café on the main drag and ordered the dinner special. It'd been quite a day. First Mrs. Lamar and then Wilbur Strain had confirmed his growing hope, but the make-or-break-it encounter lay just ahead. What did he really have to go on? Recollections, perhaps distorted by time, and two photographs in an old yearbook—one taken at the sorority house and the other of a group of admiring coeds clustered around Matthew Reeder, champion long-distance runner. In the picture Ellie Lloyd stood closest to the athlete, beaming at him with undisguised adoration.

Russ spooned bland gravy over the lumpy mashed potatoes. He didn't feel like eating. He was too nervous. What right had he to barge in and upset Matthew Reeder's mother? What if he was wrong? His questions could be construed as nosiness at best, slander at worst. He checked his watch for the third time since entering the café. Would seven o'clock never come? Elizabeth Reeder had been civil on the phone, but nothing more. All he'd told her was that he had some information about her son that might be of interest. That would get him in the door. Then what? He choked down several more bites, swigged the dregs of his coffee and grabbed up the check.

After making one wrong turn and doubling back, he found the Reeder home on a bluff overlooking the Illinois River. It was a modest ranch house, freshly painted, and in the picture window the lights of a Christmas tree blinked on and off. He stood for a moment outside his truck, filling his lungs with the cold night air. Now or never. He pushed the doorbell.

The sprightly woman who answered the door was short and plump. Her thick salt-and-pepper hair was coiled into a bun at the nape of her neck. But her eyes were arresting. Huge and deep-set, they dwarfed the rest of her face. Right now they were wide with surprise. "Mr., er, Coulter?" She stood in the doorway. "I was expecting someone older."

"I'm Russ Coulter. Look, I know how this must seem. I didn't intend to sound mysterious on the phone. It's just that it's very important to someone I love that I ask you a few questions about your son. I don't want to be insensitive or intrusive. It'll only take a few minutes."

She stepped aside. "Very well. Come in."

The living room was spotless. She indicated that he should take a seat on the sofa, and she sat in a wooden rocker. "I can't imagine what brings you here. My son's been dead a long time, Mr. Coulter." She gestured at the faded photograph on top of the television set. A handsome army lieutenant.

When John Travis had gone to the files to look up Matthew Reeder, Russ had learned that the young man had attended O.U. on an ROTC scholarship, gone into the service immediately after graduation, been posted to Vietnam early in 1968 and killed by a sniper on May 15 of that same year. This information made what he had to do here even more difficult.

"I know." He swallowed. "I'm very sorry. From all accounts, he was a son to be proud of."

She sat very still. "Yes, he was."

Russ paused. "Let me begin with this question. To your knowledge, was your son involved in a romantic relationship his senior year at O.U.?"

He detected a shadow passing over her features. "Yes, I think he was very much in love. But something must've happened. When he came home on his first leave from Fort Benning, he wouldn't talk about her. He seemed hurt and very sad."

"Did you know her name?"

"No. He was pretty closemouthed about her."

Russ's heart sank. But he had to persevere.

"Then why do you think he was in love?"

She folded her hands in her lap and rocked back and forth for several minutes. "Because he wrote to me from O.U. his senior year and asked me to send him something. An heirloom."

The creak of the rocker was the only sound in the room. Blood rushed to his head. "A necklace?"

The rocking abruptly stopped and Mrs. Reeder's hand flew to her mouth. "How did you know?"

"Because the woman I love has in her possession a beautiful *oochalata* necklace engraved with Cherokee letters."

"*Jigeyu?*" The syllables hung in the air.

"Yes, *jigeyu*. Beloved Woman."

Tears filled Mrs. Reeder's eyes and trickled down her cheeks. "But...but...I don't understand. Your sweetheart, why would she have...?"

Russ leaned forward. "There's no gentle way for me to say this. I think there's a strong possibility that she's Matthew's daughter."

Mrs. Reeder sat stunned, then suddenly stood up, cradled her abdomen with both arms and began pacing. "I don't understand. How could that be? Matthew never said a word about anything like that. All he did was ask for the necklace. It was a betrothal gift from Matthew's Cherokee grandfather to his wife, then from Matthew's father to me, and then…" She stopped pacing and turned toward Russ, wonder flooding her face. "Do you think— I mean, I could be a grandmother?"

"I think it's quite likely."

She smiled, then laughed quietly, and all the while tears ran down her face. "But…could it be?" She sank back into the rocker.

Quietly Russ began the story of Ellie Lloyd, Matthew and the gift of the *oochalata* necklace to the infant girl. At various points, Elizabeth Reeder nodded. When he finished, she spoke. "But why didn't he tell me she was pregnant?"

"I've thought about that. He probably never knew. I think Ellie's father cut her off from any communication."

"Matthew would never have run out on his obligations."

"I believe that. I also believe Ellie loved him more than life itself. Let me ask you something. When Matthew was killed in Vietnam, did the story make the papers around here?"

"Oh, yes. It was all over the sports pages."

Russ nodded, his fears confirmed. Ellie must've seen the account. His death had to be what had deepened her depression and sent her out into that awful Fourth of

July night. "Is there any chance there could be another *oochalata* necklace like the one I've described?"

"No. It was specially made. I've lived in Tahlequah all my life and I've never seen another."

"In that case, would you have any interest in seeing the necklace again and—meeting Mary?"

"Mary? That was my mother's name." She smiled. "I've been a widow for many years, my son is dead and my daughter lives in Oregon. Would I like to meet Mary?" She got up and pulled Russ to his feet. "Dear man, how soon can you bring her? All I want in this world is to hold her close and love her. And for starters, since she's not here, you'll have to do." She threw her arms around him in the warmest of motherly hugs. "What a Christmas present you've given me! Flesh of my flesh, bone of my bone. When can you bring her?"

Then, under her breath, he heard her whisper, "Thank you, Lord, for this miracle."

CHAPTER NINETEEN

LATE CHRISTMAS EVE, Mary sat pensively in her living room waiting for Woody Higgins to pick her up. When she'd offered to drive herself, he'd been intractable. He would pick her up in his prize vintage Lincoln, no ifs, ands or buts, as he'd put it. This party was the only celebration she'd have, since she couldn't justify taking more time off work to go to St. Louis. Though disappointed, her parents had understood.

She smoothed her hand over the soft nap of the red velvet skirt, then rearranged the red-and-green plaid taffeta bow tied at her waist. A high-necked emerald green moiré blouse completed her holiday outfit. She smiled reflectively. Last year she'd worn it to the country club tea dance; this year it was the Sooner Arms. What a difference a year makes.

Or even a few days. Less than a week ago she'd been feeling an awkward estrangement from her father. Now the burden he and her mother had endured for so many years was lifted, and she could relax, knowing she'd made it clear that no one else could ever take their place—they would always be her family. Her father's bear hug before they left to return to St. Louis had said it all. No icy reserve, just spontaneous, overwhelming love.

And what about her search? She was moved by the uncanny conviction that forces beyond her understanding had been involved—putting her in the right place, introducing her to special people, setting coincidence in motion. Maybe that was part of the pull she'd felt, part of the compulsion to penetrate the mystery of her birth. She smiled. Maybe the guardian angel of her childhood had heard her prayers, after all.

She knew these thoughts were illogical, but now she was more willing to admit that some circumstances defied logic. And maybe... some feelings did, too.

There was nothing logical about the images that kept running through her head. Russ sitting tall in the saddle on a windy fall day; Russ dancing her crazily around this very living room; Russ carrying her to his bed; Russ, weary and smoke-begrimed, slumping into a kitchen chair. And Russ standing in Sal's doorway the last time she'd seen him, his soft gray eyes vulnerable with longing.

"Put yourself in his shoes." When she had, she'd found it uncomfortable. Perhaps the motives she'd assigned to him weren't accurate. Had he truly gone back on his promise? He had said he'd help her, then he'd asked her to drop the search. But did that mean he'd stopped helping? She'd gotten her answers, hadn't she? Why? Mainly because of Russ's intervention. So even her twisted logic returned to the starting point. Had he really ever broken his promise? And the quiet voice in her heart whispered the only possible answer. *No.*

A booming knock on the door interrupted her reverie, but left her heart quivering as she put on her coat and allowed Woody Higgins to escort her to the silver behemoth sitting at the curb. Would Russ be at the party? Her mouth went dry. What could she say to him? Was there a way back? She wanted him out of any pigeonholes she'd tried to put him in. She wanted him just as he was.

SAL ARRIVED EARLY at Chauncey's apartment so she could select a seat that would provide maximum viewing pleasure. While she wasn't absolutely certain her plan would work, she had great faith not only in the Sooner Arms matchmaking crew but, more importantly, in the undeniable power of love. And if Russ and Mary weren't in love, she'd renounce Saint Valentine himself.

Russ arrived first, the hint of blue in his eyes enhanced by the cobalt of the turtleneck he wore under his cream-colored sweater. He looked good enough to give an old lady salacious ideas. On his way across the carpet to greet her, she watched his eyes dart quickly around the room. *Patience. She'll be here.* He bent down and gave her a big kiss on the cheek. "Merry Christmas, Sal."

"Hit me again," Sal said as she turned the other cheek. "Merry Christmas to you, too," she murmured as he kissed her a second time, then sat down beside her.

Bertha and Rose arrived next and bustled around the tiny kitchenette arranging the hors d'oeuvres. "How's a man supposed to fix the libations with you two hogging the kitchen?" Chauncey asked.

Bertha slapped his hand. "You'll have to wait. Our other guests aren't even here yet."

As if on cue, Woody and Mary entered the apartment. Russ leapt to his feet, and Sal noticed that his hands were clenched at his sides. Mary, her cheeks flushed from the cold, smiled engagingly and distributed gaily wrapped gifts to each of the old people. Chauncey impishly pulled a sprig of mistletoe from behind his back and kissed her cheek.

Then Mary's eyes landed on Russ. Sal could barely restrain the cackle that rose in her throat. Mary was right; she'd never be a poker player. Those eyes said it all, and if Russ didn't pick up on her feelings, he was dumber than dirt. Bless Mary's heart, if she didn't look like the Spirit of Christmas—black hair shining under the ceiling light, cheeks rosy as cherries and a holiday outfit that showed off her warm brown eyes, smooth skin and tiny waist. Sal sat back, a satisfied smile on her face.

In the background she could hear Chauncey taking orders for his special highballs. Just then, Sal saw Mary smile at Russ as if they shared some private joke. Woody ushered Mary to the dining room table where the appetizers had been carefully arranged—and rearranged—by the two women.

"Here, Russ. Made this one special for you." Chauncey handed Russ a highball the color of motor oil.

Mary, carrying two plates, sat down beside Sal. "Happy holidays, Sal. I brought you a sample."

"Thanks, honey." Sal took the plate and set it carefully in her lap. "You look just like a picture tonight, Mary."

"Thank you." Mary scooted closer and whispered, "I hope so."

Sal cocked her head to scrutinize Mary, whose eyes shone like tinsel. "Any particular reason?"

Mary blushed and bit her lip, obviously to hold in a grin. "I hope so."

"Is that all you can say? 'I hope so'?"

Mary let the smile loose. "Let's just say I've reconsidered the spit and the fire. I've thought of a much better use for all my fire." And, bigger than life, she winked at Sal. "At least—" she giggled "—I hope so."

"Honey, I don't think you have anything to worry about. Look at that young man. He can't keep his eyes off you. If I were you, I'd wade right into any friction between you and get it all smoothed out." She patted Mary on the knee. "And don't forget the fun part."

Mary gave Sal a kiss, stood up and walked to the other end of the room, where Russ was talking with Bertha.

Sal sat back in her chair, radiant. It was going to be all right. And with any luck at all, she'd persuade Buck he was a damn fool not to enjoy this. He'd sputtered and fumed when she'd called him to say the cat was out of the bag. She'd told him in no uncertain terms that the secret wasn't going to stay secret very long, so he could either set aside his gol-durn pride or turn into a mummy in that stuffy museum of a house. Before she'd hung up, for the first time in many years, she'd heard a crack in his voice.

Damn, she'd gone off into her thoughts and missed something. Everyone was laughing and looking at Woody. "What's so funny?"

Bertha rolled her eyes. "Count on Woody. He's got the tact of a steamroller."

Woody seemed mystified. "All I said was 'Hope you can take Mary home, Russ. I don't see so good at night and you'll foul up the plan if you say no.'"

Russ draped an arm around Woody's shoulders and spoke with mock solicitude. "I understand, Woody. I wouldn't want you to jeopardize your safety or Mary's by driving at night. Let me help you out." His warm eyes locked with Mary's. "I'd consider it a very great pleasure to see her home."

"Well, I'll be damned," Woody exulted. "It worked!"

Chauncey rapped on his glass with a spoon. "A toast, a toast. To old friends, pardon the pun, happy holidays and new beginnings."

"Hear, hear," Russ said as he clinked his glass with Chauncey's and then turned and raised his drink toward Sal in a gesture of salute.

MARY'S CONFIDENCE shriveled as she and Russ scurried through the cold toward his truck. She'd said some pretty awful things to him. She couldn't expect him just to forgive and forget. But if they could talk...

"Mary," Russ said after they'd driven for a block in silence, "I have a beef tenderloin and potatoes in the oven at the ranch and a salad in the refrigerator. Enough for two. Would you join me?" There was no mistaking the warmth in his voice.

"I'd like to." She sat beside him, her heart constricting with the pain of not touching him. His eyes were intent on the road and his strong hands gripped the steering wheel. The nearer they got to the ranch, the more palpable the tension grew. So much depended upon this one night.

At the house, Russ lighted the fire laid in the massive fireplace, the Christmas tree lights twinkled cheerily and the mouthwatering aroma of the tenderloin filled the air. When he took her coat, his hands lingered on her shoulders—the first time he'd touched her. A lump formed in her throat.

"I poured most of my highball down the sink when no one was looking," Russ said. "Could I interest you in a glass of wine before dinner?"

"That sounds wonderful." Mary wandered over to the fire and warmed her hands while Russ uncorked the bottle and poured two glasses of merlot. He crossed the room toward her, his eyes never leaving her face. Her hands shook. He stood very close to her, their fingers brushing as he handed her the wine. For a moment, neither of them spoke.

"Russ, I—"

"We need to—"

They laughed nervously and he gestured for her to begin. She strolled to the sofa, her back to him, considering her words. Then she turned, a flush rising over her shoulders and up her neck. "I have been a one-track-minded, opinionated, selfish know-it-all." He opened his mouth to protest, but she raised a hand to forestall him. "No, let me finish. I owe you more than an apology." Through the prism of her tears, she recognized his look of vulnerable anticipation. "I owe you my eternal gratitude. You pledged to help me and you did. You gave me my birth mother, a wonderfully wise character of an aunt and a new understanding with my parents, the best family a woman could have. And—" She faltered, then began again. "You gave me, I hope, a more loving, *trusting*—" she emphasized the word as she stared into his eyes "—peaceful me."

Very deliberately, he set his glass down, walked toward her, took her wineglass and set it beside his own. Then he enclosed both her hands in his. For a crazy instant she thought she might faint. "Do you remember the last words I said to you that day at Sal's?"

She lowered her lashes. "Yes."

He tilted her chin up. "What were they?"

She was so apprehensive, it was difficult to speak. "That you did what you did because…because you love me?"

He let go of her hands and clasped his loosely behind her back. Then he whispered huskily, "And what do you think has happened to change that?"

"I was hateful. You might want out."

He grinned crookedly. "You mean old love-'em-and-leave-'em Coulter?"

"Well, there is precedent." One of his hands began trailing gently up and down her back. She couldn't help herself. She laid her palms on his chest, the soft wool of his sweater warming the tips of her fingers. She was close enough to smell the spicy-clean scent of him. Her body ached with unfulfilled needs. "I wouldn't blame you."

"Since we're playing twenty questions, let me ask you one." He brought her closer. Her head was almost resting against his shoulder. "Do you remember what you said would happen when you found your identity?"

"I...I said that when I knew, I could think about...us."

His hands slid up over her shoulders, smoothed her hair back, then framed her face. He looked at her with burning intensity. "And...?"

No logic, no reasoning, no rationalizing, no prudent consideration—just blinding, spontaneous certainty. "I love you!" Her arms went around his neck and she felt herself being pulled into the sweet, swooning wonder of his kiss. Dimly she was aware of his fingers running through her hair and his hands cupping her head. Everything in her reveled in the feel of his lips on hers, the passionate insistence of their tongues, the heady sensation of body pressed against body.

He finally released her and slid his hands down over her shoulders and arms. "Mary, I thought I'd lost you."

Something plaintive in his voice caught her attention. Then she understood. She picked up his hand and placed it over her heart, covering it with hers. As tenderly as she knew how, she said, "I am not like your mother. I will never leave you."

He put an arm around her and walked her to the Christmas tree, alive with red, green and white bubble lights. "I was hoping you'd say that." He turned her toward him, stroking her hair with his free hand. "Because I love you more than I ever thought possible." His words and the hope in his eyes set up a humming throughout her body. He kissed her lightly, poignantly, and then pivoted her so that she stood facing the tree, nestled in the protection of his embrace. "See anything different?"

She found the toy train, the cowboy Santa, the ornament Russ'd given his grandfather, and . . . a new one. A sterling silver angel. She leaned forward, cradling it in her hand. She began to tremble as she read the words engraved at the base. "Mary—Christmas 1996." She turned in the circle of his arms, scarcely daring to speak. "Russ, I . . ."

He placed a finger on her lips. "We were going to start a tradition, remember?" She nodded, eyes glistening. "A Coulter family tradition." His voice caught. "Mary, will you be my wife?"

A warmth like moist spring air radiated through her body, and she lost herself in the earnestness and love in his brimming gray eyes. "You mean it?" she managed breathlessly.

His smile was tremulous. "Are you going to make a reformed Casanova say it twice? Hell, yes, I mean it."

She stood on her tiptoes, ran her fingers through his hair and then entwined her arms around his neck. "You are all I'll ever need. Yes, yes, yes." She felt him lift her off the floor as his lips touched hers.

Slowly he set her back down and pulled away. "There's one more thing I think we need to settle." He grabbed two oversize pillows from the sofa and positioned them on the floor in front of the fire. "Come here." They stretched out, his arms encircling her, her head on his shoulder. Casey padded in from the kitchen, gave a few contented snorts and sprawled beside them.

"One thing?" She looked up at him.

"Your father. How important is it to you to finish the search?"

She placed a hand on his chest. "I've learned some things through all of this. Being adopted is only a part of who I am—like black hair or stubbornness or growing up in St. Louis. But I've let it control me instead of integrating it with all the rest of me. With a rich past and a promising future." She paused, considering. "Someday, if it's meant to be, I may pursue it. But you've taught me an important lesson. There is no day so important as *this* one—no moment more precious than right now."

She snuggled against him, her heart full. He stared into the fire, gently combing his fingers through her hair. A log shifted, embers flew. Finally he spoke. "I was so afraid I'd lost you. I couldn't think about anything but how to win you back. I wanted to give you the best gift I could think of—"

"Shh." She sat up and slowly withdrew from her blouse the *oochalata* stone. "You've given me the best gift—your love." She bent her neck and slipped off the necklace. "You're the one who helped me find myself. I want you to take this—" she put the necklace in his hand "—as a symbol of my everlasting love."

He picked up the stone between his thumb and forefinger, rubbing it gently. "You need to know something about this necklace. The gift I wanted to give you...it was your father."

She felt a crack run through her heart. "My father?"

"Mary, I hate telling you this, but he's dead, too. Killed in Vietnam a month before your mother died."

"How...?" A thousand questions flooded her mind.

"This necklace is an heirloom. A betrothal gift given by a Cherokee man to his beloved. Your father must've given it to your mother." He spread the chain with his fingers and gently settled it once more around Mary's neck. "So I think you should keep it for—" his voice broke "—our son."

She ran her fingers tenderly over his face as she searched his eyes. "Our son? Oh, Russ, I hope so. I can't believe all you've done. My father, how did you find—"

"It's a long story, and I'll tell you all of it. But, most important, there's someone very special who wants to meet you. Are you free to take a little trip with me tomorrow?"

"Christmas Day? Russ, who? Where—" He stopped her with a kiss that began at the base of her throat, moved up her neck, along her cheek and then found completion when his lips nudged hers open and he drew her body into a warm embrace.

Then he released her, and, with love and mischief lighting his eyes, smiled broadly. "Beloved woman, have you ever been to Tahlequah?"

EPILOGUE

Buck Lloyd sat in his study on a snowy Sunday in late January, the Ewing *Herald* spread out on his desk, a cigar smoldering in the leather-padded ashtray. He buttoned up his cardigan. Damn barn of a house was a bitch to keep heated. He hated the weekends, especially in the winter. Couldn't do much business, couldn't play golf, couldn't even line up a good poker game. And the house was so damn empty, although he should be used to that. Nobody but him rattling around in it for nearly thirty years. He didn't know why he kept it. Memories, he guessed. Ellie playing quietly with her dolls in the corner of this room, Ellie bringing her Girl Scout troop home to see his collection of barbed wire, Ellie's sixteenth birthday when the backyard had been filled with paper lanterns, music and laughter.

Lord almighty! He was getting as senile and sentimental as those poor souls in Sal's retirement center. Maybe that was why he kept the house and the housekeeper. By God, he'd never go into one of those octogenarian holding pens.

He set the business section of the paper aside and turned to the society pages. He scowled. 'Course, now, they called it some damn fool thing—he consulted the masthead—oh, yeah, ''Ewing Living.'' Call a spade a spade, damn it. Nothing but garden hints, recipes and pictures of brides. He scanned the first page, flipped through the next few and was about to lay that section aside when one picture caught his eye. An engagement photo. That girl—he'd seen her somewhere before. Then he read the caption. He clutched at his chest as a knife-like pain sliced through him. "Fleet-Coulter Engagement Announced."

He swiveled his chair and stared out the window at the soft, wet flakes floating down from a gray sky. His vision blurred. For a moment, just for a moment, the photograph had reminded him of... Damn Sal and her stubborn insistence. How could she know if this Fleet girl was Ellie's child? Ellie and that... that... damned Indian. That was all he'd needed thirty years ago—some half-breed brat.

But... he turned back around, drawn to the picture. She looked pretty—had Ellie's chin. He began reading the article. Bad enough that she might be his grand-daughter; even worse, she was marrying young Coulter.

A cold tremor shook his body. He heard a branch scrape across one of the dining room windows. Like chalk on a blackboard. The print ran together. He took off his reading glasses and rubbed his eyes, then replaced the glasses. There. That was better.

Lonely? Vindictive? Bitter? Sal had spared nothing when she'd flung her accusations. He chafed his hands together. *Forgive? Atone?* A chunk of snow slid off the roof outside the window, startling some cardinals and disturbing the quiet.

He was lonely. Much as he hated to admit it, Sal had a point. The future loomed as a dismal progression toward death. At least some people had the comfort of...family. He'd never let on to Sal, but he'd done a lot of thinking since her visit. Still, he'd never expected to be jolted the way he'd just been. That photograph. He looked again. The face. Something about the shape of the girl's eyes.

What if he wanted to reach out? How could he begin? That girl'd probably never be able to forgive him. Because—in his heart of hearts—he couldn't forgive himself. *So what are you afraid of, old man? I thought you weren't afraid of anything.*

Before he could change his mind, he yanked open the desk drawer and drew out the phone directory. Finally he located the number he wanted. Nobody was going to call *him* a coward. Hell, it wouldn't hurt to give it a try. He couldn't end up any worse off than he was. He hated to give his bossy older sister the satisfaction, though.

He dialed the phone, waiting impatiently, his fingers tapping on the desk. "Landon, that you?... Hell, yes, I know it's Sunday, but I pay you lawyers handsomely, and when I want some work done, I don't give a damn what day it is. Now get this down." He peered through his glasses to be sure he read the name correctly. "I want to deed over fifteen hundred acres of property. That land out west, next to Coulter's. Yeah.... Damn it, Landon, I know exactly what I'm doing. Now spell this name right. Mary Phyllis Fleet. F-L-E-E-T. Got it? Send the paperwork to me as quickly as you can." He slammed down the receiver.

The first step. Ought to make a hell of an engagement present. He unbuttoned the sweater. It was getting warm in here. He stood up, strolled around his desk, then picked up the phone again. This call would be harder. "Sal? Listen. I need a favor." He waited while she let him have it.

"A favor? I thought you could handle everything yourself."

"Usually can."

"I'm on pins and needles, then. What is it?"

He stubbed out the cigar and wiped his hand across his mouth. "I've been thinking."

"That's a start."

"Could you try to arrange a meeting between me and—" he choked on the words "—my granddaughter?"

"Well, I'll be damned, Buck. Welcome to the human race!"

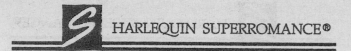

HARLEQUIN SUPERROMANCE®

EMERGENCY!

Does medical drama hold you spellbound? Are you glued
to the TV, watching "ER" and "Chicago Hope"?
Then our medical romances by bestselling author
Bobby Hutchinson will bring you to fever pitch....

St. Joe's is the hospital where it all began, and
Side Effects—coming this January—is the first
enthralling episode. Look for the second book
in our Emergency! series this summer!

Side Effects
by Bobby Hutchinson

Dr. Alexandra Ross works in a hectic emergency department
in downtown Vancouver when her whole life begins to fall
apart. Her brother is brought in on a stretcher nearer death
than life, and her husband, RCMP officer Cameron Ross,
is facing a crisis of his own.

Alex can no longer depend on the security of their marriage to
keep her world intact. It takes a different kind of healing in a
different kind of place to put the pieces back together. But will
the picture be the same?

Intense emotion, heart-pounding excitement,
flashes of humor—you'll find them all in *Side Effects*
and other upcoming Emergency! books.

EMER-197

HARLEQUIN SUPERROMANCE®

WOMEN WHO *Dare*

They take chances, make changes and follow their hearts. They're women who know what they want, who know what's important in life. They're not afraid to risk *everything* for what they believe in. They're *Women Who Dare.* And you'll meet them *only* in Superromance novels!

In January, meet Day Sutter, a thoroughly nineties woman who lives near Moab, Utah. Day is half owner of Rapid Riggers, a river-rafting company. She's in love—has been for years—with Nick Colter, her partner. But Nick insists she's not his kind of woman. She's not an adventurer, he says. Not a risk taker.

Day knows he's wrong. She *is* Nick's kind of woman. And he's certainly her kind of man. All she has to do is prove it!

Nick's Kind of Woman by award-winning author **Margot Early.** Look for it in January, wherever Harlequin books are sold.

WWD-197

You are cordially invited to a

HOMETOWN REUNION

September 1996—August 1997

Bad boys, cowboys, babies. Feuding families, arson, mistaken identity, a mom on the run... Where can you find romance and adventure? Tyler, Wisconsin, that's where!

So join us in this not-so-sleepy little town and experience the love, the laughter and the tears of those who call it home.

WELCOME TO A
HOMETOWN REUNION

Sheila and Douglas are going to spend their honeymoon in a wigwam, by choice. But rumor has it that Rosemary Dusold may be *forced*—by runny-nosed babies—to live in one if the new pediatrician follows through on his intention to renovate her home as an office. Don't miss Helen Conrad's *Baby Blues*, fifth in a series you won't want to end....

Available in January 1997
at your favorite retail store.

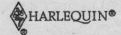

HARLEQUIN®

HTR5

Ring in the New Year with babies, families and romance!

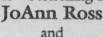
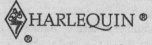

HARLEQUIN ®

Scandals

A passionate story of romance, where bold, daring characters set out to defy their world of propriety and strict social codes.

"*Scandals*—a story that will make your heart race and your pulse pound. Spectacular!"
—Suzanne Forster

"Devon is daring, dangerous and altogether delicious."
—Amanda Quick

Don't miss this wonderful full-length novel from Regency favorite Georgina Devon.

Available in December, wherever Harlequin books are sold.

Look us up on-line at: http://www.romance.net

The collection of the year!
NEW YORK TIMES BESTSELLING AUTHORS

Linda Lael Miller
Wild About Harry

Janet Dailey
Sweet Promise

Elizabeth Lowell
Reckless Love

Penny Jordan
Love's Choices

and featuring
Nora Roberts
The Calhoun Women

This special trade-size edition features four of the wildly
popular titles in the Calhoun miniseries together in
one volume—a true collector's item!

Pick up these great authors and a chance to win
a weekend for two in New York City at the
Marriott Marquis Hotel on Broadway! We'll pay
for your flight, your hotel—even a Broadway show!

Available in December at your favorite retail outlet.

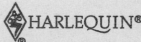 

1997
Reader's Engagement Book
A calendar of important dates
and anniversaries for readers to use!

Informative and entertaining—with notable
dates and trivia highlighted throughout the year.

Handy, convenient, pocketbook size to help you
keep track of your own personal important dates.

Added bonus—contains $5.00 worth of coupons
for upcoming Harlequin and Silhouette books.
This calendar more than pays for itself!

 Available beginning in November at
your favorite retail outlet.

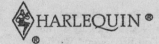